After Finding You

Britney Coon

Luna Bella Publishing

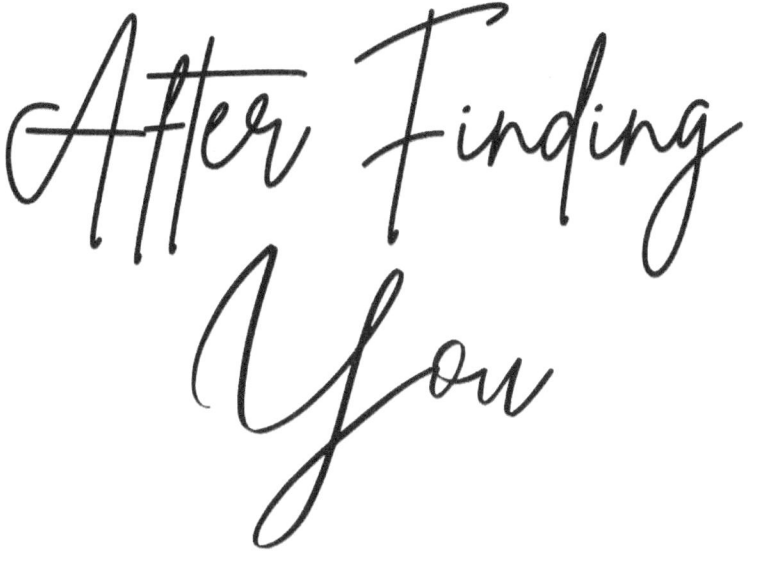

After Finding You

Brittney Coon

Luna
Bella
Publishing

Cover Design by Artscandare Book Cover Design

Page Edges Designed by Painted Wings Publishing

First Edition, 2025

Printed by Luna Bella Publishing in the United States of America

For Within Temptation—

Your music lit the spark that became this story.

Thank you for the haunting beauty, strength, and emotion in every note.

I would not wish any companion in the world but you."
The Tempest, Act III, Scene I

Chapter One

"ARE MERMAIDS REAL?" ARTHUR'S voice cuts through the chatter, amplified by the speakers mounted in every corner of the restaurant, each word rippling like a wave through the air. The question hangs, quieting the room and daring diners to believe in the impossible.

I run my hands over my blue-and-green-swirled silicone tail, ensuring the fit is snug before sinking into the water. With a deep breath, I dive under, the water muffling what Arthur says next. "We searched all the oceans, and you're in luck! We managed to find a mermaid right here in Los Angeles, and after negotiating payment...in sand dollars, of course..." He pauses for the audience's laughter.

I use the extra seconds to sneak a breath from my oxygen mask hanging discreetly by some fake seaweed.

The rescue diver, hiding in the corner where the audience can't see him, gives me a thumbs up to show everything is safe and ready for the performance. I nod my thanks as Arthur wraps up his big speech. "She's agreed to show you some of her *mermazing* skills right here at The Pearl Kingdom! Without further ado...here's Mermaid Veronica!"

As Arthur's voice fades, the deep crimson curtains around the water tank part, and the warm light chases away the darkness. I inhale one last deep breath, push my oxygen mask into the seaweed, and swim toward the center of the glass.

My usual routine is swimming from one side to the other before mixing in some spins and twirls. People stop eating to watch me whirl and wave.

Children of all ages rush to press their cute faces against the glass. I smile and blow them bubble kisses and form hearts with my hands. They giggle and point at me like I'm something exotic they found in a zoo.

A man stands up from his table and takes a photo using the flash. For a moment, I'm dazed but shake it off. Blinking away the red spots. Security darts toward the man and asks him to turn off the flash. I nod my thanks and continue the show.

The cheers and applause never fail to lift my spirits. As the curtain closes, I glide to the surface, breaking through with a deep, refreshing inhale. Hauling myself onto the platform, I settle in, my tail shimmering in front of me.

Arthur walks up the stairs and steps onto the platform to join me. He cracks the knuckles in his massive hands and swipes at his nose. "You ready to meet those grubby little kids?" he asks with a smirk.

"Isn't one of those monsters yours?" I mock, craning my neck to look up at him. His dark beard is growing back in, giving his jaw a sharper edge. His arms are toned and scarred from his days in the armed forces.

His dimples deepen as his smirk turns into a cheesy grin. Arthur raises a shoulder and drops it. "What's a man to do?"

I laugh, rolling my eyes. Arthur gently lifts me, placing his left hand behind my tail, which is actually behind my knees, and his right hand on my back. I wrap my arm around his shoulders to keep myself balanced. "You're my favorite mer-handler, you know that?"

His hazel eyes cut me a look. "I'm the only one you got."

I pucker my lips in an exaggerated pout and toss an overly dramatic air kiss at him. "Just makes you even more special."

He playfully smacks my scale-covered thigh. "Yeah, yeah."

"Do you ever want to get out of here?" The question slips through my lips as I trace the tip of the eagle wing tattoo on his neck with my finger. It's a bit faded from age, but it still stands out against his tanned skin. His reply is a confused glance like I lost my mind, so I add, "You know. Start a new life. Do something different."

He swallows, and his Adam's apple bobs. His hold on my legs stiffens. "I like it here. It's peaceful, and I always feel better when my life runs like clockwork. Plus, my wife and daughter are from here." As soon as he says that, we turn the corner, and ten children scream in unison, killing the conversation.

I wrinkle my nose and flick my fin. Arthur chuckles, the sound reverberating through me before he sets me down on the white inflatable seashell set up for photos. I wave to my young audience, flashing them a bright smile.

As the kids crowd around, Arthur's sharper edges melt away. He laughs, but it's deeper and more soulful. On the outside, Arthur might look like an intimidating bouncer, but on the inside, he's a sweet guy who loves his family.

"Hello, everyone! I'm so happy you could come over to my shell and talk. Say hello to my friend, Arthur." I motion to him.

The kids all say hi except his daughter, who stands and proudly boasts, "That's my daddy!"

He bites back a laugh and steps away. I pat my lap, encouraging the children to come closer. They ooh and ahh over my tail, touching my scales and giggling. I run my fingers through my dirty blonde curls and speak in my sweetest voice. "What are your names? I'm Mermaid Veronica."

My best friend, Alice, walks into the backroom while I'm wiggling my hips out of my silicone tail. She bites her tongue, but the corners of her mouth curl upward in a smirk.

"If you're just going to laugh, you can leave," I say, tugging harder on my tail. It's always easier to slide into than to get out of. The material clings to my legs like a second skin.

Alice wipes her hands on the bar rag she's holding and tosses it onto the bench beside me. "What happened to that bubbly mermaid attitude?" She leans against the wall as her cocky grin grows. "How will you make a career of being a professional mermaid when you can't escape your own scales?" Humor dances in her blue eyes as she tries and fails to suppress her laughter.

"How about I bitch slap you with my tail?" I joke, flopping my fins on the concrete floor. "But I need you to step closer so I can reach you."

Alice ignores me and grabs the bottom of my fin, giving it a good yank. After a few tries, it finally releases me. I stand, pulling up my blue leggings that slipped down my hips a little during the struggle. "Freedom at last."

My fingers massage the tight muscles in my legs to stop the tingling. Swimming in a mermaid tail might look easy and fun, but it's a hell of a workout on your body.

"And just an FYI. I have a business plan in motion. After I get my professional pictures taken in a few weeks, I'll be applying to cruise lines and landing more gigs. Once I have a company sponsor to back me with some money, my options are as deep as the ocean."

She lifts a pierced brow. "Mermaid puns? Really?"

"Can't take the sparkly mermaid out of me even with a knife."

"But I could try." She flashes a wicked grin.

"How was your shift?" I don't mind discussing my future, but Alice doesn't always take it seriously. But at least she understands it's what I love, unlike my mother, who thinks I'm wasting away at a dead-end job.

Alice sighs dramatically and stretches her arms out to pop her shoulder blades. "I'm not sure if you noticed during your show, but a tall guy who eats steroids for breakfast threw up all over my bar. Some splashed on Hannah's heels. Damn nasty! And they wanted me to mop it up! Me! The only bartender who knows how to mix drinks correctly and when to call a customer a rideshare." She unties the black apron and opens her locker, tossing it inside. "The nerve!"

My head bobs, showing I'm listening but not daring to interrupt. I did that once, and the conversation lasted three hours. Ranging from rude customers who don't tip to problems with our healthcare. When Alice falls into a rant, anything on her mind goes, and it could take all night.

"Almost forgot, I have a surprise for you," she says, digging into her purse and grabbing a brush, as she attempts to tame her long black mane of hair.

"Are you going to leave me in suspense or what?" I change out of my shell bra into a black, lacy one.

"Sorry. You know me and my hair." Alice laughs and grabs her pink, blinged-out phone. She pulls something up and hands it over. "Check it out."

I set my mermaid tail on the bench and drape the towel I was about to dry it with over my shoulder. Her phone is open to a ticket app. I read the name of the artist she has tickets to and scream.

Alice covers her ears and laughs. "Girl, you got siren lungs." She pokes my chest with her long, pink fingernail.

"Is this for real?" I glance at the date. The show is tonight. "What the hell? It's tonight? Why didn't you—"

"Because I didn't want you to somehow find a way to get out of it. You've been locked up in the apartment for weeks since—"

"The incident. I know." I sigh, wishing my ex didn't pop into my mind and rain on my parade. "This is amazing, but you're mean for keeping it from me," I joke, sticking my tongue out at her.

My phone buzzes with a text. The name "ASSHOLE" in all caps causes my stomach to drop. Speak of the devil, and he appears. I sink my teeth into my bottom lip to keep it from quivering, but Alice must see the panicked expression on my face because she steals my phone.

"What the hell? He who doesn't have a name anymore is texting you? I don't think so."

She unlocks my phone. I curse under my breath. Why did I let her know my passcode?

"Give it back!" But it's pointless to fight her when she's on a mission. Alice is five inches taller than me, and I swear she has the arms of an elegant tattooed dancer that could reach the heavens. Where my phone currently is. The roses and skulls inked on her skin mock me, knowing I could never be brave enough to stomp on her foot to get my phone back.

She types something and gives a satisfied nod, handing me back the device. "You need to block his ass for good."

"I know." I slip on a gray oversized T-shirt and step into my flip-flops. What happened between him and me is still too fresh to talk about.

Alice runs her hands over her tight black jeans. "He's yesterday's trash. We need to go home and change. The doors open in two hours."

"Yes!" I allow the excitement to push away the thought of my ex and whatever Alice replied to him.

Tonight, I will see my favorite band, Scarlet Failure, live. Because Alice always finds a way, even into a sold-out concert.

She hooks her arm with mine and pulls me toward the exit. "Let's go!"

Nothing cures a broken heart faster than a loud, head-banging concert. I can't wait to be standing at the base of the stage right in front of their sexy bass guitarist, Sully Graham. This is the push I need to get out of my funk and finally be myself again.

Chapter Two

"THE WAIT IS KILLING me," I say, twisting my silver mermaid-tail ring, the amethyst catching the dim light as it spins around my finger. "Are there too many people in front of us?"

For the third time, I step out of line, scanning the crowd, my pulse ticking higher with every extra head I count. Were there always this many, or have some sneaky line-cutters wedged their way in? My jaw tightens. If I lose my spot at the base of the stage because of some entitled wannabe front-row thieves, there will be consequences. And by consequences, I mean a few bruised ribs, an "accidental" elbow to the face, or a well-placed stomp on some unsuspecting toes.

"Will you *please* stop counting?" Alice sinks her fingernails into my arm, pulling me back against the brick wall beside her. "You're making me anxious." She pouts as a mom and her son walk down the sidewalk with ice cream cones. "I can't believe you got me standing here before the doors open. I'm starving."

"We just ate pizza bites, and I'll buy you something after the show." I check the time on my phone and click off the screen. It's hard not to scroll through it mindlessly, but I forgot my portable charger in all my excitement, and I need to save the battery for pictures and videos.

Alice mutters curse words as she searches inside her purse for a pack of gum. She finds a piece and throws it into her mouth like it's her salvation. Within seconds, she smacks her lips, blowing bubbles before loudly popping them to dig under my skin. I can suffer her little meltdown because soon I'll be only a few feet away from Sully Graham, and maybe, just maybe, I'll catch a guitar pick from him.

✳ 🎶 🐚 🎶 ✳ 🎶 🐚

Thankfully, arriving a little early worked in our favor. We're in the perfect place at the railing, a few feet from the stage. I'll have a professional photographer-like view of Scarlet Failure. If I'm lucky, I might earn some eye contact or a brushed hand by Sully as I nearly throw myself at his feet. Usually, I'd have more self-respect, but when it comes to concerts of my favorite bands, I'm a total fangirl who screams until my voice is gone the next day.

The opening band, Haunted Dreams, is one of Alice's favorites. She screams along and almost whacks my head when their drummer tosses drumsticks into the crowd, and she catches one.

Unfortunately, the guy behind us also catches the same stick. They fight over who grabbed it first and who has a bigger half and therefore deserves the entire thing. There's a brief tug-of-war laced with insults until Alice stomps on his foot and holds the stick to her chest like it's priceless. The man mutters under his breath and walks over toward the bar to drown his sorrows.

Near the end of Haunted Dreams' setlist, they sing more thrashy songs, and it causes a bunch of people to form a mosh pit directly behind us. One guy jumps into the air, and people pick him up, crowd-surfing him toward the stage. He drifts over my head, and I panic. I can't hold his weight, so I duck, but then this girl in a black dress and spider web leggings tries to elbow her way into my spot. I stand up too fast and it messes up the crowd-surfing and the guy falls backward with a loud smack on the concrete floor.

I grimace as a buddy of his helps him to his feet. The guy looks dazed, but thankfully there's no blood. At least none that I can see in the low light.

Alice misses the entire scene by jumping up and down, trying to reach for the lead singer's hand when he runs side to side on stage. She has no idea how close I came to losing my head. But at least she's enjoying the show and no longer grumbling about her hunger.

After the band says their farewells, the lights flick on, and house music fills the ringing silence. I roll my shoulders and stretch my stiff spine, biting back a painful groan. My feet burn, and my legs ache. I glance at the people in the balcony sitting in booths drinking and relaxing, not a care in the world. A small pang of jealousy stabs my heart, and I force myself to look away.

But they don't have a chance of catching a guitar pick from Sully. That hope pulls me out of the darkness that still lingers from my past. If I catch a pick, score a setlist, and/or touch Sully's hand, then all my pain will be worth it.

"I'm going to buy us some water. Wish me luck!" Alice says, squeezing herself through the crowd creeping closer inch by inch. Soon I won't have enough room to inhale and exhale, let alone move my arms up and down.

People eye Alice's spot, nodding toward their friends. I clench my teeth and hold my ground, trying to save her space from being taken by the people I deem vultures. They look for any way to get close to the stage without standing nearly half the night to get a good spot. Luckily the guy next to Alice is cool and helps me keep her spot safe. He also stood in line with us outside, and we hardcore fans tend to stick together to ensure no one cuts in front or pushes us out of the way.

Anticipation hums in the air as roadies set up Scarlet Failure's mic stands and drum set. I feel people pressing in on all sides as discarded cups crunch underneath my sneakers. Alice pushes her way back to our spot and sighs as she hands me a cold bottle of water. "There's a girl with spiky blue hair that's super pissed at me right now for elbowing her in the ribs. But she wouldn't let me through." She chuckles, taking a sip of water. "It's insane. The crowd goes all the way to the bar."

"Really?" I stand on my tiptoes and crane my neck to look behind us. All I see is a sea of heads. I knew the concert was sold out, but to see it is always surprising. No wonder I'm sweating like it's a sauna with all this body heat trapped inside one room.

As soon as the house music cuts off mid-song and someone kills the lights, people push in an immense wave, a humanized hurricane. I move my elbows around and stick my butt out more to preserve some room as I lean against the metal railing. I'm going to have bruised hands and arms, but that's the price you pay to be up front.

Ben Katz explodes onto the stage first, swinging his drumsticks over his head like a champion, a wild grin plastered across his face. The crowd roars. A heartbeat later, Sully and Lars Elrod rush out, guitars slung low, tuning knobs spinning as they lock into place. Sully is barely three feet away, and the sight of him sends my heart into a wild rhythm. Heat blooms under my skin as his eyes briefly find mine.

The screams around me go feral—high, sharp, desperate. Everyone's fighting for Sully's attention, and it's no surprise. He's the only single member left, and it's almost a frenzy to catch his attention as he strums his guitar.

Their lead singer, Charlotte Katz, makes her entrance to roaring applause. She blows a kiss to her husband, Ben, who playfully flips a drumstick in the air and catches it between his teeth, making her laugh. She waves at the crowd, her voice bright as she grabs the mic. "Greetings, LA! It's so nice to be back," she says in a sing-song German accent, sweeping a hand through her long chestnut hair. True to her signature style, she's rocking a pair of towering black seven-inch heels. From my spot, the view is incredible—I can see the intricate details of her purple dress and the way her diamond earrings catch the light.

The zoom on my phone's camera catches the artwork on Sully's guitar. It's navy blue with white lightning.

"How's your night going so far? You ready to rock?" Charlotte shouts, taking her mic out of its cradle.

Everyone screams in reply and a few whistle. I wince at the sharp sound stabbing my left eardrum.

"Our first song is 'Winter Heart,'" she says, nodding to Sully. He starts playing the melody, and I swear my heart bursts open.

The entire concert feels like an out-of-body experience. As if my soul floats above my body while watching one of my favorite bands perform. For nearly two hours, I'm in heaven. I sing along and take pictures. People behind me shove and almost force me to drop my phone over the barrier. I elbow them and fight to keep myself from being pinned to the rail.

When Scarlet Failure finishes their last song, Sully tosses out five guitar picks. One bounces off my breast and falls inches away from me. I search the floor, but with all the feet and debris, it's hard to find a little plastic pick.

It's hopeless. Someone else...

My eyes lock on a spot a few inches away. I squint, and it's the green pick on the edge of someone's phone light. Just as I'm about to step on it, a guy snatches it up.

Damn.

I look to the stage hoping maybe Lars still has some picks or Ben has a drumstick to throw. Instead, Sully stands in front of me. He smiles, showing me a green pick in his hand. Instinctively I hold out my cupped hand and he flicks it into my palm. Before he turns to join his band in the lineup to bow and say their final goodbyes, I swear he winks at me.

My heart skids to a sudden stop, and it physically hurts when it starts pounding again. Like it's trying to escape my rib cage.

Once the band waves farewell and leaves the stage, fans flock to the doors, but I remain at the barrier. Alice moves to leave and I grab her arm. "Wait a sec," I say, keeping my eyes on the stage.

She presses her lips into a thin line but doesn't protest. As the roadies tear down the set, I wave one over and point at a setlist taped to the floor. It's the one Sully used.

The roadie with shaggy brown hair and a scruffy beard sees the paper and carefully peels it off the ground, folding back the black duct tape. At least ten other fans eagerly wait for the same thing. There are four setlists in total and two were already handed out farther down the stage.

I reach my arm for the setlist and smile at the roadie as he dangles it in front of us like a fish on a hook.

The corner of the paper touches my fingertips. I lean forward and snatch it, nearly balling the page in my grasp as I hold onto it for life and bring it into my chest before anyone can steal it.

As Alice and I walk out of the venue, there are vendors right out the doors selling food and bootleg tour shirts.

"You want a hot dog?" I nod toward the cart, watching as a couple of brave—possibly reckless—souls buy food and eat it without a second thought. Bold move, considering those mystery meat tubes could be teeming with E. coli or whatever other horrors lurk in questionable street food.

Alice gags as we pass by the vendors. "I'm working tomorrow night. I don't have time for explosive diarrhea. How about we hit the Korean BBQ down the street?" She points at the restaurant a few yards away with her drumstick.

"Maybe later. They're open late, right?" I ask, pausing when we reach behind the venue where the tour buses are parked. "I want to hang around and see if we can meet the band."

She sighs heavily and reluctantly follows me toward the growing crowd near the venue's back door.

Chapter Three

THERE ARE AT LEAST thirty people waiting for the band at the entrance of the venue's alley. I hope to squeeze in and meet every band member before they are whisked away to their next destination, but if I only speak to Sully then that is still a win in my book.

People around us clutch magazines, posters, and records for them to sign. I dig out the album artwork I carefully put in my purse and hold it along with my new setlist.

Alice chuckles, hitting my shoulder with hers. "Of course you brought something for them to sign."

"Girl Scouts taught me to always be prepared," I joke, pulling out a black Sharpie from the back pocket inside my purse. "This isn't my first meet-and-greet."

"Most people read or sew as a hobby. Then there's you and concerts. I hope he's not a jerk. You know what they say about meeting your idols."

"What do you mean?" I'm honestly puzzled.

"Sorry to be a downer, but everyone knows Sully usually brushes fans off. He barely signs anything and never smiles for photos."

"Oh...yeah." I bite the inside of my cheek. My brain must have shoved that fact into a box and hid it from me. But Alice is right. Sully is wonderful on stage, but stiff as a board and cold as ice in person. People say he's like a robot, with no moving facial features, and doesn't like to talk much to fans.

In my concert-going lifetime, I've met super sweet musicians who ask you questions and wrap an arm around your shoulders for a photo, and I've met the don't-look-at-me-I'm-only-here-because-I-have-to-be rock stars. You'd think the latter would chase off their fans, but it rarely does.

Fans have a way of turning famous people into gods in their minds. Not me. But it will be a crushing blow to have the man featured in my dreams brush me off as another face in the crowd. Or worse, he drifts by and ignores me altogether.

Fear closes my airway just as I catch the back door of the venue opening. My thoughts die because all four members of Scarlet Failure walk out together.

People swarm each person, thrusting things to sign and smiling for selfies.

Charlotte stands closest to me, and I'm about to hand her my setlist when a girl around my age steals her attention. They take a few pictures, and then the girl gives Charlotte a colorful beaded friendship bracelet she made and explains how their music saved her life and goes into this whole story.

Don't get me wrong, I'm happy for her, but there are a lot of people wanting to speak to Charlotte, and a woman, who I'm guessing is their manager, is leaning against the building, looking annoyed and sighing as she looks at her watch.

The girl wraps up her story and hugs Charlotte. It's finally my turn, and I hand Charlotte my album cover and setlist. She signs them, and says, "Thank you so much for coming. I hope you enjoyed the show."

"It was great. One of the best concerts I've seen in a while," I reply, before raising my phone and snapping a selfie with her.

"That's wonderful," she says, smiling at me before shifting her attention to Alice.

I use Charlotte as my buffer to get over my jitters before walking toward Sully and asking for his autograph. My nerves coil tighter with every step. He's signing a magazine cover for an older guy, but his gaze keeps darting to the tour bus like he's ready to escape at any second. I swallow hard, pushing down the anxiety creeping up my throat, and wait for my chance to step in.

The man thanks Sully and pats his arm. Sully stiffens instantly, his whole body going rigid, as if the touch burned him.

Another girl jumps in to meet Sully as I gather my strength to approach him. My heart flips seeing her glossy lips mouthing things. But I can't make out her words because I'm staring at Sully. His jaw clenches as he lazily signs her magazine. As she babbles on, he "hmms" but doesn't reply with words.

The girl then dares to shrug her band tee down her shoulder and ask Sully to sign her collarbone so she can have his autograph tattooed. He signs her skin with a quick signature and pays more attention putting the cap on the marker than he did her plunging neckline. She asks for a selfie. She makes a kissy face and he looks uncomfortable, mouth closed, his eyes unfocused. I notice she's touching his back, but he's not touching her at all. His hand is open and he is holding it out so anyone can see his palm.

The girl thanks him and wanders off to stand under a street light to take a selfie of her autographed flesh.

Then Sully looks at me and it's like the entire world stops. Silly I know. But honestly, did God accidentally hit the pause button? Because everything is frozen in place when Sully waves me over. My brain disconnects. I'm on system failure. My thoughts drift away, and all I can do is lift my arm to hand him my setlist and album artwork.

"Hello," he says in a husky voice, brushing a loose piece of dark hair from his forehead before taking and signing the setlist and album artwork. His ocean eyes never leave mine.

Thankfully, my five-foot-six height gives me a perfect look at his six-foot-two body, but my eyes lock on his perfectly shaped lips.

What do they taste like? I shake off the thought. This is no place to fangirl.

"Can I have a picture too?" I find my voice. It's hoarse, almost a whisper.

"How about a hug first?" he says in his seductive, panty-dropping foreign accent. All I can do is nod before his strong arms wrap around my waist. I was wrong before; this is what heaven feels like. I inhale his spicy scent of sweat mixed with body spray and peppermint. It's now forever my standard of how every guy I hug needs to smell.

My arms wrap around his torso, and the heat of his body against mine sends shivers dancing along my spine. The touch of his muscles moving under my fingertips, his hard chest pressed against my breasts, it's all too overwhelming.

What's going on? He never hugs people. At least I've never heard about it, and I'm in a lot of fan groups online.

"I was staring at you all night. You had such a lovely smile when I gave you that pick," he says into my hair as he releases his hold on me.

"Oh?" I say, losing my balance, and he saves me from falling backward and breaking my tailbone on the asphalt.

"Careful," he says, a small grin flashing across his face. One blink, and it's gone. "What's your name?"

Every word I have ever known falls out of my head, leaving me dumbstruck. Starstruck.

My mouth goes bone-dry, and my tongue feels like a useless weight, heavy and uncooperative. Alice comes to my rescue, standing behind me. "She's Veronica, and I'm Alice."

Sully doesn't look at her. His eyes stay only on me. The fear of something on my face crosses my mind. *Do I have a zit between my eyebrows? Is my makeup messed up? Why is he staring at me like that?*

I don't know what to say or do. Honestly, I want to run away so I can scream my lungs out and do a little happy dance. *Sully Graham hugged me! I saw him smile!*

Then my dark thoughts flood in and ruin my joy. *He probably says that to all the girls he wants to screw. A few words to make the fans blush and giggle. To keep them happy and coming back for more.*

And yet...what if he doesn't? What if he means it? After all, Sully wasn't interested in the fangirl he met before me. And he's never seen with anyone...publicly.

Sully's warm hand on my arm pulls me back to reality. I can't believe this is actually happening. "Veronica, what a gorgeous name. It suits you." His voice is rich and velvety, its quiet warmth brushing over me like a soft caress.

Heat creeps up my neck and floods my cheeks. I lower my head, letting my hair fall like a shield. "Thanks," I manage to say, my throat tight and uncooperative. I try to swallow my nerves, but they sit heavy in my chest, making it hard to breathe.

He reaches forward, tipping my chin with his long, slender fingers. "Don't hide your pretty face from me. I want to see those dazzling green eyes. Let's take that picture now."

A spark ignites beneath my skin the moment he touches me, a heat that lingers even as his hand pulls away too soon. The loss of his touch carves deeper into the emptiness inside me, widening the hollow ache in my chest.

"Yes." I thrust my phone at Alice, the sudden movement catching her off guard. She flinches, barely managing to catch it before it slips from her hands.

Sully drapes his arm over my shoulders, and it takes everything in me to keep from slipping back into the out-of-body experience like before during the show. I don't want to push this feeling off as a dream. I want to remember every damn second. How the weight of his arm feels around my shoulders. The way he smells and his warmth seeps into my bloodstream. The way my heart summersaults. The way that his dimples deepen with his heart-stopping smile.

Yes, another smile! Did I win the lottery?

My usual celebrity crushes aren't this intense. But my usual crushes don't wrap their strong arms around me and say sweet things.

Alice snaps some pictures and hands the phone back to me. My bubble of perfect pops.

"Alright. We need to get out of here," the stern woman who was leaning against the wall says. A black limo pulls up. Charlotte, Ben, and Lars wave their goodbyes to the remaining fans and climb into the car.

Sully steals my phone and types something into it before giving it back. "We're staying local tonight. Text me. I'll be up. I never sleep after a show." He jogs to the limo before that woman snaps again.

Alice grabs my wrist and pulls my phone closer to her face. "Holy shit. Did you get a rock star's number without trying?"

I glance at my phone and see his name and number. "Looks like it." I shove my phone into my bra and bite my lip to keep myself from shrieking in joy. "Let's go home."

My best friend hooks her arm with mine as we walk toward our car. "And to think all this happened because of me." She bumps her hip with mine. "The universe told me we had to be here. My Tarot cards are never wrong."

"Yeah," I say. Honestly, I'm still in shock. I open my photos and stare at Sully and me smiling on the screen. Alice's voice and the radio turn into a low hum as I zoom in on Sully's face. He's leaning into me, and it's like we're friends or maybe something more.

Part of me wants to share the picture everywhere, to prove Sully can smile, and he did so for me. But then I want to keep it hidden. A secret treasure for my eyes only.

Do I have the nerve to speak to him? To say more words than, "Can I have a photo?" I have no idea. Sure, I've met famous people before, but it's always in a quick blur. The problem is, whenever someone I'm crushing on gets too close, my nerves go haywire, and my tongue feels like a heavy, useless lump in my mouth.

And yet...I'd do almost anything for Sully to flash his grin at me one more time, to hear him say my name in that sexy German accent, to inhale his spicy scent again, just to make sure my brain remembers it correctly. Maybe earn another hug. But the memories of my messy, very public breakup still linger like an unwanted shadow, holding me back. I'm not ready to let anyone in—not yet. Still, how many times does your crush want to see you again before it becomes impossible to ignore? I bite my lip, staring at his number. The possibilities are endless, if only I could force myself to hit the message button.

Chapter Four

WHEN WE RETURN HOME, I hang my signed setlist on my bedroom wall and snap a photo, sharing it on social media with a picture of Alice and me before the show, waiting in line. But I don't post my picture with Sully. Not yet. As I type out a list of hashtags, Alice leans against my doorway, scrolling through her phone. "Emily's back!" She smiles, texting her girlfriend. "I'm meeting her at The Rainbow Pony. You wanna come?"

My post is already gaining hearts and comments from jealous fellow fans. A smirk steals my lips. Some followers post it's nice to see me not as a mermaid since my page is usually about my alter ego, Mermaid Veronica.

Alice flicks the back of my phone. "Did you hear me? Emily. The Rainbow Pony. You in?"

My gaze falls onto my comfy bed. "No. You haven't seen her in two weeks. Go be with your girlfriend."

She eyes my setlist and then gasps. "Are you going to sext Sully? Booty call him? I need to know."

A blush burns its way up my neck. "What?"

She rubs the skull and rose tattoo above her elbow. A laugh slips out, and she coughs to disguise it. "Come on. I saw how he looked at you. Sully brushed everyone else off but you; he wanted to eat you with a spoon. He didn't even look my way and I'm hot shit." Her eyes blaze into me like she can see right through me.

"Not sure yet." I don't want to make a fool of myself. What if I freeze and go completely mute? What if I drop dead at his feet?

She bites her lip, gently tugging on her golden hoop earring. "Maybe it's for the best. He flirted with you, and you acted like a weirdo. Tripping on saying your own name. You're definitely out of practice." She walks into my room and pushes open my closet door. "Now if we dress you in something sexy, maybe you won't need words. And a steamy one-night stand would—"

"Stop." I grab Alice's arm and pull her away from my closet. "I'm not your Barbie and I'm not even sure I'll message him."

"Okay. I'm sorry for being so pushy. I only want the best for you and rock star sex sounds like what the doctor ordered. Especially after—"

"The incident..." I mumble, toeing the carpet.

"The best way to get over your shitty ex is to get under someone else. Food for thought. Text me if you change your mind." Alice kisses my cheek and rushes into her bedroom to slip on her heels and grab her purse.

The apartment is too quiet in her absence.

After tying my hair into a tight ponytail, I pull my workout mat from under the couch and start setting up in the living room. Tonight's supposed to be my mermaid training session—building core strength, flexibility, endurance—but for a minute, I just stand there, twirling the hem of my workout tank between my fingers.

Am I seriously getting ready to stretch and swim-train after standing in the front row of the best concert of my life? I met Sully Graham—the freaking bass player of Scarlet Failure—and he *gave me his number.* He said things that made my skin burn and my heart race. It made me feel like I was the only girl in the world. And what am I doing? Rolling out a yoga mat instead of texting him.

My phone burns a hole in my back pocket, like it knows I'm being ridiculous.

Would Sully answer if I texted him? Would he notice if I don't reach out? Then again, what if Sully's waiting for me? I don't want to disappoint him.

I exhale hard, the tension buzzing under my skin.

"Screw it," I say, tossing the water bottle aside and kicking off my slides. I'm not ready to text him yet, but I'm sure as hell not going to waste this energy. A run around the apartment complex sounds better than sitting here overthinking. The night's cool and quiet—the perfect backdrop to clear my head and maybe figure out what the hell I'm so scared of.

Ten minutes later, I find myself sitting in a lounge chair staring into the glittering water of the pool. My phone is a heavy brick in my hand.

The night air kisses my face as I pace the length of the pool to calm my racing heart. I glance at Sully's number on my phone. One text won't kill me. I can send it and wait. Or I can send it and throw my phone into the deep end.

It's now or never. Do I want to live with what-ifs? No. I don't.

> **Hey, Sully. It's Veronica. You gave me your number after the show tonight. Just wanted to reach out.**

That sounds terrible. But what else should I say? I don't want to look desperate or like I'm asking to screw a rock star. I'd be cool with talking.

Really Veronica? You can't be this lame.

Why is this so hard? I'm being ridiculous. It's a text. If he doesn't answer then fine. But if he does...well, I'll never know if I don't hit send.

With my eyes squeezed closed, I send the text and feel like throwing up. The back of my throat burns, and my eyes sting.

My stomach tightens into a hard ball of nerves. Tonight has been a lot. Maybe I should take a shower and call it a night. As I walk to the apartment, my phone buzzes with a new message.

I clutch the phone, looking at the little message symbol mocking me.

Could it be Sully? Or maybe it's Alice checking in.

My finger clicks on texts and opens the message.

> **Hey! You wanna come over?**

Do I want to meet a rock star in his hotel? Yes. No. My pulse quickens, sending my heart into overdrive. If only I had Alice here. What would she do? Probably steal my phone and tell him I'd be over ASAP. Maybe even add a winky face because she's evil.

What would be the harm in meeting with him? I could prove to Alice and myself that "the incident" didn't ruin me forever.

I need to stop overthinking and act.

> **Yes. What's the address?**

My breathing is too loud, as if I climbed ten flights of stairs to my apartment instead of one. I step into my living room and lie on the couch, waiting for his response. He sends the address and his room number. I sit up too fast, causing a dizzy spell to spin my vision.

Am I doing this? I scan our lonely apartment. Being with a rock star is a hell of a lot better than binge-watching a TV show or falling asleep only to dream of what could have been.

I change into tight jeans ripped at the knees and a formfitting gray Jack Daniels shirt. It's casual but gives the vibe of being open and willing to hang out. At least that's what I'm telling myself as I grab my keys and walk out the door.

✳ 🎵♪ 🐚 🎵♪ ✳ 🎵♪ 🐚

This hotel is one of the fanciest ones in Los Angeles. The floor is bright white with glittery swirls, and the walls are gray marble. There is a giant statue of a horse in the lobby, and above my head is the third chandelier I have spotted since coming inside.

Thankfully the people at the check-in desk are too busy processing a couple to notice me sneak past. I overhear them talking about *Twilight* and which team everyone is on. Out of curiosity, I glance over my shoulder to see the female guest wearing a *Twilight* shirt from the movie. She's in a deep discussion about being on Team Edward with the girl behind the desk, and the bellhop isn't having it. The male guest shakes his head and fiddles with the hotel keycard, patiently waiting for his companion to stop gossiping. I chuckle while walking down the hall and hit the call button for the elevator.

The elevator door slides open, and no one is inside. With this level of grandeur, I half thought there would be someone in here to work the elevator like in the movie *Titanic*.

I hit the top floor button, but nothing happens. That's when I read the sign saying you need to tap your keycard to reach your floor. A flurry of nervous butterflies invades my stomach. How will I explain who I am to Sully at the check-in desk? Maybe I can text him and he will come get me. That wouldn't be embarrassing.

As I argue with myself, a gentleman in a blue blazer steps inside. He flashes me a grin. "Floor?" he asks politely.

"Top floor please..." I say, offering a shy smile.

"Same." He taps his card and hits the button.

I sigh in relief and stare at my shoes to avoid my reflection in the glass walls around me.

It never stops on another floor, which gives it the speed needed to fly to the highest floor as if it's a rollercoaster. The gentleman lets me step out first and he turns left down the hallway, knowing where he's going.

After a few seconds, I follow the signs until I'm standing at Sully's hotel door. Out of nowhere, I'm lightheaded, and my knees buckle. Maybe this wasn't the best idea. There are other things I could do to prove I'm not turning into a sad, boring person instead of meeting a guy in a hotel that I met for five minutes in a venue's back alley.

My hand remains halfway up, ready to knock. I step back, in the middle of chickening out and fleeing to the elevator, when the door swings open.

"Oh, hey!" Sully says, flashing me a grin with two darling dimples and turning my words into mush.

"Are you leaving?" I ask in a voice almost too low to recognize.

"Thought I heard room service, but you're even better." He opens the door wider, inviting me inside his bright, charming hotel suite. The scent of fresh laundry and lavender soap swirls inside my nostrils. He must've taken a shower. Thinking of him wet, standing only in a towel, sends warmth pooling in my belly and causes tingling between my thighs.

Stop thinking about it. Just smile and nod. You can function like a normal woman.

Sully offers his hand, and I place mine in his. He gingerly tugs me inside. There's no worming my way out of this now. I stand tall and pray I don't get tongue-tied when I look into his ocean-blue eyes as I step farther into his room, and the door closes behind me.

Chapter Five

SULLY'S WEARING BLACK SWEATPANTS and a white tee that clings to his broad chest, hinting at the sculpted physique underneath without quite hiding it. I've seen photos of him without a shirt, and it's marvelous. There's a recent cologne ad where his abs glisten and appear hard and perfect like he's a Greek god statue come to life.

I shouldn't be ogling him in the privacy of his hotel room. He's not a piece of meat, but damn, he's so much sexier in this light. Only the two lamps on either side of the bed are on. Their glow is a halo of yellow light. And my mind can't stop wishing he'd peel that damn shirt off.

He pads over to the dresser barefoot and grabs a bottle of whiskey. *Why am I still standing two feet away from the door gaping at him as if I've never seen a handsome man before?* I force my eyes to inspect the small polka-dotted pattern in the carpet and shuffle toward Sully. But it also means I move closer to the bed, and alarms scream inside my head, ringing louder than my pounding heartbeat.

Now I can worry about being this close to a king-sized bed *and* Sully.

"Do you want a drink?" His smooth-as-butter voice snaps me out of my thoughts. He lifts the whiskey bottle. "You drink, right?"

"Yeah...Sure," I say quietly, sitting on the edge of his bed, an overwhelming urge to get up and run pulsing through me.

He pours the amber liquid into two tumblers and grabs them before sitting beside me. The bed dips under his weight and forces me to lean closer to him. His warm thigh touches mine and it sends my heart into overdrive as something flips inside my chest. Suddenly I'm transformed into a shy high school girl when her crush asks her to prom and she's nothing but nervous smiles and millions of butterflies in her stomach. I'm giddy and scared out of my skull. What a silly feeling this is. My palms are clammy and I keep wiping them on my pants in the hopes he won't notice.

"Are you okay, *Schatz?*" he asks in his deep, seductive accent. The word hits me like a jolt—*Schatz*, the German term for "sweetheart," something I remember from high school classes—and my already racing heart stumbles. Is he trying to drive me insane?

"Mmm-hmm," I answer, not trusting my voice. He offers me a glass. I accept it, taking a swig.

Please let my liquid courage be swift so I don't have an anxiety attack.

Truth be told I haven't been this close to a man since my ex. He'd be romantic one night and cold as a dead fish the next. I never knew what mood he'd be in or if it was me. If I was sexy enough. But before I could figure it out, "the incident" happened, and he left me alone to gather the pieces of my shattered ego.

Sully sips his drink and then rests the glass on his knee. "You don't seem okay. Are you—"

"Nervous?" I say in a rush, running the tip of my finger over my glass's rim. "No...Yes...I'm sorry."

He stands and leans against the dresser. "I don't want to scare you. What can I do?"

"Not sure." I twirl the liquor in my glass. "I broke up with my boyfriend a few weeks ago. It was messy and it's been hanging over me since."

"Understood. Relationships know how to fuck us up, don't they?" He makes a deep raspy sound like a sorrowful laugh. "The pain helps me write songs. How do you use the pain?"

"I toss myself into work to avoid how it makes me feel."

Why do I feel like I can be honest with him? It's as if his gaze sees straight through me, unraveling something deep inside, and before I know it, the words spill out.

"We can talk if you want or watch something. The remote's somewhere." He moves a pile of folded shirts and looks underneath them then starts opening drawers.

"You don't need to find it. I could—"

A knock on the door keeps me from rambling on. "Hold that thought," Sully says, rushing away to open the door.

Chills bite into my flesh. I ache to be close—feel his warmth beside me, his pulse beneath my fingertips, and the softness of his cupid's bow lips on mine. But the fear of rejection and abandonment wraps around me like chains, holding me back, keeping me trapped in this cage of doubt.

Sully greets a man wearing a hotel uniform and allows him to enter the room. He's pushing a cart with an ice bucket holding a bottle of champagne and something covered by a silver lid.

"Thank you," Sully tells the room service man, handing him a tip. The man nods and leaves without looking in my direction.

"Maybe I should go and let you eat." I hop off the bed and set my glass on the dresser. "It's late and I—"

Sully pulls the lid off, revealing a bowl of fresh strawberries, and my next words die on my lips.

He lifts a fat strawberry between his pointer finger and thumb, inspects it, and sets it back down. "I saw this in a movie once and thought it would be nice to order in real life." He laughs at himself, replacing the lid. "But maybe it's not as—"

"Romantic?" I chuckle, tugging on my earring. "I always wanted to feel like I was in a rom-com. Just for one night."

"Will you please stay, *Engel*?" He grabs the flutes by the champagne bucket and offers me one.

I want to, but I should leave before putting my foot in my mouth, and he forever remembers me as the strange fan in LA who was too on edge to hang out in his fancy hotel room.

But he keeps calling me such lovely words in German. I want to hear him say my name over and over in his accent.

My hand shoots forward, deciding for me. "Yes. I'll stay." I nod toward the cart. "You can't eat all those strawberries by yourself. You'll get a stomach ache."

A stomach ache? Really? I sound like his damn mother. He's going to throw me out. I should toss myself off the balcony for that line.

He chuckles and sits on the bed. "I'd like to get to know you better."

The tips of my ears burn. "There's not much to know about me."

"A beautiful woman like you? I'm sure you have stories." He motions toward the chair near the desk, offering me another place to sit.

33

If I take the chair, that's it. All the heat will fizzle out and I'll spend the night with a hot rock star talking like I'm interviewing him for a blog. Or I could swallow my fears and forget my past discretions. Why should I be haunted by "the incident" when my ex isn't? He's who ruined everything, not me.

"What else can we do besides talk?" I sip my champagne and sit beside him on the side of the bed. His arm gently slides around my waist. Gravity tips me closer to his chest, and suddenly I'm engulfed by his delectable essence of mint and aftershave.

I'm never washing these clothes again. Maybe I could find a way to bottle his scent.

His eyes sparkle in the dim light cast by the lamps. "Veronica, there are so many things I...er...*we* could do." His words rumble in his chest. He caresses my cheek and touches my amethyst stud earring, admiring it.

Between my thighs buzzes. I want his hands to caress me everywhere. I want his mouth on me, tasting me...

His fingers trace my jawbone and his thumb gently tugs on my bottom lip. "But I'm following your lead."

My lead? No man has ever cared about what I wanted. Just as long as he was satisfied, that's all that mattered.

Releasing a shaky breath, I finish the rest of my drink. "I'm not sure what I'm doing..." I admit, pressing a hand to my face, hiding my scarlet cheeks. "I'm not a groupie or anything. I just—"

"Let's go slow and tell me when to stop, *Schatz*." There's that word again, making my heart flip-flop.

Sully stands and pulls the cart with the bowl of strawberries and champagne closer to us. I can't help but notice how his shirt clings to the muscles of his biceps and chest, and the proximity of him makes a tight, nervous flutter stir deep in my belly.

He picks up a strawberry and lifts it in the air, hitting the strawberry I grabbed with his. "*Prost!*"

"Cheers," I reply, biting into the sweet fruit.

My breath catches in my throat as Sully bites into the strawberry and red juice drips down his chin.

Without hesitating, I wipe it from his mouth before it falls onto the snow-white sheets.

"Sorry," I mumble, curling my fingers into my palm and wishing I could bury my head into the mattress and hide.

His steely blue eyes wash over me as a smile tugs on his lips. "Don't be."

We sip our drinks and eat a couple more strawberries in silence.

When I finish my drink, I reach for the bottle, but Sully beats me to it. He fills my glass, but his eyes never leave mine.

The bubbles must be going straight to my head because why would he be this interested in someone like me? What do I have to offer? What's so special about me compared to all the other girls standing in the front row screaming while he played on stage? To all those fans who stood hours behind the venue for a chance to meet him.

Sully gathers another strawberry and offers to feed it to me. I'm about to protest, but he places the tip of the fruit on my lower lip, gently pushing it forward. My mouth opens, and I bite into it as juice runs down my throat. He leans closer, kissing my neck and licking the strawberry juice from my skin.

How am I not a melted puddle on the floor yet? The way his eyes watch me is like he can't get enough. His tongue on my skin is like warm honey. It's intense and so damn hot.

A moan claws its way out of my chest. It sounds nothing like me. Almost primal.

His nose traces my jawline until his lips meet mine. *Holy shit.* I'm struck by lightning. My hands dive into his thick black mane of hair and gently tug. Our glasses smash into each other and he sweeps them onto the floor.

My body isn't under my control; it moves by strings, and Sully is the puppet master.

I'd do anything if he whispered Schatz into my ear right now.

Chapter Six

Sully's hands cup my face. His ocean eyes are full of fervor. It's like being trapped in a dreamscape and I never want to escape. I nip at his lower lip while tugging on the bottom of his shirt. He groans and takes the shirt off in one solid motion. My eyes feast upon his perfectly sculpted and tan chest, noting a small patch of hair between his pecs leading to the firm v that dips into his boxers.

His hands slide to my sides, fingers pressing gently into my ribs, pulling me closer. A sharp wince escapes me as pain flares through my body, and I can't hold back a hiss. He immediately freezes, his gaze searching my face, concern clouding his eyes. "What's wrong, *Engel*?"

"You touched a fresh bruise." I run my hands over my arms. "At the concert, people kept pushing me into the metal railing. I'm bruised all over."

"That's horrible." He kisses my arm tenderly. "Wherever you hurt, I'll kiss." Goosebumps rise on my skin as his lips pepper my throat and shoulders with gentle kisses.

We roll over. I'm sitting on top of him with my legs resting against his sides as I toss my shirt carelessly. It collides with a lamp and I barely register the noise the lamp makes as it crashes against the wall. He rubs his cheek against mine and his scruff tickles. His fingers sink into my lower back as his thumbs find the perfect place on my hips as if they always belonged there, holding me firmly against his broad chest.

There's a loud thud outside the door like something heavy fell. I jump at the sound. Sully tightens his large hands around my waist, pulling me back under his spell. "You're safe. I promise, *Schatz.*"

His hips move a little and I'm acutely aware of how few clothes are between us. My thigh can feel how big he is. How much he wants me.

His hand wraps around my long hair as he pulls my head down to kiss my lips. It's out of hunger, a desperate need to taste each other. To devour. Our tongues tangle. He tastes like champagne and strawberries.

For a fraction of a second, we pause to catch our breath. My eyes lock with his, dark with desire. Our chests rise and fall rapidly, the air thick with tension. His nose brushes against my cheekbone as he whispers, "Can I be inside you?" His words send chills rushing down my spine, melting my heart into jelly.

My body falls onto the mattress. All thought of the pain from my bruises gone. I shimmy my butt to sit up more onto the pillows. Sully hovers over me, his knee nudges my legs to open wider, while his hands are planted on either side of my chest. His mouth is only an inch away from mine as he awaits my answer.

"Yes," I purr, licking my bee-stung lips. I'm hungry for more of his touch; I need to feel every inch of his body against mine.

A wolfish groan rips from his mouth as his fingers touch under my chin, lifting it up gently to drop a quick kiss before his mouth travels down, kissing each freckle on my right arm leading to my collarbone until finally his lips meet the top of my cleavage. Long, calloused fingers trace the hem of my lacy bra toward the back clasp. Each unhook makes my breath hitch and my nipples throb. My back arches as my hips rub against his. I don't think I have ever been this excited before, this wet.

My bra swiftly disappears, and his eyes lock on my breasts. He teases my left nipple between his fingers, the rosy bud peaks tightly. His other hand works my right nipple, until they are both hard pebbles, pulsing for more attention. I choke back a moan. Dark blue eyes cut into me. This man knows what he's doing. He's slowly unraveling me, and he loves it. The desire in his eyes tells me he wants to devour me.

Our lips crash together as his hands unzip my jeans and roughly tug them down my thighs. I kick the pants off and shove them to the floor with my foot.

"Another bruise." He kisses my thigh as his thumb gently circles the skin beside the delicate spot. "What pain you went through just so I could see you." He kisses my right breast as his fingers twist my left nipple a little harder, sending a jolt of electricity straight to my clit. Every nerve is on fire. I need him. "Thank you," he says, moving to lick the nipple he's been toying with. Until it's raw and throbbing.

"For what?" I gasp, heat swirling through me, deep and consuming, making me ache with anticipation.

Sully hooks his fingers in my soaked panties and teasingly drags them over my hips. I eagerly wiggle them down my legs and kick them to the side.

He grabs my ass and pulls me down the bed, nibbling at my thighs as he pushes them farther apart. Then he locks his gaze with mine. "For being at the foot of the stage so I could see your gorgeous smile. For being at the back of the venue so I could touch your delicious skin. For being here..."

His fingers rub circles over my swollen and aching clit. He smirks while moving his fingers around my opening. "You're already so wet." He uses his thumb to make the circles faster and harder. My hips buck in response. His fingers between my legs are enough for my clit to throb harder than I have ever experienced before. I can feel my orgasm building, teasing me, as my vision blurs around the edges. I bite the back of my hand to keep my moan at bay and brush a hand over my aching breast.

"We have all night." He smiles, and his dimple is almost my undoing as he dips two fingers inside me, stretching me as he continues to stroke my clit. I let out a soft groan as his hard cock twitches against my thigh. Between my legs aches to have him inside me.

My legs lock around his neck as his tongue replaces his fingers, swirling around my clit and making me see stars. When his tongue enters me, I moan and bite my lip. I'm so close to heaven, but as soon as I reach it, he stops. He's gradually killing me with every touch.

Sully moves his head to watch me with hooded eyes as he sinks three fingers into me. As they move in and out, I feel the most stretched I've been in years and it's about to tip me over the edge.

"Not fair," I mumble, forcing myself to sit up using my elbows. I reach forward and stroke him through his boxers. He's hard and bigger than before.

He chuckles and slowly slips his fingers out of me. He teasingly licks the juices off them. It makes me want to kiss him. He rips his boxers off and releases his huge dick. It spills into my outstretched hand. Concern tugs at my stomach seeing how big he is. Will he even fit?

I force the thoughts away as I caress the head of his cock. It already has pre-cum coating it. He grunts as my fingers work his shaft, tracing a thick vein with my thumb.

"*Schatz*, you're going to make me come if you keep that up." His accent is thicker when he's on edge. Desire darkens his eyes, and I can't help but pump him. I want to see him lose control like I did. He growls, grabbing me by the waist, and gently pushes me onto my back. He places a knee between my legs, towering over me, and exposes my core.

"The first time I come will be inside you," he says. He licks my breast; my nipple is painfully hard. He wants to drive me wild with need as his hands remain at my sides. He sinks his teeth into my other nipple before moving toward my collarbone. All my nerves are on the verge of exploding.

I lean my head back, giving him access to suck on my neck. With my left hand, I stroke his dick and eagerly guide it toward my entrance.

"Wait," he says, taking my wrist and stopping me. We lock eyes. He grabs a condom from the nightstand drawer.

"Oops..." I mumble, embarrassed. How could I be so careless? This man is making me reckless.

I can't take my eyes off his dick as he slides on the condom. Everything inside me crackles with electricity and anticipation.

The room sways around me, thick with heat and tension. His lips claim mine, and then he enters me with an intensity that steals my breath. I shift a little to make room for him, feeling the pressure as he presses against my thighs, widening me just enough. For a moment, it's a sharp discomfort, but then he slips fully inside me in one smooth motion. He slides into place, like I was made for him, only him. The overwhelming feeling of fullness intoxicates me, leaving me dizzy with desire.

His hips start rocking, going deeper and deeper. He fills me up, all the way to the hilt.

"You're perfect, *Schatz*," he moans, licking at my nipple as his fingers twist the other.

My fingernails dig into his back as he quickens his pace, pushing deeper and faster. My orgasm builds, pleasure flooding my veins in warm, liquid waves. I gasp his name over and over, like a desperate prayer.

I love this. Us. It's perfect. It's mind-fucking amazing!

Colors flash behind my closed eyelids as I fly high. A blur of watercolor, of bliss, unimagined. Never before experienced. My body shudders as my breaths turn into heaves. My heart races, trying to break free of my chest.

Sully makes a deep, tortured noise as he continues to thrust, faster and harder, like a man out of control. His body shakes violently as he comes, spilling inside the condom. I feel the rush of warmth inside me. He groans and bites my collarbone, but I feel no pain as I'm still riding out my orgasm.

He throws the used condom into a little trash can beside the bed before he collapses next to me, his arms wrapped around my naked body.

The room smells of sex, mint, and him. For a moment, the only sounds are my thundering heart and our sharp breaths in a quiet space.

The things we could do in this room. I never want to leave.

Sully smiles, tracing his thumb along my jawbone. He holds me close, and all I can think is this must be a dream because it's too perfect to be real.

Chapter Seven

THE SUNSHINE STINGS MY eyes and stirs me awake. I roll over, pulling the blanket to cover my head. It's silk and too high a thread count to belong to me. I freeze as confusion swirls in my dazed brain. "Hmm." An electrified zap races along my spine, forcing me to bolt up and look around. I'm in a king-sized bed with snow-white sheets.

"That wasn't just a wet dream?" I drop the blanket and glance at my naked body.

Not a dream! Holy crap!

My hand touches his side of the bed. It's cold. The bed is giant with only me in it.

Where did he go? Did he ditch me? Did he hope housekeeping would shoo me away?

The bathroom door opens as if to answer my questions. Sully steps out of a cloud of steam with an ivory towel tied around his delicious waist. "You sleep okay?" he asks, drying his hair with another towel.

"Yeah. You?" The sight of his rippling muscles and water droplets sliding between his pecs and down the firm planes of his chest turn my brain to goo.

He chuckles. "No complaints." He grabs a pair of boxers and returns to the bathroom.

I place my feet on the carpet, and my big toe touches my phone. After wiping sleep from my eyes, I bend forward to pick it up. The light flashes, and I type in my passcode to see over a dozen unread texts and a few missed calls from Alice. She probably came home to an empty apartment and assumed I was murdered since I'm not the type of girl who's spontaneous, let alone has a one-night stand with a rock star.

Sully steps out with a toothbrush in hand. "You hungry? We can order breakfast."

My stomach rumbles at the mention of food, but I motion to my phone. "I need to call my friend first. She probably thinks someone kidnapped me and is calling the police to report me missing."

He raises an eyebrow but doesn't say a word, just nods as he returns to the bathroom.

I inhale a deep breath, preparing for Alice to yell my ear off, and tap on her contact. She picks up on the third ring.

"My God, Veronica! Where the hell are you? I came home hours ago. I thought you went on a walk, but then—"

"Calm down. I'm good. I...umm...kind of hooked up with someone," I whisper, hoping Sully isn't eavesdropping.

"Are you kidding?" she shouts then clears her throat. "Who is this mystery person?" Her voice drips with curiosity, but I can tell she wants to wring my neck for not telling her sooner.

"Now isn't the time. But I'll be home later, okay?" I bite my lip, eyeing the bathroom. His shadow moves along the door.

"You can't leave me hanging. Who are—"

Sully exits the bathroom and pads over to dig through a suitcase lying below the window. "Do you want to go downstairs and eat at the little café or do you want to order room service?"

Saliva pools in my mouth watching him move. Knowing he kissed me. That he was inside me just hours ago. I need to keep it together.

As Alice rattles on about being worried, I pull the phone away from my ear and cover the mouthpiece with my hand. "The café sounds wonderful. I'll meet you down there." I gesture to the blanket I'm hugging to my chest.

"Perfect. See you there, *Schatz*." He pulls on a clean blue shirt and steps into a pair of shoes, before exiting the room.

I sigh in relief, falling back against the pillows then remember Alice is still on the line. "Hey, sorry..." She isn't there anymore. My phone's screen is black. Shit. It died. I hunt around the room for a charger and luckily Sully uses the same kind. I plug in my phone and quickly get dressed. If only I brought something else to wear. I feel a little slutty walking to breakfast in what I wore last night.

I make a mental note to call Alice back later. She'll want me to spill details, but I'm not ready to burst this bubble quite yet. And it's weird, but I feel lonely. Sully's been gone five minutes, and I already miss him. Damnit. This isn't good.

I stop by the bathroom to splash cool water on my face and tame the wildness of my hair. I borrow Sully's brush and try to calm my nerves.

Don't get invested in this. Your heart can't handle another relationship. This is a healthy one-night stand to get this sexual tension out of your system and nothing more. And who's a better rebound than your favorite musician?

Now I can move on and allow the past to rest. Finally, close the door on "the incident" and cast my ex into the far recesses of my mind until I forget his name and his face. Block him from my phone and mind. And one day he'll become just another stranger I walk past on the sidewalk.

✳ ♫♪ 🐚 ♫♪ ✳ ♫♪ 🐚

Fifteen minutes into breakfast, we've already devoured a stack of blueberry pancakes and a couple strips of bacon. We're sitting in the lounge on a brown leather couch watching the roaring fire. If I close my eyes, I can pretend I'm in a Hallmark movie somewhere during Christmas in a cabin in the middle of a snowy small town. Me, a serious businesswoman who is a professional mermaid, and Sully, the kind-hearted and drop-dead gorgeous small inn owner who happens to shred on the bass guitar.

Sully clears his throat and touches my knee, popping my dream world. "In an hour my band and I are leaving for our last show in Las Vegas." He grabs my hand, running his thumb gingerly over my knuckles. This is when he kindly dumps my ass. Says it was fun, and maybe he'll see me again on their next North American tour. But the blow never comes.

His blue eyes sparkle as he offers me a small smile. "This might be crazy, but I want you to come with me."

"What?" It takes my brain a minute to catch up to the fact that he changed the entire script inside my head of him giving me the brush off. He wants to spend more time with me?

"You want me to go to Vegas?" My voice comes out in a squeak, disbelief tangling with excitement. Part of me feels like I'm being punk'd, while the rest of me moves in slow motion, struggling to process if this is real.

"Of course," he says, his accent curling around the words like a slow caress. A shiver runs through me, heat unfurling low in my stomach, spreading like the first sparks of a wildfire.

"Umm..." I choke on my words and stare at him, thinking this is a cruel joke. His face is stone, his eyes dark pools pulling me under.

Would it be so bad to screw him again?

Who am I? This is insane! He might be famous, but he's still someone I just met.

But he continues to stare at me. His eyes blazing into mine. He squeezes my hand as he allows me to process his request.

"You're serious?" I whisper, my stomach flipping as a rush of adrenaline surges through me. My lips part, but the words stick in my throat, caught between shock and the dizzy thrill of possibility.

He nods, brushing his fingers along my inner wrist. Things low in my belly clench. My breasts ache for his touch. This is too overwhelming.

"Come with me. I'll buy you new clothes and whatever else you need. It will only be for the weekend."

Shouldn't this be a one-night-only kind of deal, and he sends me off? A wave and a quick thanks-for-the-memories smile. Isn't that what rock stars do?

Thinking is impossible with my heart pounding so hard it drowns out reason. My tongue feels thick and clumsy, useless as I try to form a response. The coil of tension in my stomach tightens, twisting until it's almost unbearable. I can't seem to catch my breath—has all the air been stolen, or did the fire between us burn it away?

Sully runs the back of his hand against my cheek. I close my eyes, leaning into his touch. I don't want this to end. The ghost of his touch still lingers on my face. My skin misses his kisses, his bites. One night, and I'm already hooked.

He leans in closer, whispering into my ear, "Please come, *Engel*. I don't want to go without you. I'm not a fan of Las Vegas." His fingers tuck a strand of hair behind my ear. I know deep down I'm a goner.

Sully brushes his nose against mine, his lips hovering just out of reach. "We can have dinner, take a walk...maybe more of this..." His fingers glide over the nape of my neck, sending a shiver down my spine. A slow, pulsing heat builds deep inside me, coiling tight and relentless.

"Okay," I say between his feather-light kisses. "I'll come."

What did I agree to? I've lost my mind.

He crushes me in his arms and holds me tight as if I'd vaporize if he didn't keep his hand on me. I inhale his sweet yet spicy scent.

Another concert. More kisses. More of what we did last night in that bed. My body is a little sore, but heat spreads through my veins at the idea of doing it again. Me being his and him being mine. For the weekend. I can do it. For once in my life, I'll be the girl who throws caution to the wind. It appears I'm headed to Vegas.

Chapter Eight

"PLEASE WAIT HERE, AND I'll see what the holdup is." Sully gingerly squeezes my knee and flashes a grin that awakes a flurry of butterflies inside me.

"Okay," I reply as he steps out of the limo and closes the door. The rest of the band stands in a group with their luggage at their feet next to a bright red private jet with a whiskey logo of their tour's sponsor splashed across its side.

My body trembles from head to toe. I can barely hold my phone without dropping it. While waiting, I call Alice to let her know I'm still alive and not to wait up for me. She'll rake my body over the coals in a few days for my disappearing act and not spilling any details about it.

Holy shit, I can't believe this is happening. What am I doing? Never in my life have I jumped the gun and gone on a trip with a stranger. It takes me weeks to plan anything, and I don't even have a change of clothes. This is madness.

The phone ringing in my ear grounds me back to reality. On the fourth ring, she yells, "Where the hell are you? You call, and then you hang up on me! I call back, and your voice mail comes on. Who—"

As she rants, I lean forward, checking to see if Sully is still talking with his band, then settle into the leather seat, running my fingertips over the stitching where Sully was a moment ago. "It's a long story. My phone died earlier. I'm safe." *I think.* "But I'm not coming home this weekend."

"Wait, what?" Alice screams into the phone, forcing me to pull it away to save my eardrum.

After a couple of heartbeats, I say, "I'm with Sully."

"Sully?" She pauses as the name clicks and she sucks in a breath. "Holy shit! You called him? You hooked up with a bass player? I told you he—"

"Yeah. I put myself out there, and it was..." *Thrilling? Mind-blowing?* "Rewarding..."

She snorts. "I bet. In all kinds of ways," she chuckles.

"Alice, please," I say while peeking out the window. Sully and his bandmates greet another guy dressed in black who appears to be the pilot. A nervous breath escapes my lips. My middle finger and thumb run along my eyebrows over and over, trying to help me gain control over my anxiety, but it's not working. My skin crawls as my nerves snap like livewires. My left leg won't stop bouncing, and I'm sweating too much. It's not even hot, but my bra feels like a swamp, the curse of big boobs. I can't be this spastic on the plane with the entire band in small quarters; they'll think Sully picked up a stray from the mental hospital.

The line muffles as Alice shouts, "My roommate isn't dead!" Her voice isn't directed at me. I hear a female voice in the background but can't make out what she replies.

"Who are you talking to?" I ask, trying to keep my voice from cracking.

"Oh, Emily," she laughs. I can picture her waving me off like it's no big deal. "She came over after The Rainbow Pony and since you weren't home..."

I bet she was real worried about me when she noticed I was gone. So much so that she cried on her girlfriend's shoulder. Yeah, right.

"She wants to come to the restaurant and see your show. Being a marine biologist, it's great research and—"

A frown bends my lips. "Is that a mermaid joke?"

She snorts. "Duh! But she really does want to see the restaurant. You were kidding about leaving this weekend, right? Because we're thinking of ordering in. Do you—"

"Actually...I'm at an airport right now," I say, twirling a piece of hair around my fingers until my heartbeat pulses in my fingertips. "We're going on a quick trip to Vegas." I glance out the window, watching Sully laughing with his band as the rest of their gear is loaded. He steps back, motioning to the limo. He's going to walk over here and open the door any second now.

She chokes and coughs. "What? Seriously? With Sully? You don't have anything packed. I checked your room earlier and—"

"Yes. I know..." I drag a hand down the side of my face. "But...umm...I have that handled." I hope anyway because I need fresh underwear and a new outfit. A toothbrush wouldn't hurt either.

"Okay. You're being cryptic as hell." She pauses and then gasps. "Emily thinks you're being held against your will. Say a kind of cookie if that's true."

"Please tell Emily I appreciate the concern but I'm okay. Here of my own free will. If I wasn't, would he let me call you?"

I hold the phone away as they squeal like a couple of gulls.

"Your hookup was that good? Damn, girl," Alice laughs. "But why Vegas?"

"That's where their last show is."

"My BFF and roomie is a glorified groupie now!" I hear her high-fiving Emily and roll my eyes, swallowing my reply.

The term "groupie" digs under my skin, I hate that term, but that is what I'm doing. Having sex with a musician the same night you meet them and then flying off to see their next gig. God, how did I get myself tangled in this web?

A different voice takes over. Alice must've put me on speaker. "Girl, you rock! I met bands before, but you've gone beyond the veil. Tell us what it's like when you come back," Emily says excitedly.

Sully knocks on the limo's back window, scaring the crap out of me. I open the door and step out, placing a mask of maturity over my fear. Hopefully, the band will see me as more than a fuck buddy or a devoted fan bordering on stalker.

"Gotta go. I'll call later."

"Take your time! I'll get Chloe to cover your next shift."

Shit. I spaced about working tomorrow.

"Thanks. I didn't—"

"Enjoy your *Almost Famous* movie moment!" Emily says.

Alice clicks her tongue and adds, "Be safe but have fun. Remember what happens in Vegas stays in Vegas." They laugh then the line clicks dead.

I shove my phone into my purse and give a small wave to the band as we walk up to join their little group.

Sully hooks his arm through mine. "Do you remember Veronica?"

Charlotte tilts her head, studying me. "You were one of the fans we met after the show last night."

"Yes," I say, swallowing my pounding heart. Hopefully, they can't hear its thundering beat.

"The more the merrier!" Lars shouts in his thick Irish accent, smacking Sully on the back. Sully winces but smiles at his bandmate.

Ben kisses Charlotte's cheek, holding her close to his chest. "Just in time, we're ready to board." He motions toward the plane's stairs. "Ladies first." Charlotte pinches his ass before grabbing my arm and pulling me up the stairs.

She places me beside her like I'm her favorite doll. "I love your hair color," she says, admiring a strand of my hair in the sunlight.

"Thanks." I fight the urge to hide behind a curtain of hair.

How many people board a plane with their favorite band? This is my chance to ask them anything. To get to know them on a level no one else does, not even those who interview bands for a living. My excitement lessens my anxiety a little.

"Do you usually take jets? Isn't that—"

"Expensive?" Charlotte answers, nodding. "Extremely, but our sponsor came through since the man who owns this plane happens to be wrapping up his holiday in Las Vegas." She gestures toward the white leather seats and the bar. "It's lovely in here compared to our cramped tour bus. We've been on that bus for a little over two months driving across your beautiful country, taking in the sights and tasting interesting food."

"You Americans like everything fried," Ben interjects, snorting, sitting across from us. He kicks his legs onto the couch, lies down, and places an arm over his eyes.

Charlotte shushes her husband. "Don't interrupt." She stretches her legs, kicking off her heels. "Anyway, we had two interviews this morning. One for a rock magazine and another for a radio station." She leans forward, shooting daggers at Sully, who drinks greedily from a water bottle and looks at the carpet with too much interest. "But Sully didn't bother to show up for either interview."

Sully shrugs and sits next to Lars, who ignores everyone as he hunches over and scrolls through his phone. "I texted I couldn't make it." His voice rumbles and heat creeps up my neck when his eyes lock on me.

I sink a little deeper into my seat. I'm the reason he ditched those interviews.

"Dude, say it, don't spit it on me," Lars halfheartedly laughs, wiping his arm and glaring at Sully.

Ben sits up and throws a shoe at Lars's leg, hitting his knee. "That's not how you say that."

"Hey! That hurt!" Ben shouts, throwing the shoe back at Lars, who blocks the flying object with his arms covering his head.

Sully smirks at me before turning his attention to Charlotte. "You've always handled the interviews brilliantly. I never talk anyway."

"Yes, but someone might've noticed you were missing. Rumors start as a whisper but can unfold into a nightmare if you're not careful. You're lucky Amy's in New York visiting her daughter and Mark's already in Vegas. Do you want them breathing down your neck again? You know they hate it when anything takes the focus off our music."

Sully shrugs, not caring about those people. I look between them confused.

Charlotte pats my arm. My expression must give away how lost I am. "Amy is our PR rep, and Mark's our tour manager. They're not fans of

Sully's habit of slacking off or disappearing." She narrows her eyes at him. But he leans back in his seat, unbothered, with his hands tucked behind his head.

"Don't know why they always care what I'm doing. It's not like I'm destroying hotel rooms or passing out in clubs."

"But your cold attitude gives our band a bad rap. Fans talk and—"

"I don't care about their opinions and neither should you." He rubs the back of his neck like he's had this fight before. "My private life is just that...private."

Charlotte wrinkles her nose like something smells foul but drops the subject. She grumbles something in German and drums her slender fingers on her thigh. She tsks and grabs my hand, inspecting my fingernails. They're not polished and a couple of the tips are chipped, and based on her frown, she's upset about my lack of self-care. "We're getting manicures before soundcheck."

"Okay." I glance at her hand, and her nails are perfectly polished a fiery red. I'm not going to argue.

I glance nervously at Sully. He smirks. "Looks like you're part of the family now."

Chapter Nine

THE LAS VEGAS STRIP below us is like seeing the world on a single street. Sully sits next to me with his hand pressing into my thigh. I'm too aware of him. But I ignore the pings between my thighs. I'm not the type of girl who publicly makes out with a guy, let alone does anything more than PG-13 with other people on the plane.

Sully envelops my hand in his as the limo speeds down the freeway toward our hotel. He taps on Charlotte's foot with his to gain her attention. She lifts her head from Ben's shoulder, watching us curiously.

"Can you do me a favor?" Sully sets our entangled hands on his thigh. I try not to focus on how perfectly our fingers lock together.

Charlotte puckers her lips, spinning her wedding ring around her finger. "Depends on what it is."

"Could you please take Veronica shopping? We didn't have time to stop by her place for her to pack anything."

I chew on my inner cheek, avoiding Charlotte's searching gaze. Does she think I'm trashy for jumping on a plane without a change of clothes? She probably already hates me.

Charlotte surprises me by leaning forward and slapping Sully's leg. "Shame on you for dragging this poor girl all the way here without necessities. You're lucky we already planned on getting manicures, so stopping by a few shops won't be a bother." Her tone is clipped, but there's a smile playing on her lips. I think she's toying with him.

He nods. "Thanks."

Charlotte took me to her favorite shops to buy some jeans, a cute concert dress, shoes, and underwear. She insisted on me getting this fire-red bra that she claimed made me look like a sex goddess. I also bought a few Vegas shirts, one being extra baggy and long so I can wear it to bed. We then stopped by a Walgreens for everything else essential.

She follows me into the hotel suite so I can drop off my new things. Sully's in the room, strumming his guitar. He flinches when Charlotte barrels her way in, ditching the bags on the king-sized bed, and grabs my arm to tow me away again.

"You'll have all night with him. Right now you're mine," she says.

Sully mouths, "sorry," and smiles.

All I can do is go along with her or be dragged.

We settle into comfy white chairs at the nail salon. While our nails are being filed, clipped, and polished, Charlotte gives me this cold hard look and says, "Should I be worried about you and Sully?"

The nail tech glances at me and then grimaces before moving on to another finger. The things these people probably hear.

"I'm not sure what you're referring to. I just met him."

"This is so out of character for him..." She glances at her wedding ring, lost in thought.

Confusion wrinkles my forehead. "Taking a girl to Vegas?"

She blows a curling piece of hair out of her face. "Talking to you in general. He's taken a shine to you. He's usually so—"

"Cold?" I offer.

Charlotte puckers her lips. "I don't like that word, but something like that. He doesn't like interviews or meeting fans. He's an introvert and it's hard for him to date. Especially after that last girl. She was...well..." She sniffs and shakes her head. "He should probably tell you about that. I just don't want him to get hurt." She offers me a kind smile. "For either of you to get hurt. No offense but, you don't seem like the type to—"

"Just fly to Vegas with someone I met not twenty-four hours ago?" I close my eyes. "Hard for me to believe he talked me into coming on this trip. But something about him made me say yes."

"He's good at that. It's his eyes. Ben thinks Sully can compel people with a stare, but my husband also thinks our house in Germany is haunted, so it's hard to believe him."

Charlotte's nail tech finishes her left hand and moves to her right. "Just promise me you're not using him. It's bad enough our PR rep tries to push him into situations he doesn't want to be in; my heart can't stand seeing Sully go through the heartbreak all over again and—"

"You're a good friend. I've been hurt recently too and I don't want to harm Sully. But I..." This is only a weekend fling, isn't it? Why does she make it seem like something more? A whirlwind romance in some cheesy movie. No. Sully and I are using each other to help move on from past traumas and find something better in the future.

Charlotte grabs my arm with her left hand and squeezes until I wince in pain. Her happy demeanor vanishes and her rich chocolatey brown eyes turn coppery and murderous as she leans in closer. "Don't make me regret liking you," she says between clenched teeth.

Words fail me. What the hell? I grasp for a response, but nothing comes. Before I can recover, she plasters on a bright smile. "I think we're going to be great friends." Then, as if the conversation never happened, she leans back in her chair, sighs, and closes her eyes.

The nail techs exchange glances and whisper something in a language I don't understand. But I'm pretty sure they think I'm screwed.

✳ 🎵 🐚 🎵 ✳ 🎵 🐚

When Charlotte takes me back to the hotel room, she hugs me goodbye and wanders off to her room. My entire body's exhausted between the travel, shopping, and that intense talk with Charlotte. The band hasn't even left for the club to set up or do their soundcheck.

My legs wobble as I walk toward the bed. A shoe box trips me and I fly forward.

"Whoa," Sully chuckles, grabbing my arm and saving me from face-planting into the glass coffee table. "You okay?"

"Yes," I mumble. Thank God he doesn't know what my day job is—I can already hear the jokes. *Still gaining your land legs? You'd think you were a mermaid. Do you swim better than you walk?* Five years of this, and I've heard them all. I can laugh them off, pretend they don't bother me, but deep down, each one lands like a tiny weight in my chest, pressing heavier over time.

"Charlotte tried to kill me." I'm only half-kidding. I lie back on the California king bed with my arms out to my sides and allow myself to sink into the ivory-colored comforter and stare at the powder-blue ceiling.

"I'm heading over to the club to help set up. I'll be back in a couple of hours. We can grab a quick bite before the final soundcheck."

I kick off my shoes and roll onto my side. "Okay, that gives me time for a shower." But first, I'll lie here until the bed and I become one or until my feet stop pounding, whichever comes first.

He sits beside me. The bed dips under his weight, and I tighten my ab muscles to keep from rolling into him. I sit up, using my elbows, and meet his gaze. His eyes darken as they sweep over me. "You're going to shower without me?" His voice drops into a rough husky tone. "Wouldn't it be better if I helped?"

His words reverberate in my chest and cause my clit to buzz. It's strange—I've never felt this kind of craving for sex before, this raw, urgent desire. It's almost painful to look at him, to want him so badly, and yet to be unable to reach for him, taste his lips, feel him inside me. Without warning, my body responds—an undeniable pulse of longing. I meet his gaze, and my eyes drop to the bulge in his pants, the tension between us thickening. He feels it too.

I've only been with two other guys, but with Sully, everything is different. It's new, exciting, like stepping into a world I never knew existed, one that makes everything before feel small in comparison.

"Go to the club and set up your guitars or whatever you sexy bass players do." I playfully push him toward the door. "Maybe we can shower later tonight."

He gives me a wolfish grin. "You can count on that."

As he slips out the door, I press my hand to my chest, trying to hold back the frantic pulse in my veins, the urge to run after him, to follow him anywhere.

At least Alice can't say I never come out of my shell anymore. I'd say this mermaid has gotten herself lost in deep uncharted waters.

As a teen, I always wondered what it would be like to be a roadie, following a band from city to city. I thought it would be fun and you'd meet all kinds of cool and interesting people. But after tonight, I'm thankful for never becoming a roadie.

They do so much heavy lifting, not to mention hours and hours of work before anyone lines up outside the venue. They test the lights, the sound, and check technical things I don't understand. And wires snake along the ground everywhere. I stand next to the sound booth guy and the number of buttons he keeps track of makes me dizzy.

While Scarlet Failure and the other band, Haunted Dreams, do their soundchecks, I walk around the club, getting a feel of the place before it's filled with screaming fans. This is the last show of their tour so naturally, it's sold out. I can hear the fans buzzing outside while I check out the merch table without anyone pushing or shoving me.

Something hums inside me remembering how yesterday I was on the outside, standing in line before the doors opened to be one of the first inside and stand right in front of the stage. My only goal was to catch a guitar pick and maybe land a setlist. Not only did those wishes come true, but I also nailed the bass player.

Goosebumps break out on my arms, the kind of exhilaration that feels almost otherworldly, like I'm floating, weightless in the moment. I tug on the lanyard of my backstage pass hanging around my neck, the thrill of it all sinking in. This is definitely going on my wall in my room when I get back, right next to Scarlet Failure's signed setlist and guitar pick. Maybe I'll even frame it in a shadowbox to make it extra special.

When the doors open, I hideout backstage and feel the anticipation whirling in the air, becoming more alive as each minute ticks by. I watch the show from the side stage. Even though they play the same setlist as last night, I still rock out but try not to draw too much attention from those working the stage or security.

Girls scream at Sully as he rips into his solo. He throws them picks and they dive for them like they're gold coins.

It's insane how last night I was one of those girls, and now I'm watching them from afar like I belong to Sully somehow.

A girl in the front looks around frantically and frowns. She must not have found a pick. Sully notices and nudges Lars, nodding to the girl. Lars struts over and points at the girl. She locks eyes on him and jumps eagerly up and down with her hand outstretched. He flicks a black guitar pick her way, and she catches it, smiling ear to ear.

Sully turns around, and when our eyes meet, he winks. My chest heaves like it did last night when he handed me my pick. I hope this feeling never stops. The way he looks at me makes me feel like I'm the only woman alive.

Chapter Ten

It's hard to think as blood whooshes in my ears when Sully walks off stage and kisses my lips. He's sweaty from playing under all these hot lights, but I want to kiss him on stage until all those fangirls cry.

Charlotte ties her long hair into a ponytail and takes a drink from her water bottle. She touches my upper arm and smiles. "You like the show the second time around?"

"Yes." I fiddle with the backstage pass around my neck. "I loved seeing all the behind-the-scenes stuff, and of course, your band was amazing."

A smile plays on her lips. "Maybe better than last night?" she says, her laugh gentle and low, a warm sound that lingers in the air. Ben walks over, wiping his face with a white towel. He grabs Charlotte's ass and kisses her. She lets out a soft giggle, and together, they disappear into the room reserved for artists backstage.

Lars walks over biting an apple. "Is backstage everything you thought it would be?"

"There's more tripping hazards than I thought," I joke, motioning to all the wires being coiled up by the stagehands.

"We're about to leave in twenty minutes. I'm sure you and Sully will find something to do," Lars chuckles and takes another bite from his apple.

The members of Haunted Dreams come by saying their goodbyes and walk out into the night air. I can hear fans outside waiting; they're talking excitedly.

Sully tugs on the neckline of his new clean blue shirt. "Ready? We can grab dinner unless you'd rather return to the hotel?" His eyes trail along my body slowly as he takes in every curve.

I hook my arms around his neck and kiss his lips. "We have all night. Let's start with some food and see where it takes us."

Charlotte, Ben, and Lars join us, all wearing fresh clothes and secret smiles.

"Ready to meet the fans?" Charlotte asks, opening the door.

A group of about forty people swarm in like a flash flood.

The members of Scarlet Failure move effortlessly to meet their fans in smaller groups—Charlotte with her warm, practiced smile, greeting everyone like she's known them forever. Ben and Lars jump straight into jokes and selfies, already laughing with fans like they're old friends.

I stand there, frozen for a second, trying to keep up. The noise hits me first—voices, laughter, camera clicks, all layered over one another in a dizzying mess. I don't know where to look or what to do with my hands.

No one's looking at me, and yet I feel completely exposed.

I force a smile, hoping it doesn't look as awkward as it feels. My heart's pounding, and I'm suddenly hyper-aware of everything—my clothes, my posture, the way I'm breathing. This isn't just backstage anymore. This is the other side of the glass, and I'm supposed to belong here.

But right now? I'm not so sure I do.

I look over to Sully. He's reserved, standing still like he's in pain, and told he's not allowed to leave. His eyes meet mine and I wander over.

"I can take the picture," I say to a fan snapping a million selfies with Sully.

"Thanks." She thrusts the phone into my hand and wraps her arm around Sully's waist. He doesn't smile, just stares ahead with his arm extended behind her back, not touching her anywhere.

"Okay," I say, handing the phone back. "Thanks. Have a good night."

I motion to the next fan and become Sully's unofficial photographer/bodyguard, making sure no one stays longer than they need to. Just a quick photo and a signature on one or two things then on to the next fan.

A gentleman wearing black jeans and a pressed red shirt comes out of the venue and motions toward the two black town cars that pulled up. "Alright, everyone. Time for the band to say goodnight. Thanks for coming out."

The man comes over to Sully and nods toward the second car. "Charlotte told me about your guest. Thought you'd want to take her somewhere nice for dinner."

Sully pats the man on the shoulder. "Thanks, Mark. This is Veronica." He smiles at me and turns my insides to goo. "Veronica, this is Mark, the band's tour manager."

"Nice to meet you." He shakes my hand. "With the tour over, I'm going to enjoy myself tonight as well. But don't have too much fun or Amy will give us all hell."

Sully winks. "Just enough trouble."

The car drops us off at the Paris hotel and we ride the elevator up to the top floor where the Eiffel Tower restaurant oversees the Strip. We have an amazing view of all the sparkling lights and the Bellagio fountain.

The food is a little too fancy for my taste, but at least it's edible. I love watching the fountains dance below and seeing the tiny ant people wandering around the streets. When I glance at Sully, he's staring at me, taking a sip of his wine.

"What are you looking at?" I ask, wiping my mouth with a fancy white cloth napkin.

"Just you. You're all I want to look at."

There's a flutter in my stomach as my cheeks warm. "You're being silly." I take the last bite of my lavishly weird salad. "What do you want to do now?"

He taps his finger on his glass. "Whatever you want."

Thirty minutes later, we're on the casino floor. We passed by the slots and went right for the blackjack table. At first, Sully sat beside me, but after one round, he discovered he doesn't know how to play very well.

On my fifth hand, I'm doing good. I've made at least five hundred dollars off my hundred-dollar chips.

Sully stands behind me with his hands resting on my shoulders. "Why are you so great at this?" His lips brush my ear, sending goosebumps all over my body.

"My dad likes playing cards on the weekend. He taught me everything I know."

"Here I thought you were just lucky, *Engel*." His fingers trail over my shoulder blades and press into my lower back. Suddenly this game is the last thing on my mind.

I win the next round and cash out. As we walk to the cashier, Sully's arm wraps around my hips. "Do you want dessert?"

"You read my mind."

We stop by an ice cream shop before walking out onto the Strip. We lick our treat and cross the street to watch the fountains up close.

The water dances to the music perfectly. I sigh dreamily, watching the show. "Last time I was in Vegas I got a fountain view room just so I could sit by the window all night."

He chuckles and kisses the tender spot below my ear. "That's all you did in your room?" His voice is hot, scorching my blood.

I turn around in his arms and brush my nose against his. "It was a work trip. Alice was there too, but she was at the club. I checked in early. But sadly, they do turn the fountains off."

"Bummer." He cups my chin and kisses me deeply. Our tongues tangle, fighting for dominance. The back of my legs hit the little wall as the mist from the water sprays across my skin.

He pauses, watching people wander by. "Do you want a picture?" He nods to the fountain.

"Only if you're in it too." I grab my phone and smush my face into his chest. He smiles, and it makes my knees weak.

"Do you want me to take a photo of you two?" An older gentleman asks.

"Please." I hand over my phone.

He takes a few shots and hands the phone back. "Thanks," I say as the stranger strolls away toward the Bellagio's entrance.

"They have a seasonal garden inside. It's gorgeous."

Sully plants his hands on my hips, pulling me closer. "I'd rather return to the room," he says, his voice low.

The way he looks at me—like I'm the only woman he's ever wanted—makes my breath hitch. His gaze doesn't waver, intense and hungry, as if he's already imagining exactly what he'll do once we're alone.

"I'll call the town car to pick us up." Sully nods and grabs his phone.

As we walk toward the pick-up area, a girl squeals and runs over to us, dragging her friend along. The friend trips on the curb and almost drops her three-foot-long drink. She glares at me like it's my fault.

The strange girl gawks at Sully, touching his upper arm. "You're Sully from Scarlet Failure, right?"

"Unfortunately." His voice is flat and his face turns to stone.

"I love you! Saw your show tonight. It was amazing, of course!" She waves her angry friend closer. "This is the bass player in the band we saw tonight."

Her friend nods, sipping her drink, unfazed by her near fall.

"Can we help you with something?" I dare to ask, crossing my arms over my chest.

The girl frowns, realizing I'm with Sully and not just someone walking by.

"Oh...yeah..." She grabs her phone and shoves it into my chest. "Can you take our picture?" The girl says in a rush. She tries and fails to snake her arm through Sully's. He has his arms pinned to his sides with the meanest look on his face.

"Sure. One photo." I open her camera and snap a single shot.

She's all smiles, beaming like she's just met her idol. But Sully—he's still. His face is tight, jaw clenched, eyes slightly narrowed like he's bracing for something. He doesn't even fake a smile.

He almost looks like he's in pain, like just being there costs him something he doesn't want to explain.

"Bye now." I toss her phone back and she catches it with a wild look in her eyes like she can't believe I did that. I can't either, but she's annoying me.

The girls rush off, whispering to each other. Sully sighs and rests his arm along my shoulders. "Let's go before anyone else comes."

I laugh despite myself. "No wonder people say you're colder than a fish. Your face in that photo was terrible."

"I don't like pictures. Fans are cool, but not when they're all in my face. I like my space."

"What about me?" I kiss his cheek. His scruff scrapes against my lips. What I want that scruff to rub against tonight sends my stomach into cartwheels.

"You're different. When I saw you at the base of the stage, I knew you weren't like the others. It was almost...I don't want to say it. You'll laugh."

"Come on." I bump my hip against his. "Promise I won't."

He glances down at me and caresses my cheek with his thumb. "Magic. Seeing you was like magic."

My heart turns to slush. What the hell is with this man? He's like a romance character fresh out of the pages of a book.

But it won't last. We're from different parts of the world and our jobs don't align. There's that dark voice, ruining my mood again.

Sully takes my hand and points to the black car pulling into the parking lot. "Here's our ride." He wraps an arm around my waist and leads me to our town car. His hot breath lingers on my neck, quickening my pulse and killing any negative thoughts.

✳ 🎵♪ 🐚 🎵♪ ✳ 🎵♪ 🐚

As soon as we're behind the closed door of our hotel room, Sully kisses my lips hungrily and presses himself against me, pinning my back against the wall. "You have no idea how long I've been dying to do this."

He picks me up and I wrap my legs around his waist. I can already feel how swollen he is and it makes everything low in me clench. "Only you can drive me this crazy," he growls in my ear, dropping me onto the bed.

His tongue thrusts into my mouth, desperate to tangle with mine. His kiss is deep and then his hands whisk my shirt over my head. His hungry mouth meets mine again as his fingers unhook my bra and toss it aside. My breasts pulse and ache when he cups them. I feel him smile wickedly against my mouth before his lips trail down to my breasts. He teases my left nipple, pinching the bud until it painfully puckers. He sucks on the other until it's a desperate peak of need. His tongue strokes it in punishment and I moan.

Sully pulls away and my body aches in his absence. "I need to grab a condom—"

I lock my legs around his waist, keeping him pinned. The desire to have Sully buried deep inside me ignites my blood. I can't allow him to leave for a second. "I'm on the pill."

He smirks and his warmth ensnares me again. "Good. I want to feel all of you." He nips at my left breast then the right. "This is all I want," he says, pulling my pants and underwear down over my thighs.

"What about what I want?" I ask, tugging on the collar of his shirt.

Sully rips off his clothes and grasps my bare ass, holding me closer. Our lower bodies instinctively grind together.

My hands glide into his thick hair, and our eyes lock. "You're mine, *Engel*," he breathes, rotating his hips until his shaft bumps against my clit, sending a shock of pleasure sizzling through my veins.

Words escape me as my hands move along his neck and shoulders to explore the hard plains of his chest. I kiss his left pec and nip at it. He groans and hooks a finger under my chin.

As we kiss, he slides into me, slow but deep. I moan against his mouth, and he swallows the sound, his fingers finding my clit and rubbing just right, sending pleasure surging through me.

"I'm close," I gasp.

"*Schatz*," he murmurs, lips trailing down my neck. The way he touches me—his voice, his mouth, his accent—it's too much.

"Fuck..." My vision swims. It's intense, overwhelming. Sully knows exactly how to break me apart.

"Be a good girl and come for me."

His fingers move faster, and my body shudders as everything crashes down. I come hard, clinging to him. A second later, his body jerks, and he spills into me, breathing ragged against my skin.

I lie on his chest as we both catch our breaths. The bed groans underneath us. I think we broke a few of its springs.

When we settle back to Earth, Sully leads me to the shower. I never knew it could be so erotic. As the water rains down from two showerheads, Sully presses me against the wall and forces my legs apart with his hand. His fingers enter me first, rubbing the perfect spot, sending my eyes fluttering closed.

"How sweet do you taste, *Schatz*?"

His hot mouth covers me, and when his tongue replaces his fingers, I moan his name. As his tongue strokes inside me, everything comes loose. I'm putty in his hands. My body trembles, and my hips rock against his mouth, needing more.

Sully chuckles. "You make it hard not to fuck you again."

When he stands at his full height, I grab his dick, rubbing my thumb over its tip. He's already swollen.

"My turn," I say, kneeling in front of him.

I haven't given a guy a blow job in a while. My first boyfriend said I did it wrong, and my last ex didn't like them.

At first, I'm nervous, but as he fills my mouth and I look up to meet his lustful gaze, I feel empowered. My hand gently squeezes his balls as I swallow him deeper. My tongue knows where to stroke, and Sully groans, fisting my hair.

"Shit. I'm going to come and I won't do it in your mouth. Not yet."

His hands hook under my armpits, and within a second, I'm pinned against the wall again. His mouth devours mine as water pours over us. He gingerly shoves himself into me. Our hips rock in rhythm. My heels dig into his lower back, allowing him a better angle. He slides in deeper. I want to stay in this room with Sully forever.

Chapter Eleven

SULLY WALKS ME TO my apartment door after a car picked us up from the airport. "I hate to drop you off and run, but Amy's back in town and wants us in the recording studio. She says we're collaborating with Gigi on a new song, and she's only free today."

I toy with the ends of my hair and swallow the lump lodged in the back of my throat. Of course, he's singing with Gigi, one of the hottest female artists right now.

"Thanks for a great weekend." I dig in my purse for my keys.

Alice throws open the front door with a whoosh. "Look what the cat dragged in," she mocks, eyeing us up and down like she caught us naked.

"I'd like to see you again," he says, handing me my new suitcase.

"Text me." I shove my suitcase into Alice's chest and force her inside. "See you later." I shut the door and lean against it.

Alice huffs, dropping the suitcase on the couch. "You hook up with a rock star, and he buys you a new wardrobe? Damn." She spies through the window shades next to the door. "Why didn't you invite him in?"

"Because..." I motion to our cramped, messy apartment. "We spent the weekend in a hotel room twice this size. I'm not letting him see where I live. Besides, he's on his way to the studio to record a song with Gigi."

"Oh, I love her. Her new 'Candy Heart' song is stuck in my head. I made it Emily's ringtone."

"Yeah. I know. Gigi's amazing and hot and whatever."

She scrunches her nose and follows me into my room as I drag the suitcase behind me. "Sorry. Guess it doesn't make you feel good having him record songs with her. But you don't know what the song is about. Maybe it's an angry song about hate or breaking up."

"He belongs with someone like that. Musicians usually stick together."

Alice sits on the edge of my bed and places her hands on her knees. "Do you see their divorce rate? They hate each other after a year or so."

"Not all of them. But it doesn't matter. He's probably deleting my number as we speak."

Alice tsks as I unzip my suitcase and toss my new clothes into my hamper. "Yeah. Dude who ices everyone out randomly whisks you to Vegas and buys you things is just going to dump you like that." She snaps her fingers. "I may have slight hearing loss from all the clubs and concerts over the years, but I swear he said he wanted to see you again."

I sigh and sink onto the bed. "They're recording right now. But he's not staying in LA. Why do I want to—"

My phone buzzes. I check, and it's Sully. Is fate mocking me? My stomach twists; his text could say so many things.

Alice raises her brows. "Also...for the record? I asked my Tarot cards if you two would see each other again." She gives me a sly smile. "They said yes. Strongly."

Alice laughs, standing and whisking my phone away before I open his message. "Lover boy sent you a text. It doesn't seem you're off his radar yet."

"Don't steal my phone." I snag my phone back and glare at my best friend. "And don't read my texts. You're like the sister I never had."

At times like these, I'm happy my parents never gave me a sibling.

"You're welcome." She bows and settles back onto my bed, resting her head on my stuffed pink cat. "Go on and read it."

I clutch my phone to my chest. "I will, but without you reading over my shoulder." I race to the bathroom and lock the door.

Alice pounds on it. "Not fair!" She sighs and surrenders.

"Finally." I sit on the lip of the tub and read Sully's text.

> *We're staying in LA to record new tracks. Can we meet for dinner one night this week?*

A shriek slips out and I cover my mouth with a hand, hoping it didn't perk Alice's ears. There's no knock, so I think I'm safe.

This is insane. Like a feverish dream, I'll wake up and laugh at how real it all felt. Yet when I pinch myself, I'm still here, staring at Sully's text.

What do I say? I don't want to reply right away and seem too eager. Do I want to see him again? Yes. But it's only dragging out the inevitable. He lives in Germany and my place is here.

I crack open the bathroom door and hear Alice talking on the phone in her bedroom. Tiptoeing into my room, I close the door and collapse on my bed.

My phone buzzes again. Damn, he really wants to see me again.

But when I see who the text is from, my mood sours, and anger spoils the blood in my veins.

> **ASSHOLE: V. I'm in LA for a few days. Can we meet up? I need you.**

Fucking ex thinks he can break my heart and fly to New York after "the incident" and just return a couple of months later, and I'll come crawling back? Ha. I'd rather be eaten by sharks than see his face again.

Being with Sully gives me the burst of self-confidence I need to block my asshole ex. I open my texts with Sully and reply.

> **Let me check my schedule but dinner this week sounds perfect.**

Maybe seeing Sully again is a good thing. It will keep me level-headed. Plus, I could never turn down sex with him. Not ever.

Chapter Twelve

Two DAYS LATER, I see Scarlet Failure tagged in a post on Insta with Gigi. It's a thirty-second teaser from the song they recently recorded. Gigi's wearing headphones, smiling at Sully like she's sharing some private joke with him. The camera pans toward him, but it's too fast—I can't read his expression.

A tight, uncomfortable pressure settles low in my stomach, like everything inside me just clenched at once. I shouldn't care this much, but I do. And it hurts more than I want to admit.

Because I hate myself, I doom-scroll through the comments. Fans gush over the snippet of the song. They're excited and post too many emojis. Some love Sully and Gigi together. They ship them hard.

I move on only to find another post from a media outlet stating Sully and Gigi were spotted having dinner together at a fancy restaurant last night.

Confusion tangles my thoughts as my throat closes. What is this feeling? Jealousy? Shit. One weekend with the guy and I feel like this?

What would they say if I posted my pictures with Sully? With him *actually smiling*. I open my photos and look at the picture of Sully the night I met him and flip to the one of us at the Bellagio fountain. His smile is wider and his arms wrap around my waist like we're an item. We look perfect.

Wow. I need to let this go. I click my phone off when it rings. My mom's name and picture flash on the screen.

Great. This will be fun.

"Hey, Mom," I answer, putting the call on speaker so I can brush my hair.

"Hey, Ronni. How are you?"

"Good. What's up with you?"

"Same old. I planted cucumbers in my garden. Hopefully, your father doesn't kill them. I told him he's not allowed in my garden anymore after he flooded it last summer."

I add some hair product to keep my hair shiny and not frizzy when it gets wet. "How's Bishop?"

"He's a sloppy mess." She laughs. Mom loves that dog maybe more than me. He can do no wrong.

"I'm getting ready for work. Did you call for any reason?" I hate cutting her off, but it takes forever for her to get to the point.

"Oh...well, I emailed you some job listings I thought you'd be perfect for. One is at your Aunt Sally's firm. She can put in a good word for you."

Yeah. The aunt I haven't seen in five years would know so much about me to suggest a desk job. I cross my arms, fingers digging into my side. Do I want to start this fight with her right now? No. I don't.

"Okay. I'll glance at them when I have a moment." I cringe. The word "glance" wasn't the word I should've used.

She sighs heavily like I turned down Harvard for community college. "Veronica, you need to get serious about your life. Your mermaid gig was cute in college, but you graduated four years ago. You can't stay in this forever."

Because I'll get old or be mocked or whatever excuse she's thrown at me over the years. When in truth it's her that's embarrassed by my career choice. I guess having to tell her friends that her only child dresses as a mermaid for a living makes her think I'm an overgrown child. But it makes me happy and pays the bills. Isn't that what life should be?

"I need to go. But I'll see you Saturday."

"Okay, sweetie. Look at those jobs before then and I can help you fix your resume after we go shopping."

"Love you. Bye." I hang up before I say something that can't be taken back. My body feels heavy as I finish my makeup. Talking to her is exhausting, but now I get to go swim around and act like the happiest mermaid anyone's seen. Yay me.

✳ 🎵 🐚 🎵 ✳ 🎵 🐚

A private event, for a weather convention of all things, wrapped up early, so Arthur and I decided to surprise his daughter with a mermaid lesson to celebrate her good grades this quarter.

Sarah flips her sparkly tail in and out of the water, splashing and laughing. "First, we're going to learn to swim with the tail. It's harder to move in the water with your legs pressed together. We'll go slow."

Sarah leaps into the water and I help guide her from one side to the other. "Good. Use your arms and your core." I touch her stomach. "Kick with your legs together. Very good."

She laughs and hangs onto the side, waving at Arthur who is watching on the grass sitting in a lawn chair. "You see me, Dad?"

He nods. "Yes. You're a cute mermaid, baby."

She gets the hang of it and swims from one end to the other in the shallower end of the pool. I prop myself onto the edge and let my tail float in the water. Arthur sits a few feet from me so I lean back on my hands to look at him. "She's having a blast."

"Thanks for doing this. She loves you. Maybe more than she loves us."

"I'm sure that's not true. But she probably thinks I'm cooler." My smile slips, remembering my chat with Mom and how she wants me to give this up. But if she could see how happy Sarah is, she'd change her mind. I bring joy to people and magic to a dull world, but she'll never realize that.

Arthur stands and kicks off his flip-flops to settle beside me and dip his feet into the water. We watch Sarah giggle and swim, adding an impressive twirl as she moves.

Arthur bumps his arm with mine. "What's wrong?"

I lean my head on his shoulder. "My mom. Spoke to her on the phone and she reminded me how much I'm wasting my life." I flick my fins, splashing Sarah. She laughs and hits the water with her hand, sending a wave my way.

"She has the old-school way of thinking. Once your name is out there and you have big sponsors and forget about us at The Pearl Kingdom, she'll know how important you are."

"I'd never forget The Pearl Kingdom, but you..." I giggle as he slaps my scale-covered thigh.

He pushes me into the pool. I go under and flip around to splash him with my tail. When I surface, he's soaked and cracking up laughing, lying on his side.

Sarah watches us from the other side of the pool. "You're weird," she says, swimming toward my inflatable shell in the deep end. She hops on it and floats, looking like a cute little mermaid resting in the sunshine.

I move to the side and place my arms on the cement, resting my cheek on my forearm. "It's not just my mom."

"Sully?" Arthur sits up and wipes the tears of laughter off his face.

I roll my eyes. "Alice told you."

"Hey, don't be mad at her. She showed me pictures."

"How..." I shake my head and drag myself to sit on the edge again. "Of course, she stole my phone and sent the pictures to herself."

"Never take nudes. She'll go postal."

"Right. She would." I nudge Arthur with my shoulder, getting his sleeve wet. "Sully and I had an amazing time in Vegas. Like..." I fan myself and he nods, understanding. Sarah is still in the shell, not caring about our conversation.

"But on Insta he's tagged in Gigi's post and there are reports they had dinner together. What if he's stringing me along as his side piece in LA?"

Arthur takes my hand and squeezes my fingers. "You gotta take a chance on love. I know it hurt you before, but your shitty ex wasn't worth the air you breathe. In the second picture of you two by the fountain in Vegas, he's staring at you, not the camera. I think you need to test the waters and see if he surprises the shrimp out of you."

"Those mermaid puns are terrible." I lightly punch him in the arm.

"They are dad jokes, thank you very much." He gives me this serious look and then howls in laughter.

Arthur's wife, Melissa, comes out of the back door. "Pizza! Any hungry mermaids out here?"

Sarah waves her arms. "Me!" She dashes out of the shell and swims to the edge to meet her mom with pizza on a plate.

"What am I?" Arthur asks, standing and stretching his back.

"My hungry pirate." She walks over and kisses him.

"You want pepperoni, Veronica?" Melissa asks, smiling and batting her husband's arm away as he grabs her ass.

"Please."

Melissa and Arthur walk over to the table where the pizza boxes and plates are. They've been together for fifteen years and love each other deeply. My heart aches wishing I knew what it felt like to be that cherished by someone.

Chapter Thirteen

THURSDAY ROLLS AROUND FASTER than expected. Between private gigs, kids' birthday parties, and evening performances at the restaurant, I've spent more time in the water than on dry land. But that's the reality of being a professional mermaid—part fantasy, part business. It's more than just glitter and smiles—it's lugging fifty-pound tails, squeezing into wetsuits backstage, staying in shape to swim long routines, and managing bookings, invoices, and social media.

My bookings have been steady, and for once, I'm ahead instead of just staying afloat. I've paid off my credit cards, and I'm finally able to set money aside for my next trip—something strategic to boost my social media presence. The goal is to invest in a few top-tier custom tails and hit some of the most iconic beach locations in the United States I follow other pro mermaids online to track trends—new tail designs, choreography, even waterproof makeup hacks. It's not just about playing dress-up—it's a brand I'm building, and every splash counts.

I'm sitting on the bench in the break room enjoying a chicken salad between performances when Chloe walks in to grab her pink seashell bra from her locker.

"Hey, Chloe. Thanks again for covering my shift the other weekend last minute."

She smiles, tossing her long raven hair over her shoulder. "Happy to. Alice said something about a trip to Vegas with a hot guy?" she asks, watching me with her steely green eyes, wanting me to spill the tea.

"Yeah," I nervously chuckle and take a bite of my chicken salad. "He invited me to see a concert. It was a blast."

"Sweet." She tucks her pink bra gently into her bag. "Rachel, me, and some other mergirls were thinking about going to the Mermaid Con in Maryland that's coming up. Do you wanna join? We can all share a hotel room."

I take another bite, chewing slowly to buy a few extra seconds. Chloe's the same age as me and has been a mermaid for three years. She's talented, even landed a commercial for sunscreen a few months ago. Sometimes we perform in the same shows. Rachel's about three years younger than both of us and still fairly new. She passed her deep dive certification just six months ago. Part of me knows I should be more social with the other mermaids and make more of an effort to connect with them, to be part of the team. But deep down, I'm focused on my solo career—and it's hard not to see them as competition.

After taking a sip of water, I reply, "Thanks for the invite. But I need to check my calendar." A polite way of saying no thank you.

She scratches the purple octopus tattoo on her left forearm. "No worries. Just let me know if your schedule clears up."

As Chloe walks out, Alice breezes in, smelling of violets and vodka.

"Shouldn't that be tuna?" she mocks, opening her locker and grabbing an apple to snack on.

"Don't start." I point my fork at her.

She sits beside me and takes a giant bite out of her apple.

"Can you not chew like a horse? Geez." I flick a piece of apple that landed on my leg to the floor.

She swallows, wiping her mouth with the back of her hand. "What bit your ass today?"

I scoop another bite of chicken salad onto a cracker and sigh. "I'm sorry. I like being busy, and all these events mean my name is getting out there, but it also means no sleep." I shove food in my mouth before saying more.

Alice bumps her shoulder against mine. "I hear you, girl. Respect for all this hard work you're doing."

"How are you and Emily?"

Alice turns her apple and sinks her teeth into its red skin, but doesn't bite down. "It's complicated. We're too alike."

"Dating yourself can be exhausting." I squeeze her thigh. "I think you two are cute together."

Alice shrugs, losing interest in the apple, and drops it into her lap. "There's no argument there. Did you see the pics I posted? We're gorgeous." She adjusts the arrow ring around her middle finger. "I just don't want to lose our spark if we get serious. You know?"

"Yeah." I give her a side hug. "It's fun to hook up and fool around, but sometimes the heart does want to settle and focus on one person."

She leans her head against my shoulder, scrolling through her phone. The words between us trail off, as if the air's been sucked out of the conversation, leaving it suspended in awkward silence.

Suddenly, Alice sits up so fast it makes my heart leap. She covers her mouth with one hand, her eyes wide as saucers.

"Listen to this," she says in a sing-song voice. Her lips curl in a mischievous smirk. "Playing my guitar on the beach while missing my girl." She shows me a picture of Sully with a red wooden guitar on his lap staring out over the ocean.

A sinking feeling takes over as if the bench suddenly turned into quicksand and is swallowing me whole. "He could be talking about anyone." I pop the last bite of cracker into my mouth and stand, hoping to avoid seeing Sully's gorgeous face anymore.

But I've been avoiding him. The week's almost over, and I still haven't replied to him.

"I don't know. People are commenting, asking who the mystery girl is, and he's replying. In one, he writes, *I might not have known her long, but she's the type of person who just fits into my life. Like she belonged there all along, and now the puzzle is complete. Now I sound cliché.* And in another, he talks about your eyes. *Evergreen eyes stare back at me. Full of secrets and sorrow, yet sparkle brighter than the most priceless jade when she laughs.* He's pouring his heart out on social media. Kinda sounds like a Hallmark card, but he's trying."

The floor beneath me seems to drop, as if everything around me is shifting out of place. My phone buzzes, cutting through the chaos of thoughts spiraling in my mind.

> **Dinner tonight? I can pick you up. Promise not to bite. Unless you want me to.**

Arthur enters the room and tosses a thumb over his shoulder. "You ready? The crowd is getting restless."

I have to work late. Sorry.

Where do you work? I can meet you there.

I bite my lip, feeling a little mischievous.

Wouldn't you like to know?

I lock my phone inside my locker. "See you out there," I say to Alice and climb the stairs to the top of the tank.

She waves half-heartedly. "Yeah...see ya."

⁂ ♫♪ 🐚 ♫♪ ⁂ ♫♪ 🐚

Tonight, I'm wearing my midnight blue tail that lights up. I do a quick breathing exercise before diving in and giving the people what they want.

When the curtains part and the lights turn on inside the water tank, I swim out from behind the rocks. As I do my routine, I wave to amazed customers and blow the occasional bubble kisses.

A couple is having a romantic dinner with a candle in the center of their table. I swim over to them and interact. The woman smiles and waves. After doing a backflip, I motion to the man who's now on his knee proposing. I draw a heart with my hands when she nods yes.

With everyone clapping for the happy couple, I take a moment to hide behind seaweed and take a few breaths from my oxygen mask. The diver gives me a thumbs up and I give him one in return.

As I swim out, someone catches my eye at a table in the corner of the tank. My heart thunders in my skull as the man looks a lot like Sully, but that's impossible. I never told him where I work.

But when I press myself to the glass, he smiles at me and I could never mistake those blue eyes. It is Sully! And he's holding his phone up.

Is he...is he recording my show?

I flick my fins and twist to face away from him. What the hell? I need to remain calm.

Just focus on the show. With that advice, I swim in circles and twirl. But when I do another lap, he's still there, smiling.

The tables have turned. Just a week ago, I was filming Sully killing it on stage with his bass guitar, and now he's behind the camera filming me swim.

A provocative thought slips into my mind, distracting and tempting. I beckon him closer and press my forehead to the glass. He moves forward, zooming in on me. I do a backflip, letting my hair float wildly behind me. I wink at the camera and swim away, surfacing for a breath and a short break.

I'm giddy thinking about my video in his media library, and later, we can exchange autographed pictures. I laugh at myself. Maybe having this fling last longer than a weekend isn't so bad.

✳ 🎵 🐚 🎵 ✳ 🎵 🐚

Arthur scoops me up and carries me to the meet and greet like we do almost every night. My fins sway as Arthur cradles me against his chest. I gather my hair and rest it over my left shoulder to keep it from getting tangled in his gold chain necklace.

"My daughter hasn't stopped talking about you giving her a private lesson. She keeps telling her friends how her dad's friends with a mermaid," he chuckles, smiling like a proud papa.

"Awe, that's precious." I place a hand over my heart. "She's a natural. Maybe in a few years, she can be my trainee."

He lifts a brow. "There's no way I can afford those fancy tails. Don't get my girl hooked." His laughter is deep, making his chest rumble.

When he turns the corner and the kids spot me, they gasp and giggle. I turn on my Disney princess voice and prepare myself to answer all their burning questions.

"Can I touch your tail?" A little red-headed girl, around six, asks, already reaching out to touch my fins.

"Of course," I say with a friendly smile, flopping my tail closer.

Ten hands shoot out. Some are brave and pet my tail like they would a dolphin. Others are shy and keep jerking their hand away as if they're about to touch a snapping turtle.

"How can you live out of the ocean?" A boy with wild blond curls asks.

I brush a piece of hair out of my face and say, "Mermaids have a special ability to stay out of water for a little while."

After about fifteen minutes, Arthur claps his hands, cutting the meet and greet off. "I think it's time to say goodbye to Mermaid Veronica. She needs to swim on home and visit her family."

The kids mutter in disappointment. I blow them kisses as their parents come to collect them. "I loved meeting all of you little guppies. Farewell."

"How about one last question?" Sully asks, leaning against a column with a smirk that kills me a little inside.

Arthur steps forward, thinking he's a creep. We've had a few before. "He's harmless," I say.

"Hmm." Arthur moves back but doesn't leave.

"How did you know I was here?"

Sully pulls up a chair and straddles it backwards, draping his long arms around the back of it. God, to be that chair.

"What the question should be is, why did you never tell me I was with a mermaid? Sounds like something a guy should know about."

I twirl a lock of hair around my finger, teasing. "You worried I put a spell on you?"

"Maybe," he says, his voice low. "Are you a siren?"

A soft laugh escapes me. "Something like that." I shift slightly in the inflatable seashell, trying to ignore how long I've been sitting still. "Since you've come all this way...I suppose we can have dinner."

"Great. I have the perfect table." Sully stands and waves his phone in the air. "I also have a lot of fantastic footage." With that, he leaves.

"Was that Sully?" Arthur asks, picking me up.

"Yeah." I hook an arm around his shoulder.

"And you didn't tell him about this place?"

"Nope. Guess who did."

He chuckles. "Your best friend."

"Who's going to be fed to the sharks."

Arthur sets me on the bench in the break room and glances around. "Looks like she's hiding at the bar."

"I know where she lives." I grab a towel and dry my hair.

"Don't be so harsh on her." He waves before exiting.

I shimmy out of my tail and hang it up before exchanging my seashell bra for a nice cotton one paired with a solid black shirt. Then I trade my pink scaled leggings for a fresh pair with leopard print. After tying my hair into a ponytail, I grab my phone and purse from my locker. Out of curiosity, I read over my texts with Sully, and sure enough, Alice sent him one during my show inviting him to the restaurant.

For our first date I'd rather not smell of chlorine and have my eyes sting, but what can a girl do? After adding pink gloss to my lips, I leave to meet Sully.

He sits at the bar with two wine glasses in front of him. When he spots me, he picks them up and offers me one.

"Thanks." I take a sip. It's my favorite. Alice already knows she's in deep water.

"Hope you don't mind I ordered chicken wings and fries. Your friend said you'd love them."

I eye Alice across the bar. She's busy shining the whiskey bottles with a rag, which she never does.

The food arrives, and I grab a chicken wing, rip it in half, and take a bite. Damn, this is good.

Sully grabs a fry and watches me, his gaze amused and a little curious. "Who knew swimming caused such an appetite," he chuckles, eating the fry.

"Sorry." I lick my fingers and dip the other half of the wing into the ranch.

"When were you going to tell me about this place?" He waves his finger around in a circle. "It's incredible."

"Usually I have to know someone longer than a weekend before I tell them about my career; otherwise, people usually laugh." I stare at the bar as my finger traces the rim of my wine glass.

"For the record, I'd never laugh at you. And we may have only met last week, but I know you better than just about anyone here." He takes my hand, flipping it over. His thumb traces the lines on my palm, sending tingles straight between my legs. "They don't know how good you taste," he whispers in my ear and lifts his wine glass, tapping it with mine.

Wow. I might've just cum a little.

My grasp on the glass increases but thankfully it doesn't shatter. "No..."

"Good. Keep it that way."

He bites into a wing when his phone buzzes. He reads the screen and mumbles something in German under his breath.

"Worst timing for a band meeting."

I glance at the time on my phone. "Isn't it late for a meeting?"

"Not when it comes to Amy. She takes being our PR rep to a whole new level—like she's running a political campaign, not managing a band. Everything's about the brand, the image, the next headline. She's obsessed with pushing us harder in the States—bigger interviews, strategic pairings, the works. She wants us headlining festivals in a year or two, like we're some packaged product she's fine-tuning for mass consumption."

He runs his thumb along the edge of my hand. "I usually just tune her out. It's easier than arguing. She talks like everything she's doing is for the band, and maybe some of it is, but it never feels like we get a say. Especially me. I'm the easy target—I'm the one who doesn't push back, so she steamrolls me."

He meets my eyes, something softer there now. "Dinner tomorrow night? Let me make it up to you."

His pout mixed with his gorgeous blue eyes makes me a goner. "Yes. Dinner tomorrow."

"*Wunderbar*." His German curls my toes. He stands and cradles my face in his hand. "Looking forward to it." He kisses me deeply, his tongue stroking mine. My hands sink into his hair, pulling him closer. A small moan slips out when he breaks away.

When he's gone, Alice leans against the bar finishing Sully's wine. "Damn, girl. You're hooked on that boy."

I flick a fry at her head. "Don't think I'm not mad at you for breaking into my locker and taking my phone."

She tsks, stealing a handful of fries. "If not for me, you wouldn't have that kiss and probably whatever dirty dream you'll have tonight." She giggles and moves farther down the bar before I toss something bigger than a fry at her head.

Sadly, she's right. I needed that nudge, and now I'm officially seeing Sully again. Am I ready for that? Things tighten and throb inside me. I believe the answer is yes.

Chapter Fourteen

"Come on, girls. It's time for cake." The hostess of the party, and mother of the twelve-year-old birthday girl, sends the kids through the double glass doors of the house, leaving me alone in the pool. I pull myself out of the water in the shallow end and motion for Arthur to carry me into the pool house, so I can transform back into a human being and not ruin any magic for the children.

The last few girls in the group turn around to catch a glimpse of me. Their faces squished by pouts. I blow them kisses, waving goodbye. The mom pulls the chocolate brown curtain over before closing the glass doors, hiding us from prying eyes. She gestures around the backyard to the hanging mermaid decorations and my white inflatable seashell. "Thank you for such a wonderful party. I'm sure this will be one of her most memorable birthdays."

I bring my tail to my chest, wrapping my arms around it. Arthur hands me a towel and stands behind me with his arms hanging to his side, waiting for his role as mer-handler to kick start.

"It was a joy to see their faces light up. That's my favorite part of the job," I say, brushing a leaf off my arm and drying my chest with the towel.

She pulls out her phone. "Who should I send the money to?"

"He's your guy." I nod to Arthur. "Mermaids don't have pockets," I joke, patting my hip and tapping my fins against the concrete edge of the pool. I'm not a fan of the prolonged small talk after shows. I want to leave before the kids stuff their faces full of sugar and return, running a thousand miles an hour, and won't let me go. Or worse, ruining the magic by them seeing me without my tail and proving I'm not a real mermaid.

She laughs into her cupped hand. "Right. Sorry."

Arthur walks over and they discuss the matter of payment. After it goes through, she eyes the curtained covered glass doors. "I should get in there before they rip that cake apart before singing happy birthday." She waves and walks toward the house.

We patiently wait for her to slip inside before Arthur picks me up. "I'm just muscle to you, aren't I?" he laughs as his hands carefully secure me under my tail and around my torso.

"You're also pleasant to look at. That's a bonus." I scrunch my nose while hooking my arms around his veiny neck.

He swallows, making his Adam's apple bob. "Just another pretty face then." He shifts my weight, holding me with only one arm and forcing me to hold on tighter so he can open the pool house's door. "It's cool. Not everyone can deal with mermaid drama."

I gasp in mock horror. "What drama?"

He sets me on a wooden chair and checks his phone. "You better hurry before those kids attack," he says, avoiding my question.

I shoo him toward the door. "Give me some space." I hug my chest, pretending to be shy. "I'll be ready in a few minutes."

After playing tug of war with my tail for a few minutes, I free my legs and take a moment to stretch them and wiggle my toes. In a perfect world, I'd take a quick shower, but I'll just have to wait until I get home.

I check my phone, but there are no missed texts. Out of habit, I open Insta and do a quick check on my notifications, reading comments on my newest post of me unboxing my red and black tail. When I return to the main feed, a story catches my eye. There's a picture of Sully and Gigi, along with the bold white words reading, "Confirmed to be dating by insider."

My stomach falls to my feet. What the hell? I click off my phone and toss it into my purse. No. This is not going to ruin my mood. Despite the mule kick to my heart, I slip on my mask of indifference and pack away my tail.

When I step outside, Arthur is wandering around the pool, admiring its rock fountain. I lift a brow, adjusting the bag strap on my shoulder. "You having fun?"

He motions to the pool. "Melissa wants to add a fountain to our pool. Just checking it out." He jogs over and takes my bag before eyeing the back door. Laughter and screams of "Open mine, open mine!" pour out of the house. Arthur nods toward the gate. "Sounds like the kiddos moved on to opening presents."

Arthur drops me off at home and honks as he drives away. I wave and force a smile. He didn't notice my mood shift because I let him play his country station, and he sang the entire way here.

As I walk toward the stairs to my apartment, an unfamiliar black SUV with tinted windows catches my eye. It doesn't look dangerous, but something about it feels off, like it's out of place.

I take a calming breath and pull my pink pepper spray from the front pocket of my purse, holding it in my palm. I create a tight fist with my other hand. Thanks to my self-defense classes, I know how to land a solid punch. My parents taught me to go down fighting if anyone messed with me, and I guarantee there will be DNA under my fingernails to land the asshole who killed me in prison.

Dread prickles my spine when I'm forced to turn my back on the SUV when I reach the stairs. If I wasn't worried about falling and breaking my neck, I'd climb the steps backward. It's hard to keep looking over my shoulder, so I rush to my apartment. My nerves tell me to run, but again, I don't want to fall and be one of those victims who always die in horror movies. I've already fallen down a flight of stairs while at college, and it caused me knee cap problems. If I could, I'd like to avoid that. Especially if I'm just being paranoid.

A figure moves out of a palm tree's shadow, and I have the pepper spray aimed and ready.

Sully holds his hands up to shield his eyes. "Wait! Don't shoot!"

My arms fall to my sides, and a wave of confusion crashes into me, almost knocking me over. "Are you trying to give me a heart attack?" I roll my shoulders, releasing the tension, but keep the pepper spray close because you never know.

He pulls the rim of the baseball hat down to cover his face while a blonde girl passes by walking her dog and talking on her phone. Once she's gone, he steps closer and says, "Sorry. I wanted to see you in person to explain."

"Explain what?" I fire back, placing a foot on the first step leading to my apartment. "That you're involved with Gigi but still want to have me on the side?"

He shoves his hands into his pockets. "That insider was Amy. She did that without the band's knowledge, thought it would help when the tour is announced. I'm not with Gigi. She's not my type."

I drop my bag near my feet and plant my hands on my hips. "What tour?"

He stares at his shoes, kicking a rock off the sidewalk. "Next month we're going to open for Gigi's European tour."

"Oh. Just that." I bend down to grab my bag. "I'm too tired for whatever this is."

"What about our date?"

"My ex took all my patience. I can't play these games."

Sully rubs his chin and eyes my bag that's straining my shoulder but quickly averts his attention back on me. "Scarlet Failure will drop out of the tour."

Heat creeps up my neck. I lean a hip against the stairs' metal railing and rest the bag on my thigh. "What?"

Sully presses his hands together like he's praying. "Please don't let Amy's stunt ruin us. There's still so much I want to do with you, especially knowing your secret." He flashes me that wolfish grin again, and a dimple peeks through his clean-shaven cheek.

"What secret?"

A smile tugs at his lips. "You're a magical mermaid." He closes the distance between us. "Let me take that." He grabs my bag and tosses it over his shoulder like it weighs nothing.

He's left me tongue-tied. For some reason I believe him. Why would he ambush me and insist he's not with Gigi, if he secretly was? But I've been burned before. I can't be made a fool again.

"How can I believe you?"

He makes a cross over his heart. "I swear you're the only girl on my mind. Hell, you should hear what you did in my dream."

A guy on a bike rides past us, and I shush Sully. He cracks a smile.

"Fine. But you're on probation." I motion toward the front door.

He steps up to follow, his breath warm on my neck as I unlock the door.

"Nice place," he says, stepping inside and dropping my bag on the floor. He runs a hand over the couch, as if testing its comfort level.

"Where are you taking me on this date?" I grab my bag and flick on a light to not trip over the heels Alice leaves around the house like random landmines.

"It's a surprise." Sully follows me down the hallway as if we're attached by a string. I hold a hand up once I reach my bedroom door, and he halts.

"That doesn't help. I've been in a pool all day. I need to shower."

He steps between me and the bathroom. "Can I help?"

My lady parts say yes, but he's on my list, so I shake my head. "Nope. Part of your probation means no steamy showers."

I slip into my room to grab some clothes and then lock myself in the bathroom before I change my mind and tug Sully inside with me. It's not fair I'm being punished too.

Sully leans against the door. "We're going to the studio for a bit. I need to lay down a few riffs but then we'll grab dinner. Whatever you want." His voice slips through the door and wraps around me like a warm weighted blanket.

Studio? I'm going to see the band again? At least I'm going to see Sully in his element, since he snuck into mine.

"You know, you're sexy as hell in a tail. How long have you been doing this?"

"About six years. I turned my childhood fantasy into a career. It's a lot of hard work, but it's rewarding."

Knowing Sully's alone in my house snooping through my things makes me take the fastest shower of my life. I slip on my bra and panties, but frown looking at the jeans and band tee I grabbed. Wearing my Evanescence shirt to a recording studio for another band seems wrong.

I open the bathroom door a crack and peek out. Sully isn't anywhere in sight. I dash into my bedroom and smack into his chest.

"Whoa." He catches me by the arm before I tumble backward. "You're a fascinating creature, Veronica." His dark eyes roam over me as if I'm a statue on display.

"Oh?" I press my tongue to the roof of my mouth to keep from biting my lip again. "Maybe I'm just a tease."

"No." He traces the lace on my bra strap. "You're amazing." He sits on the foot of the bed and pulls me toward him. I'm trapped between his legs. "There's a song in you. I can almost picture the lyrics when I look at you." He kisses my collarbone and stares up at me. "My gut tells me it'll be the spark we need for our new record."

A nervous laugh bursts from my chest. "Do you use that on all the girls?"

He cups my face in his palm as he traces my eyebrow with his other hand. For a moment, I feel like I'm made of porcelain, and he's memorizing every detail of my painted face. "Most of the songs I write are from past experiences, people I've known for ages, but with you, there's something more." The hand touching my eyebrow moves to grasp the nape of my neck. His eyes are deep sapphire pools. I press my hands into his chest to keep from drowning. "I can't quite place my finger on what it is, but I know it's something alluring."

Wherever his touch connects with my skin is scorched in flames, but I crave more. I want to push him onto the bed and feel his warmth on my chest.

I pull away and move toward my closet. "I need to get dressed. Don't want to keep your band waiting."

"When we return, I'm fucking you on that bed."

"Is that so?" I challenge, meeting his eyes.

He hooks his finger under my chin. "And after tonight I'll no longer be on probation."

"Hmm. We'll see about that." I turn to look through my closet and feeling a little devilish I wiggle my ass as I reach for a purple dress.

Sully's hands press into my hips while his thumbs lower my panties. I press my back into him and can already feel how much he wants me. I grind against him as I remove the dress from the hanger.

He moans and twirls me around to face him. "I can't wait to take that off you." He grabs the dress and gently pulls it over my head. "But first I want you to hear this new song."

"I have high expectations on songs. I'm quite opinionated," I say, grabbing the brush off my dresser and brushing my hair.

Sully pins me with a heated look. "I welcome all feedback." He grabs the keys from his pocket. "I'll drive."

"You don't have a driver?" I drop the brush onto my bed and slip on a pair of black ballerina flats before grabbing my purse.

He shakes his head. "I'm not that big of a celebrity."

I lock the door and follow him toward the SUV I thought was shady and slide into the passenger's seat. All my nerves are on high alert. My palms are sweaty, and I should focus on breathing to avoid hyperventilating.

I should be cautious. I've been burned before, trusting someone only to end up with my heart in pieces. But everything about Sully feels different—right, even. Still, I can't ignore the nagging voice inside me. Amy and Gigi are already stirring up trouble, and I haven't even met them yet. I don't want to be the one to cause a rift in the band, but there's something about Sully that makes me want to believe him. I want to trust him; I really do.

He's not just the best sex I've ever had; there's something deeper, something real between us. He's the calm to the storm inside my mind, the only thing that makes me feel grounded when everything else feels chaotic. But if he's lying to me...if he's playing me like everyone else has before...this could destroy me. I'm terrified of trusting him completely, but a part of me hopes I'm wrong. I hope he's the one who won't break my heart.

Chapter Fifteen

WHEN WE ARRIVE AT the studio, Ben and Lars fist bump Sully as he walks in. Their smiles grow when they see me behind him.

"You have a hot shadow," Lars jokes.

Sully drapes his arm around my shoulders. "Don't I know it?" He nods to the sound booth where Charlotte is singing.

"You wanna hear?" Ben hits a button and Charlotte's heavenly vocals filter into the room.

Sully pulls out the chair and gestures for me to sit. I'm afraid of touching anything. This board looks like it can launch a NASA rocket. How do producers figure out how all these switches and computers work?

After a couple of minutes, Charlotte stops and pulls the headphones on her ears down around her neck. "How was that?"

Ben hits an intercom button. "It was perfect. Sully's here so we'll do his riffs and vocals now."

"Thank God. I need a break." Charlotte exits the sound booth and instantly hugs me when she sees me. "I didn't know we had a guest."

Sully grabs his bass guitar from its case and steps into the sound booth. He strums a few warm-up chords before Lars taps a few buttons, starting the recording.

His fingers dance over the strings, and something deep inside me aches, wishing those fingers were strumming something else.

Charlotte chuckles and leans her arms across the back of the chair I'm sitting in. "He's exceptional, isn't he?"

"Yes." I can't take my eyes off of him. He shreds and it's hauntingly dark. Some chords make me want to weep. Then when he sings the first verse, my heart skids to a stop and melts away.

"Don't tell him I said that. It'll go straight to his head."

A smile curls my lips. "Your secret's safe with me."

Sully plays the guitar too aggressively and a string snaps. "Shit," he says.

Ben face palms and hits the intercom button. "Dude, I told you that pick wasn't going to work."

Lars shakes his head as he grabs a box of strings and walks into the sound booth.

Charlotte snags my wrist and pulls me outside. "I need fresh air. Being in a band with those three can be a lot."

"But you like being in a band, right? You never thought of going solo?"

She leans against the brick wall and crosses her left ankle over her right. "When I was younger, I wanted to be solo. But I like being in a band. Not all the focus is on you, even as the singer. I know my boys will back me up, and it's nice to have others to bounce ideas off of. And it's a bonus to travel the world with my husband." She spins her wedding ring around her finger. "Even if he can be annoying now and again." She smiles. "What about you? Seeing you with Sully after Vegas must mean something."

"Oh." I hug myself. "He found where I worked and asked me to dinner."

"And then brought you here?" She tsks. "Boys."

"He came by my apartment because of the Insta post about Gigi." I stare at the crack in the sidewalk. Not wanting to see her reaction and fear Sully really is playing both sides.

Charlotte touches my shoulder. "Sweetie. He only has eyes for you. Trust me. He never talks to anyone outside of the band, Mark, and Amy." She makes a face. "Thankfully, you haven't met Amy yet. She's...good at her job, but she's a lot. She's basically the reason we even stayed afloat after the third album. She knows how to sell a story to the media. Problem is, now she thinks she owns the band's image—including Sully's."

I blink at her. "Owns it?"

"She acts like it's all about protecting us, but it's really about the money. Sully's the only single member left. Amy sees dollar signs when she looks at him. She wants a picture-perfect romance to sell tickets, merch, anything she can put a price tag on."

"That's what he told me. That it was all a PR stunt he didn't agree to."

"Yes. Gigi asked us to record a track for her new album, and Amy thought it'd be great press. I was against it, but I got outvoted." Charlotte sighs, rubbing her palms down her jeans. "And now Amy's pushing for us to tour with Gigi in Europe. We're still ironing out the details, but it's looking more and more like a done deal."

The word *Europe* lands like a punch to the ribs. I don't want to imagine Sully leaving—but what right do I have to ask him to stay?

Charlotte watches me, her mouth pulling into a soft frown. "And Gigi...she's another story. She's used to getting her way. Always has been. She loves the spotlight, and she's smart enough to know pairing herself with Sully will give her fresh attention, boost her tour numbers, sell this fantasy."

"She sounds awful."

Charlotte nods. "She is. She barked at Sully like he was an intern the first time they met—ordered him to fetch her green tea." She shakes her head. "The sad thing is, Sully's too easygoing. He hates drama. He thinks if he stays quiet, people will leave him alone. But it's the opposite with people like Amy and Gigi. They see him as this prize they can polish and parade around."

I chew the inside of my cheek, the anger and sadness tangling up inside me.

Charlotte smiles, just a little. "But you...you're the first thing that's broken through that ice around him in a long time. I've known him for years and I've never seen him smile so much until you."

She opens the door, ushering us back into the studio.

Sully's guitar is fixed, and he's laying down his part of the track. His eyes are closed, and the melody fills the air. Damn, he's breathtaking, and all I want is to have those hands all over me and see what kind of music we can make together.

After Sully's finished with his part, we walk a couple of blocks north to this hole-in-the-wall pizza and ice cream place I never heard of. He holds the door open for me, and a cow moos to welcome us instead of the usual bell ringing.

"How did you find this place?" I ask, looking around. It's small, maybe two hundred square feet, with only a few tables. In the corner are two pinball machines that use bouncy balls. There's a TV hanging in the corner of the room playing *Friends* with the volume low and closed captions on.

"I read reviews and found this hidden gem." He wraps an arm around my hips, and I have no clue if he's messing with me or not.

We both order a slice of pepperoni pizza. The slice is huge, needing two plates to support its weight.

We sit at the table with a giant Marilyn Monroe poster hanging on the blood-red wall. For a few moments, we're quiet while enjoying our dinner.

"Dessert?" Sully licks grease off his fingers.

He read my mind. I've been eyeing the ice cream menu since we sat down. They have endless options.

I order a cookie monster munch, which is cookies and cream flavored ice cream with extra Oreos crushed on top. Sully gets dirty love, which is rocky road ice cream with gummy worms.

Sully licks his purple plastic spoon and stabs at a gummy worm, slicing off its head. "Tell me something you've never told another soul."

I wipe my mouth on a napkin. "And why would I do that? Do you want to run for the hills?"

He makes a show of glancing around then leans forward to whisper, "You're not a serial killer, are you?"

"Ha!" I snort and ice cream burns my nose. "I'd be the worst serial killer. I pulled a muscle putting on my tail last week."

"Come on. It's easy to open up to someone who doesn't know you."

"You go first then," I say, taking a bite and chewing thoughtfully. "Need to rate how honest I should be." He needs to give me some range because there are some scary skeletons locked in my closet.

He leans back and cracks his knuckles, treating this like a contest of sorts. "Right before the tour started, I almost walked away from the band for good."

A heavy weight crushes my chest. My favorite band almost broke up, and no one knew. No music magazine or social media outlet posted a peep about it.

"Wow..." I clench my jaw to keep from gaping at him like a fish and poke at a cookie piece with my spoon, lost for words. "How...when..."

He sucks a gummy worm into his mouth like it's pasta. "Now you go."

"You're not going to elaborate?" I sit back in the booth, trying to focus on Sully's face to keep the room from spinning.

"I will after you share your secret."

"How can I beat that?" I say louder than I mean to.

His blue eyes are soulful as they pierce into me. "Be honest. I want to know the real Veronica."

The cozy little restaurant melts into an interrogation room with a metal table and I am handcuffed to cold steel as my brain rolls around with something deep to share that I can live with having someone else know.

The scraping of my empty cup is deafening. I take a final lick and chew on the end of my spoon.

He rests his chin in the palm of his hand, not giving up on me spilling my guts to him.

Do I tell him I shoplifted a shirt once in the fifth grade? Sometimes I wish I could be a real mermaid and be left alone in the quiet ocean where I'd never have to worry about money or my next post on social media. Reveal how my high school boyfriend dumped me because I wouldn't sleep with him. Or should I tell him about "the incident" with my ex?

I can't sound pathetic. What should I confess? Steal a story from a TV drama or a novel and hope he doesn't notice.

He crumples a napkin and tosses it into his empty cup. "If you don't want to share, it's cool." He checks his phone and says the words that mean the death of any date. "It's getting late, maybe—"

I'll never ask you out again because you're dull and terrible and I don't feel connected to you anymore. I guess the rest of his sentence as he shifts his weight to stand up.

"Hold on." I slide the mermaid-tail ring up and down my finger. "Two months ago, the guy who I thought would be my future husband publicly humiliated me. He reserved a table at the then brand-new French restaurant in town. He made this show of how fancy it was. How the chef was from Paris and would help prepare our taste buds for France. To me, all the signs of a proposal were there. Romantic atmosphere, check. He hinted around about wanting to know what kind of rings I liked the month before. So, thinking he had a diamond ring, check. He liked putting on a good show and a public proposal was right up his alley, check. But no..." My lungs forget how to function as I choke on my tongue.

All the blood in Sully's face drains as he sinks into the booth, running a hand over his jaw. "Oh...I'm sorry. I shouldn't have—"

"It's okay." I tap my fingernails on the table. "I never talk about it. Alice knows the basics, but I never shared the entire story. He set up this entire scene and even got down on one knee and took my left hand. He kissed it and told me he wanted to break up. Then he laughed as I burst into tears. My former college roommate filmed the entire thing across the way. He'd been screwing her for months. They posted the ruse online to tank my career."

Sully frowns. "Holy shit, what an arsehole."

"Yeah. The real joke was I taught him how to be a social media influencer and connected him to people who could help him. He wanted to do stupid pranks and he got famous fast. He and my college roommate met at my birthday party and hooked up while I danced with my friends." I toy with my spoon to avoid looking at Sully's face, not wanting to see the pity in his eyes. "Then he strung me along because he needed my contacts to help him have a solid fan base. My reward? Him trying to ruin me in every way someone can destroy another human being." My voice stutters as a sob closes my throat.

Sully offers me a napkin and I dab my eyes with it.

"What happened after?"

"Last I heard, they moved to New York. But he recently texted me, saying he's in LA and wants to meet. I blocked him. I can't see his stupid face or even say his name."

"If he shows, let me know," Sully growls. His face twists in wolfish rage, and it honestly makes me hot. I like having someone fight for me.

"Thanks." I sigh, tearing my napkin in half. "The only bright spot was my lawyer, who helps me with the business side of my mermaiding, has a husband who deals with defamation cases. He threatened to sue them if they didn't delete the video and issue a public apology. But it's still in the dark corners of the internet."

"People are terrible. I'm leery of dating too after my ex. Thought she liked me for me, but it was the band life she wanted. When she realized we were not super famous around the world or shitting out gold, she dumped me in the middle of our last European tour to shag another bass player who was headlining a show in the same city we were in. She hopped onto his bus and vanished."

"What a bitch," I say, sniffling and rubbing my hands together. My skin is itchy when I overshare. "Guess we both have good reasons for being bitter."

He offers me a hand. "Let's make a deal to never look back. They're the past and we will never allow them to ruin our future."

His ocean-blue eyes sparkle as he leans in. I inhale and take his hand. "Deal."

We shake on it.

"I'll be right back," Sully says and goes to the register. He talks to the cashier and returns only to flash me with a handful of quarters.

"How are you at pinball?" He nods toward the two machines.

We walk over to the spaced-themed pinball machines. "I haven't played since I was a kid, but I'm game."

After a few good hits, I lose, but Sully is a secret pinball master. When it spits a second ball out at him, he gets sloppier and finally, a ball loses control and they both fall into the gutter.

I can't resist grabbing the blue bouncy ball and tossing it against the wall. It flies above my head, and I catch it before it smacks into the new customer walking in through the door. I glance at the people working, and they're watching me like I'm a kid on the loose from their mother, and they want to kick my ass outside.

Sully holds his green ball like it's a lucky stone, rolling it between his fingers in thought. He nods to the booth we were sitting in before. "I shouldn't have pushed you. It—"

"Don't worry about it." I hand him the ball back before I bounce it off the wall again and get us banished. "I'm glad I finally told someone."

He pockets the toys and nods toward the door. His shoulder brushes against mine. I run my hand along the wall with a painted mural of Hollywood actors who we lost a long time ago.

"Thank you for sharing that with me." He turns the corner, walking toward where he parked the SUV. "Do you want to get out of here?"

Chapter Sixteen

On the way home, I send Alice a text and confirm she's spending the night at Emily's. She replies with a winky face emoji. Being alone with Sully leaves the night open to endless possibilities, hopefully involving us being naked.

"Do you want to watch a movie?" Sully sits on the couch and turns on the TV like he already lives here.

"Sure. Go ahead and find something. I'm going to change into something comfier."

I slip into my bedroom and rummage through my dresser. If Alice was here, she'd shove sexy lingerie in my face while wiggling her eyebrows. But I don't want Sully to think all I want from him is to jump his bones. The extra-long shirt I bought in Vegas to be PJs and never wore catches my eye. It's perfect. The hem hugs my thighs. I'm feeling naughty and slip out of my bra and panties before padding back into the living room.

Sully has *Die Hard* paused on the screen and ushers me over. I sit next to him and lie against his chest. He's a firm yet comfy pillow. "I love this movie."

"It's a classic." At least he picked a movie we can make out through and not worry about missing anything.

Thirty minutes later, Sully's engrossed in the film and I can't fight my fluttering eyelids anymore and bury my face into the crook of his arm. Right before I drift away, I swear Sully kisses the crown of my head. He places his cheek on top of my head and in his embrace I fall asleep.

My nap doesn't last long because John McClane is still running around barefoot, but a nightmare scared me awake.

Sully pauses the movie and reaches for my arm as if keeping me from bolting out of the apartment. "What's wrong?"

"Bad dream." I move to my side of the couch, bring my legs up to my chest, and pull the shirt over them.

Sully lays a hand on my knee. "Do you want to talk about it?"

"It's okay. I don't remember it."

His hand trails up my thigh. "I'm always here to listen."

The honesty in his words cracks my heart. "Thank you. You don't know what it means to have someone listen. My ex constantly pushed everything I felt to the side. Said I was just being dramatic."

Sully wraps his strong arms around me, burying my face in his chest. "Whatever you feel is important to me. All I want is to see you happy."

I raise my head and kiss his lips. His hand slides down my back to cup my ass. The shirt rides up and his hand grazes my bare cheek. His blue eyes widen and darken.

My hand strokes the stubble on his cheek. He dips his face into my neck and licks my collarbone. "What am I to do with you, *Schatz*?" His accent makes me wet.

I climb onto his lap and rub myself against the bulge in his pants. "Whatever you want."

He pushes me against the arm of the couch and slides his hand along my inner thigh until his fingers tease my clit. "You like this?"

"Mmm." I buck my hips, trying to increase the pressure. My nipples harden underneath the shirt as my left foot falls to the floor to help open my legs wider.

"I need to see all of you." He takes my hand and tugs the shirt off in one smooth motion. He cups my right breast and gives it a loving squeeze.

A moan slips out as I hungrily grab his shirt and pull him into a kiss. "Off," I order, and his shirt goes flying. My hands study the hard planes of his chest until they find the perfect V above his waistline.

Sully surprises me by grabbing my thighs, yanking me onto my back, and planting my legs on his shoulders. His nose hovers above my vagina, and I know he can feel the heat radiating from me. He smiles as he dips two fingers inside me, and his tongue wickedly sweeps over my swollen bud.

"Oh, Sully. Shit. Yes." I lose sense of words and my body when a third finger sinks in and he flicks my G-spot over and over until the air in my lungs turns to fire and my bones melt into jelly.

My body spasms around his fingers and he pushes them in deeper. He sucks on my clit until it's nothing but nerves. He lets me ride my orgasm out on his hand before gently removing himself.

"You smell sugary sweet." He licks the stickiness off his fingers. There's a glint in his eye and then he's on his feet, pulling me up with him. My legs wrap around his waist and my arms tangle around his neck. "This is my favorite view." He licks my nipple and gazes into my eyes.

He carries me into my bedroom and sets me on the mattress. His pants and underwear are kicked to the side and he nudges my legs open with his knee. "I hope you don't plan on swimming straight tomorrow."

"Don't work," is all I can say. My hand strokes his dick, my thumb rubbing against the head.

"Good." He plunges into me. All I can hear is skin on skin and my heavy breathing.

Sully whispers in German, and I grab his balls, and he spills into me.

He falls next to me onto his back, his chest heaving. "Fuck. I gotta write a song about your body."

I nuzzle under his arm and listen to his heart pound and slowly return to normal rhythm. "You want to write me a song, my sailor?"

He twirls my nipple gingerly between the pads of his fingers. "Sailor? Huh? Then you're my mermaid?"

"As you wish." I close my eyes and press my body to his, molding to him. The room smells of sex. I don't think I've ever felt this satisfied.

The only light in my room peeks around the royal purple curtains as the sun rises, turning the sky cotton candy pink and chasing away the stars. I sit up and yank the blanket off before realizing I'm still naked.

"Are you hungry?" I ask, turning to Sully, but all that's on his side is a pillow.

After a few seconds of searching the apartment, I learn I'm alone.

There's a freshly brewed pot of coffee and a box of doughnuts on the kitchen counter. A note half hides under the box. I unfold it and read.

Had to leave for an interview with the band. Lame excuse I know. But if I missed another interview I'd be gutted by Amy or Charlotte. Hope you like the doughnuts and coffee!
I'll make it up to you. I promise.
— Sully

I fall into a kitchen chair and glance at the time on the oven's clock. It's eight in the morning. I touch my thumb to my ring finger to spin the mermaid ring I never take off, but it's gone. I stare at my blank hand. *What happened to my favorite ring?*

My stomach growls, and I bite into a fluffy pink sprinkled doughnut. After, I shower and pull on some oversized sweats and a Kiss t-shirt. I refuse to check my text messages. Instead, I drink coffee while standing on my tiny balcony and enjoy a crisp California morning. The smog is minimal, and I can almost make out the Hollywood sign in the distance. A day off is sacred with my busy schedule, and I won't allow anything to ruin it. I push my missing ring out of my mind and try to remain positive as I sip my delicious coffee.

Chapter Seventeen

WITH MY SECOND CUP of coffee gone, I decide to tear the place apart, searching for my ring. It might not be worth a lot of money, but it was the first gift I bought myself with the money earned from my first successful mermaid gig. It's a promise to never give up and to do anything for my dream. I've had it for years and my finger feels incomplete without it.

First, I search the couch, between every cushion and underneath it. Nothing. I grab a flashlight and look on the ground. I move random things and search behind them. Not sure how the ring would slip off after wearing it all these years, but something happened to it. Finally, I search my room and the bed. Nada. Where the hell could it be?

Did Sully take it?

My phone buzzes. *Is that him admitting his crime?*

Unfortunately, the text is from my mom reminding me of our shopping date today. I look at the time. Shit. I'm late.

I rush into the bathroom to brush my hair and put on a little makeup. With fresh clothes on, I slip on my shoes and fly out the door with my purse.

Mom's sitting in the bookstore's Starbucks at a table with a coffee in hand as she leafs through a magazine.

"Hey, Mom. Hope you weren't waiting long." I sit in the chair across from her.

She glances up from the article she's reading. "It's fine. How are you? Your hair looks a little dull."

I run my fingers through the hair lying on my shoulder. It looks fine to me. "Must've forgotten to condition last night. But I'm good. How are you?"

She's still studying my hair. "It's all that swimming. Those chemicals are not good for your hair."

Of course it's because of my swimming and not running out the door without more than a few strokes from a hairbrush.

Mom closes the magazine and takes a sip of her coffee. "I'm well. Your dad bought a new grill. I'm afraid he's going to burn the house down. Had to have him move it far away from the back porch."

She finishes her drink and tosses it in the trash as we leave the bookstore and enter the mall. For a while we walk side by side in silence. It's nice and peaceful. She motions to a clothing store and we duck inside.

"What do you think of this dress? It would be lovely to interview in. Cute but professional." She lifts a black and white dress with a sweetheart neckline that's knee length.

"It's cute. But I don't need anything to interview in." I sift through a rack of jeans, waiting for her to blow up again over my terrible life choices.

She sighs, hanging the dress back up. "Oh, Ronnie. I wish you'd expand your horizons. You can do your mermaid hobby on the weekends, but you really should get serious and—"

"Mom. I told you, mermaiding isn't a hobby. It's a career." I grab my phone and type in my website to show her it's more than a silly waste of time. "Let me show you my website."

She shakes her head and grabs a shirt, pressing it against her chest and checking it out in the mirror. "That's fine, dear. I believe you." Her flat tone clearly saying the opposite.

A little while later, we grab pepperoni pretzel bites and continue to walk around the mall. She stops by a jewelry store looking at diamond rings in the case.

I eye the salesman warily, hoping he doesn't come over thinking we're going to buy something.

"Do you remember Stacy?" Mom asks, still studying each ring.

"Yeah." How can I forget Mom's best friend's daughter? She's the same age as me but does everything better. Rode her bike without training wheels first. Won the spelling bee in high school. Went off to law school and graduated top of her class. She doesn't do it on purpose, but I've always lived in Stacy's shadow.

"She's getting married next spring to a partner in her law firm."

"Glad she found someone." I don't know what else to say. I haven't physically seen Stacy since high school, but Mom always shows me pictures.

"He proposed in Hawaii at sunset. Very romantic." Sure enough, she's searching for photos on her phone and shoving it under my nose.

There's Stacy, beautiful, successful, and now with a giant rock on her finger. Then there's me, a silly mermaid who's single and slumming it in LA, according to my mother.

"Where are they getting married if he proposed in Hawaii? Already made the stakes quite high," I joke, turning to look at a pearl necklace to avoid my mother's hate-filled glare.

"Veronica, honestly." She tucks her phone away. Thank God. "You need to settle down soon too. I know you were with...what's his name?"

I flinch. My ex only met my parents twice. He didn't like family gatherings. Mom tolerated him because his grandparents went to Harvard and are successful doctors. Sadly, he fell far from that tree. But naturally I'm attracted to rotten apples, hence why I'm not dating anymore. Just laser focused on my mermaiding.

"Not important. I'm happily single."

"But you live with a roommate." Her nose scrunches with disgust.

"So do most people in LA. Actually, I'm lucky to live with just one roommate and not five."

"Sweetie, I'm just looking out for you. Don't you want to have kids?"

Here we go.

"No." I sigh and tug her away from the jewelry counter as the salesman wanders over. "I don't want kids. I don't need a man. I'm perfectly happy with my life."

"As a mermaid," she says in a huff, tossing her pretzel bites away half-eaten.

"Yes."

She checks her smart watch. "I should go home and take Bishop out on a walk. You need to come over for dinner sometime. Your dad misses you."

"I'll check my calendar and get back to you."

She kisses my cheek. "Love you."

As she walks away, a weight yanks me down. It's exhausting being around her. If only she could take the time to understand the mermaid-ing industry, she wouldn't think of me as a joke anymore. But she hears that word, and it triggers her.

When I open the front door, Alice is cleaning. "Am I in the wrong apartment?" I snicker, running my finger along a bookcase and it's clean. Haven't seen that in forever.

"Very funny. When I got here it looked like a Veronica tornado hit. The couch was crooked. Every cabinet door was open. The remotes were in the bathroom. It was insane. After fixing everything, thought I'd tidy up since Emily's coming over later to watch a movie."

"Oh, shit. I forgot about the mess. I had to go shopping with my mom and...it went how you're imagining."

She frowns. "Went to hell."

"So fast. I have third degree burns." I look at my empty finger, remembering my mermaid ring is missing.

"You didn't happen to see my ring anywhere? I lost it."

Alice fake gasps. "The ring you never take off even when showering?"

I roll my eyes. "Yeah. That ring."

"Haven't seen it. Sorry." She eyes my bedroom and then me. "Maybe someone took it."

"What?"

She flips her hair dramatically. "I don't know. Looks like someone had some fun in the sack and maybe he took it."

"Maybe..."

Alice laughs. "Text him and see. Emily should be here soon." She gives me a look as if asking me to disappear.

"I'll be in my room doing orders from my website. People really love the pillow and new shirt options I added. And don't worry. I'll have my noise cancelling headphones on the entire time."

After finishing my one hundred and forty orders and setting them against my closet since Alice would skin me alive if I put the packages in the living room, I lie on my bed and stare at my naked hand.

Thinking back, I do remember having the ring while watching *Die Hard* because Sully commented on how cute it was when I reached for popcorn. So, it's in the apartment...or is it?

I lie across the bed on my stomach, kicking my legs in the air. He's going to think I'm weird asking him if he ripped a ring right off my finger while I was asleep, but I have to know. It's that or there's a ghost who is vicious enough to watch me run around with my head chopped off.

Before I chicken out, I type out a quick text and hit send. I roll over onto my back, clenching my teeth. My stomach twists with nerves, tight and fluttery, like it's trying to fold in on itself.

What are you thinking? Why would a rock star want your damn ring that's not even worth a hundred bucks? When did you become the center of the universe?

I press my fingers into my eyes as a bitter laugh cuts through my teeth. The phone vibrates with his reply.

You mean this?

And he shares a picture of my ring on his thumbnail.

Fucking bastard!

Sudden rage spikes through my veins. I bolt into a sitting position with my feet planted on the floor. After inhaling a breath, I type my reply.

Why did you take my ring!?

To ensure I'd see you again. Come over. I'll send a car.

Kinda feels serial killer-like now.

You can strip-search me if it makes you feel better.

Going to do more than that when I get my hands on you

Can't wait. Car will be there in 15 mins!

What am I doing? I brush my hands over my torso. *Getting your ring back of course. What's the harm in flirting too?*

Chapter Eighteen

It's a frivolous problem, but I'm not sure what to wear. My outfit can't scream "groupie in need of another fix," but I don't want to appear like a stick in the mud, annoyed and waiting to collect what was taken and then turn and leave. Maybe a black and red plaid skirt with a black spaghetti strap crop top. Simple but nice.

As I change, my eye catches the red leather jacket lying haphazardly on my bed. It wouldn't hurt to try it on and see if it will make or break the outfit.

A boot hidden underneath a pile of clothes trips me and I go flying into a bookshelf. It wabbles but thankfully doesn't tip over. Unfortunately, a dozen books rain down from the shelves, forcing me to cover my head for protection and wince as random sharp edges of hardcovered books strike my body.

Alice bursts into my room wearing a thin nightshirt that comes to her thighs. "What the hell are you doing?"

"What are you wearing?" I ask, rubbing my head where the corner of a book hit me. I check for blood on my hand and am happy to say I don't see any. But I'm going to have a giant knot on my head. At least my hair will hide it.

"Emily and I got comfy on the couch," Alice says, pushing the door open wider. She scratches the back of her leg with her right foot. "Did a bomb go off in here?" She kicks a pile of shoe boxes, and they tip over, spilling their contents.

"I tripped and was almost killed by books."

"Sounds legit with the number of books you hoard." She leans against the doorway.

"Hey, books are important," I reply, while unburying myself from the books and standing on shaky legs.

Alice coughs when she smells one of the many perfumes on my dresser. "If I don't need to rescue you, I'm going back to my movie." She scrunches her nose as she replaces the perfume.

"I'm going out," I say too fast, grabbing my leather jacket and pushing past her. "Turns out Sully did steal my ring." I grab my phone from my bra and show her the picture he sent. "And he wants me to come get it."

She forgets about my perfume collection and snatches my phone, zooming in as if I'm lying. A whistle sails through her lips as she taps a pink fingernail on the screen. "Of course he does." She snickers. "You got him good."

"Please. He's stealing jewelry off my person as an excuse to see me again. Isn't that borderline psychopath or something?"

She shrugs. "Depends on who you ask." She clicks her tongue and grabs the jacket from my grasp. "This is a no. Are you trying to look like Lzzy Hale?"

"At least I'm not wearing sky-high boots," I say, glancing down at my outfit.

She shakes her head, tossing the jacket onto my bed. "Maybe at a concert you can look all rock glam, but you're meeting him at his place. You need to be more subtle." She dusts invisible lint off my shoulder and walks around me with a finger pressed to her lips. "If you want, I can be your fairy godmother like what Cinderella had. I'll dress you up before—"

"No. I'm not a princess and never will be." I push her away and walk toward the living room. She's hot on my tail and is about to argue when a car horn honks outside. I check my phone. It's my ride.

Emily stands up, holding a mostly empty popcorn bowl. "What's going on?"

Alice bats her eyelashes at me. "Veronica here has bagged a sexy bass player who stole her favorite ring to get her back into bed."

"Damn. Sounds ripped out of the pages of a steamy romance novel."

Alice snort laughs. "It does."

"I can't believe you two." I sigh. "My ride's here so—"

"Go nail that rock star." Emily loops her arm around Alice. "We approve."

Alice giggles, yelling, "You're being safe, right?" as she makes a dick motion with her hands. Emily is cry laughing, slapping the top of the couch.

"I'm not a teenager. We're good. Thank you, *Mother*." I snag my purse and slip on a pair of flats and hightail it outside before she tries fixing my hair or adding lipstick to my bare lips.

Alice means well, but I don't need her to be my big sister and dress me for a "hot" date nor do I need any advice from her or Emily. I like that Sully has seen me without a mask. He's seen the real me and wants more.

I slide into the back seat of the waiting town car and dig inside my purse for my strawberry lip balm. The driver is the strong silent type, following the GPS while playing classical music on low. It's awkward going to a place I've never been. Maybe insane. My stomach turns on itself as doubt gnaws at my brain.

What if I'm making a huge mistake? But what if I'm not?

Guess I'll see.

Chapter Nineteen

THE DRIVER PULLS INTO the driveway of a hotel. When the driver passes the passenger drop-off area and keeps driving along the road that winds behind the hotel, I get lightheaded as my heart lodges in my throat. Where are we going?

Out the window are little houses. I squint to read the plaques in front of them. The house with ivy covering most of its cream-colored face with a fire engine red door is called The Garden Private Casitas.

Damn, Sully is staying in one of these casitas? I've heard how nice they are. Like little homes but with the luxury of being in a fine hotel. Could he be in one alone or is the entire band with him?

Anxiety bubbles within me as we stop in front of the casitas known as The Star. The building is red brick with a light blue door and flower boxes under the windows with pretty little purple blossoms inside. The path toward the front door is cobblestone steps cutting through the greenest grass I've ever seen in California.

"Thank you," I tell the driver and slip out of the car. As he drives away, my panic surges. What am I doing? My legs stiffen as I make my way to the entrance. For a moment, I pause, glancing at the small patio and swing bench between two arched windows.

After taking several deep breaths, I knock on the door, and its rough wood scrapes my knuckles. It swings open, and Sully greets me with a smirk, wearing a tight white shirt and low-hanging jeans. "Welcome." He flashes my ring on his pinkie and beckons me inside with his other hand. His blue eyes hold a glint of mischief. As soon as I step inside, freshly brewed coffee fills my nose.

"What do you think of my place?" He opens his arms wide, walking toward the open-space kitchen area.

"It's nice." I place my purse on top of the brown leather couch. "Are you staying here alone?" I peek down the dark hallway with closed doors.

"Yeah. The rest of the band is crashing in a house in Beverly Hills, but I wanted more personal space." He grabs two mugs from the cabinet and sets them on the shiny black marble counter. "You want coffee?"

"Sounds good." I watch him pour the coffee and grab the creamer and milk from the fridge, my ring catching a glint from the fluorescent overhead whenever it hits the right angle, shining on his pinkie like it belongs there.

"I don't know how you like it." He places a spoon next to my mug as he drinks his black.

"When are you planning on giving me my ring back?" I pour milk into my mug and stir it with the spoon. "And why did you steal it in the first place?"

He taps the ring's silver band against the side of his green mug. "Steal is such a strong word. I wouldn't go that far." He downs the rest of his coffee and pours himself more.

"What would you call it then?" I watch him over the rim of my cup.

He pulls a blue and white checkered dish towel off a square object, revealing a package of blueberry muffins underneath as if it's a magic trick to change the subject. "You want a muffin?" He rips off the sticker and opens the container. They smell amazing and almost distract me enough from my ring, but not quite.

"You're avoiding my question." I place my coffee next to the muffin he gave me on a paper towel.

Sully bites into his muffin, and crumbs tumble from his mouth all over his shirt. He mutters something in German.

"You should know I don't like mind games." I break a small piece of muffin off the top and squish it between my fingers. "Especially when it involves my stuff. I'm an only child and—"

"Eat first." He licks his fingers and brushes them on his shirt.

Why am I getting a fifty shades vibe from him?

I remove the wrapper and inspect the muffin.

"Do you think I poisoned you?" he asks, voice soft and eyes cast down. He sounds offended.

"What should I think? You take my ring while I'm sleeping then have the world's quietest driver drop me off at your little casita. The first thing you give me is coffee and muffins. It's all a little suspicious."

Sully plucks the ring off his pinkie and takes my hand, placing the ring in my palm. "I meant it as a joke. Guess it wasn't funny."

I slip the ring onto its rightful finger and spin it. "I'm not into pranks or being teased." A terrible memory of my uncle always teasing me the summer I stayed with my cousin floats to mind. If I said I was bored, he'd reply, "Hi, bored, nice to meet you." He'd steal my library books and hide them in places, usually too high for me to reach, and forget, and then I wouldn't have enough time to finish the book before it was due. He once hip-checked me, and I tripped on the sidewalk, scraping my knee. My cousin chuckled. She liked it when her father wasn't on her back for once.

Closing my eyes for a moment, I lock those memories into the box they came from and bury them deep inside my mind.

Sully pouts, sulking into his muffin, taking tiny bites.

To show good faith, I bite into my muffin. It is moist and smells amazing with juicy blueberries baked inside the golden-brown batter. "If you would've invited me over for coffee, I would've said yes. There wasn't a need to pull this is what I'm trying to get at," I say, taking a big bite. Crumbs fall from my lips and chin, but the taste is so out-of-this-world I don't care.

He doesn't look at me. Instead, he closes the plastic muffin container, pushing it away. "I can call another ride if you want to go. It's cool. I didn't—"

"No." I close the distance between us and place a hand above his heart. "Can we enjoy our coffee?"

He nods, topping me off and pouring another for himself. "There's a deck out the sliding glass door. Let's check out the view."

I follow him outside, and he isn't lying. The view is breathtaking. I was too nervous in the car driving here to realize we were driving up the side of a hill. As far as the eye can see is Los Angeles.

Sully sits on the railing and nods toward the horizon. "That blurry grayish-blue thing is the ocean. Quite a sight, right? Way better than the condo the band is renting. Their view is of a wall."

"My last apartment had a view of a wall. Couldn't see an inch of the sky from any window. It was depressing." I rest my elbows on the railing and sip my coffee.

Sully's hand grazes my hip and settles on the small of my back. Heat blooms in my chest and spills upward, dizzying and sweet. I turn into him, breathing in the warm scent of coffee, blueberries, and sandal-wood—softened by just a trace of mint.

His fingers slide into my hair as my lips skim his jawline and find his mouth. We pause, catching our breath. He tips my head back with his finger. "Do you want to see the bedroom?" he asks in a silky-smooth voice.

A pulse of want stirs low in my belly, humming through me like a lit fuse. But I manage a small smile and shake my head. "I'd like the coffee to settle in my stomach first."

"Oh. Right." He motions to the couch and we sit down. "I'm not using you for sex or anything." The tips of his ears redden as I watch him sweat out his next set of words. "I just wanted your company. I like you and..."

"It's not your fault. My ex liked to use sex to kill an argument. It killed the thrill of it. And with you..." I run my fingers through my hair, using it as a curtain to hide behind. "I know you're going to leave LA to go home and I don't want those bad feelings to return."

"Abandonment issues," he says softly, dragging a hand down his face.

My spine stiffens. "Excuse me. I'd call it—"

He waves his hand in the air like he wants to erase his words. "Sorry. I didn't mean to offend you. I know how you feel. Before the girlfriend who left me for a different bass player, I had a woman leave me because I was never around. Said I loved the road more and probably cheated on her. Turns out she just wanted to fuck her neighbor."

"Who needs a relationship? Right now, my focus is on my career. I'm going to continue to grow my social media and land more gigs. There's a mermaid show coming up in Miami next year and I'm super close to landing a cruise line as a sponsor."

"I love your drive. It makes the green in your eyes shine like emeralds."

"Says a songwriter." I playfully punch his arm and bite my cheek to keep my smile in check.

"No. I'm serious. It's good to love what you do in life, but don't you want someone to spend it with? I want someone to share my life with. To be there for the good times and console each other through the tough times."

"After reading enough romance novels, you start to think love only exists in fictional worlds," I say, lowering my head so my hair veils my face.

He gently brushes it back. "If that's true, then what is life but a bleak countdown to the end?"

I shrug. "With random bursts of happiness, but yeah, pretty much."

He captures my chin with his hand and brushes his thumb over my lower lip. "How can someone who's a mermaid for a living and brings such joy be so sad and dark?"

"Talent," I mumble, looking past him to the painting of weird black and white lines tangling together in a gold frame. Whoever decorated this place has odd taste.

"Nein. Du kannst mich nicht täuschen, Schatz," he whispers into the shell of my ear. His lips trail kisses along my jawline.

"What did you say?"

He smiles. "You can't fool me." He stands and takes my hand, pulling me to my feet. "I have an idea."

He ushers me to sit on a chair at the kitchen table as he disappears down the hall. He comes back with his guitar.

My heart skips a beat as he takes a chair across from me and sets the guitar on his lap.

"You're going to sing?"

He nods. "I'd call it serenading."

"Oh?" I rest my elbow on the table and cradle my cheek against my hand. "Go on."

He strums the strings and clears his throat. The melody is plucky but slowly becomes softer. "I hear the birds singing, as my tears sting. I've lost my north star. I don't even know who you are. My heart's racing, my thoughts turn into a pinwheel of color. Reflected in the mirror, who am I facing? Thunder rolls with a howling wind." Sully closes his eyes as his fingers glide over the guitar's strings. I lean closer, resting my knee close to his.

"Life's bitter. How I long for sweet death. No matter where I go, we'll meet. I have more tears than the sky has rain. No matter what I do, I'm always in pain. Lightning lights up my window, all my marks become aglow. I look away to see a sparrow. She flies away, I wish to follow. For you my dear, I give my soul. For you my love, I relinquish all control."

He stops and lets his guitar drop between his legs. His eyes catch mine and I'm drowning.

"Wow. That's amazing."

"Thanks. I wrote it for you last night. Kinda came to me. Not sure where it's going."

"It's dark and beautiful."

"Like you." He reaches for my hand and gently kisses the back of it. He turns my wrist and kisses up my inner arm. His scruff tickles. I can't conceal my giggle.

"I love your laugh. It's my favorite music."

"You say that to all the girls?" I grab his guitar and place it on the table so I can sit on his lap. His arms circle my waist, his warmth sends pains of desire through my stomach.

Sully brushes his nose against mine. "No. When I first saw you, it was like someone lit a fire in my icy chest. And seeing you again behind the venue, it was magic. I wanted to see you. To touch you." He trails his fingers along my ribs. "And now that I have, it's like I can't get enough."

My heart flutters. Is he saying these pretty words as a musician or does he mean them? Right now I don't care. No man has treated me like I'm the only woman in the world. Looked at me like I'm priceless. I don't want this to stop.

I capture his mouth with mine. Our tongues dance as I sink my hands into his hair and gingerly pull. My hips have a mind of their own and buck against him. He moans.

"You can show me the bedroom now...if you still want to."

His stands and I instinctually wrap my legs around his torso. "*Schatz, ich gehöre dir.*" His accent sends electricity through my blood. I nip at his neck as he carries me to the bedroom.

Chapter Twenty

WE SHED OUR CLOTHES and fall onto the bed in a tangle of naked limbs. Sully licks my collarbone and sucks my nipple into his mouth, giving it a teasing bite that drives me insane. I buck my hips higher as his mouth travels down my stomach. He forces my thighs apart with his hands and takes his time, kissing his way up. At first, his thumb rubs against my clit.

"You're already so swollen and wet for me." He dips a finger inside, and I curl my fingers around the metal iron bars where the headboard should be.

"You're such a *braves Mädchen*," he murmurs, voice low and reverent. Then he glances up at me, eyes dark with heat. "Such a good girl."

Usually, it takes me a while to get going, but Sully knows the right combination to unlock my body. To make me feel things I've never experienced before.

He hooks his hands under my knees and pulls me closer. His blue eyes darken with desire as his gaze pierces into me. My breath hitches when his face dips between my legs. "You smell incredible..."

I bite the pillow as his mouth finds me, and a scream rips from my throat with the first stroke of his tongue. He moves deeper, more deliberate, each motion unraveling me.

When I reach the peak—every muscle tightening, hips bucking, pleasure rolling through me in waves—he pulls away and sinks his teeth into my thigh, marking me. A shiver rockets down my spine.

He plants his hands on either side of my torso and pulls himself up, hovering over me. I wrap my arms around his neck as he kisses my lips.

Using all my strength, I force him to roll over and straddle him. My hips line with his perfectly. "My turn," I murmur, running my nails down his chest.

He's already stiff and large when I reach down to grasp his penis. I pump the base a couple of times, and he groans in pleasure.

A sinister smile curls my lips as I get into a better position, sitting back on my legs. There's a bead of moisture on his tip already. My thumb rubs it away, circling him a few times before easing him into my mouth. My tongue traces the thick vein underneath his cock and he grabs handfuls of sheets as I close my lips around his shaft. He's big, but I'm able to fill my mouth with him to the hilt. It doesn't take long before he comes. I swallow and lie beside him as he tries to calm his breathing.

"That mouth of yours is something," he says, resting his head on his arm.

"Hmm." I lay my cheek on his chest and lazily trace the spider tattoo just below his belly button.

The air is thick with the scent of sweat, skin, and satisfaction. My hair is tangled from fingers and friction, clinging to my neck in damp waves. "I'm taking a shower."

Sully follows, completely naked, not even pretending to hesitate. "Allow me." He turns on the hot water and we step inside together. Warm streams cascade from the ceiling while the detachable showerhead rests on the wall, filling the space with steam as the heat sinks into our bodies.

I look at his shampoo; it's the basic kind hotels offer, but squirting some in my hand it smells like lilacs and honey. As I lather my hair, Sully snags my wrists with each hand. "Let me wash you."

He pumps some shampoo into his palm and focuses on each strand like he's trying to make my hair shine. He has me lower my head back and gingerly runs his fingers through my hair until all the suds are gone.

He grabs the conditioner and his brow crinkles. "I never use this."

"It's for the ends."

He smiles and lathers it between his hands before adding it to my hair.

"As that sits for a bit, let me wash your hair," I say.

Sully lowers himself to his knees, allowing his head to be the same level as my chest. I lather his hair and create a mohawk on the center of his head. I bite my tongue, but he can feel my laughter with his hands planted on my hips.

"What did you do?" He reaches up and feels the spikes.

"I couldn't resist."

"You're going to pay for that." He stands and snags the showerhead from the wall. "Now be a good girl and place your foot here." He points to the soap dish and turns the setting on the showerhead to a more singular and powerful water jet.

Oh, fuck.

My foot fits in the soap dish perfectly. He hooks his right arm around me to keep me steady as he nudges my thighs open wider with the back of the showerhead. When he turns it around, the water hits the perfect place on my clit and I bite his shoulder.

My legs weaken and he supports my weight as the water moves farther down and back up. He finally drops the showerhead, allowing it to smack hard into the wall and plunges three fingers inside me. "This belongs to me."

"Yes..." I feel myself tighten around his fingers. As he moves in and out, the orgasm hits me like a train.

Sully hangs the showerhead back up and grabs a washcloth, adding some body wash, and washes me. He's careful around my sensitive bits; a little too handsy on my breasts, but I won't complain.

After we rinse off, he grabs us each a towel. I bury myself into the fluffy white cloth and pad to the bed. I'm too sleepy to get dressed; this towel dress will have to do.

Sully grabs a small remote from the nightstand beside him. He hits a button, and the window blinds close, erasing all light.

I drape a leg over his and use his torso as the perfect pillow, listening to the steady rhythm of his heartbeat. His fingers gently flow through my hair, making it easy to fall asleep in his embrace.

Chapter Twenty-One

THE BEDROOM DOOR BANGS open. I jump and burrow deeper into the bed as the curtains fly apart, pouring in blinding sunlight. I roll onto my side, but all I can make out in the bright white light is a dark figure surrounded by red dots.

"Sully? What's going on?" I mumble, blinking through the haze of sleep and smudged dreams.

"What the fresh hell is this?" A female voice stabs through my eardrums and pierces my brain.

I sit up like a metal rod is shoved into my spine and grasp the sheet to my bare chest. "Who are you?" My heart plummets into my belly. Never taking my attention off the invader, I nudge Sully harder and shake his shoulder. He snores and mutters something before rolling out of my reach.

The woman in a pale blue blouse and black pencil skirt frowns at me before typing something on her phone. I narrow my eyes. I've seen her before. She looks like the annoyed woman waiting by the wall when Sully and the rest of the band were doing meet and greets after the show in LA.

She ignores me and walks over to Sully's side of the bed, smacking his leg repeatedly. "Get up! You're late!"

Sully grumbles and moves again. His arm searches for me. He grabs my wrist, tugging me back into his warm body.

"A woman is here," I hiss, nudging his chest.

His eyes fly open. They're wild and blue like a hurricane in the ocean. He leaps out of bed as if he drank a pot of death coffee and got tased in the ass. In a blur of motion, he grabs his boxers from the floor and shoves them on in a blink of an eye. If there was a race to get dressed, he'd place in the top three.

"What are you doing in my bedroom?" he demands, grabbing the pillow that fell on his foot and tossing it back onto the bed. "Didn't you see the closed door? Not only that but the front door was locked!"

"You wouldn't answer your phone," Amy says, deadpan, as if that explains why she invaded our privacy like a bomb was about to go off. "I figured you found a nice side piece to distract you and..." She nods at me.

Horror prickles at the base of my skull. They think I'm a side piece of ass? *Am* I just a side piece? I hang my head, hiding behind the curtain of hair to conceal my blush.

"Fuck you." Sully strides forward and shoves Amy's shoulder, but she doesn't budge. "I'll get to the damn studio when I'm ready. Now leave," Sully orders, pointing at the door.

I lift my gaze briefly to see the muscles straining in his back as tension rolls off his skin. I'd give anything to rub his shoulders while he whispers into my ear that this is all some big misunderstanding. That I'm not just another hookup and being strung along like I always feared would happen.

Amy whips her head to the side, moving her long black bangs out of her eyes. The haircut oddly works with her sharp nose and square jaw. But her eyes are dull pinpricks, like a shark's. She sighs, the sound is harsh. I feel like this woman sighs a lot. Her lips bend into a permanent frown. "Sully, you—"

"Out," Sully orders, standing firm with his arms across his chest.

She tsks and finally moves a couple of steps toward the door before her shark eyes land on me again as if I'm a little fish she could swallow whole. "I'll wait out here while you get dressed," she says, never removing her glare from me. I'm pinned into place, stuck in the bed naked with only a sheet to hide me as if she's some wicked witch who cursed me to stay still. Maybe she's related to Medusa and I'll turn to stone by the end of the day.

Just as fast as she blew into the bedroom, she's gone. But my heart remains hidden in my belly, too afraid to move back into its correct position. All my nerves are on edge as fear trickles down my spine.

Sully kicks the door closed, the wood rattling against the frame. He paces for a moment at the foot of the bed, shoving his hands into his messy hair. "I'm so sorry." He grabs his clothes, pulling on his pants and shirt. His palms smooth over the wrinkles, but they stay creased. "Give me five minutes. I'll get rid of her."

I swallow hard, the lump in my throat thick and unmoving. He's fully dressed—except for his shoes—and I'm still naked under the covers, while a stranger waits outside, ready to burn me at the stake for daring to tempt her rock star.

"What about the studio?" My voice sounds stronger than I feel.

He shrugs, forcing a smile that doesn't quite reach his eyes. "They can wait while I drop you off at home."

I nod, slipping on my practiced mask, trying to look cool and unbothered. But inside, everything is tight and knotted, my stomach churning with dread. A sick, twisting tension coils in my gut, like I'm bracing for something to break.

Is he dropping me off...and that's it? Goodbye forever? Should I ask? No—don't ask questions if you're not ready for the answers.

Sully slips out of the room, closing the door with a loud click. It's like a bullet to my soul. While alone, I gather my clothes and piece myself together. Their voices carry through the thin wall, and I can't help but overhear.

Amy's heels scrape against the wooden floor. One well-placed match would make this condo go up in flames and this whole awkward situation would be over in a flash.

"Sully, really," she sighs but sounds like it's more for effect than anything else. I can picture her as one of those helicopter PR reps who must fix everything just so. Straightening a picture here or moving a flower vase there. "You had to find a groupie when you need to be focusing on recording the new album. We booked studio time here to keep you on track and you're—"

"How do you expect me to write without inspiration?" Sully spits back. His voice sends my stomach into a summersault.

"It's not just the record. You're performing at the Rock Music Awards in a few days and you need to practice your set."

I cover my mouth to snuff my gasp. Could he be thinking of bringing me to the red-carpet event where Hollywood icons walk and talk? People I'd never dream of seeing in flesh and blood instead of on billboards, bus stops, and TV screens? What if I sit next to someone super famous? Should I prepare talking points?

"Practice? We're playing one song. Why do we—"

Amy cuts Sully off with a tongue click. I can't see her face, but in my mind's eye she's scowling and daggers fly out of her shark eyes.

"Forget it. Oh, and Gigi is all set to be your date. She's super excited and already looking for the perfect dress. This is excellent timing for fans to see you two mesh before the European tour. This could also add a nice buzz for the record release next year."

"What? No." Sully's voice is cold as steel.

My heart shatters on the floor. Of course, I'm not allowed to go. Why did I think there'd be a chance in hell I'd be invited? It's for the pretty people and I don't belong.

"Come on. The fans love your duet and want more. She's blowing the charts up right now. Don't you want Scarlet Failure on everyone's radar?" Amy's voice drips of sugar but deep down it's poison.

"Humph." I plop my ass onto the bed and close my eyes. Gigi isn't that great. So what if her new album is soaring and blowing up on Spotify? She mixes rock and pop with a breathy voice and loud bass. In her videos, she mainly dances and screams. Last year she won three Grammys. Her newest single is about breaking up with a guy and setting his house on fire. Though if it was to escape a situation like this, I'd understand.

"No!" Sully's voice bursts my thoughts and forces me to jump off the bed as if tased. "Veronica's my date."

My skin is too hot at the mention of my name. I couldn't be happier there's a door between Amy and me.

My phone vibrates in my hand. I unlock it and see five missed texts from Alice. I need to cover Chloe's shift, and here I am hiding in a room like a mistress almost caught by her lover's wife.

With a deep breath and double-checking my reflection in the mirror, I dare step out into the chaos. They both look my way like I'm disturbing a church service.

Chapter Twenty-Two

"Hey...I need to go." I lift my phone. "I ordered a ride." I hit the final button to finish the rideshare before Sully argues, insisting to drive me back.

"You can wait outside." Amy points to the door with her chin. She places her hands on her hips as she stares me down, probably wishing she could toss me out herself.

"Okay..." I skirt past her and steal a glance at Sully. He clenches his jaw and moves toward the door, pressing his hand against it. Blocking my exit and keeping me in this hell. Terror prickles my spine knowing Amy is only a few feet away.

"No. She's not some whore you can toss out. She's my guest and she can wait inside until her car gets here." His voice is harsh and sharp enough to cut glass. I'd feel more honored if Amy would stop staring at me with her shark eyes. My hand flutters to my throat, the need to protect my jugular comes as if by instinct. Maybe Amy is a vampire. That would explain so much.

Sully's hands cup my hips, gently guiding me away from the door, but I'm too uncomfortable to sit anywhere in this room. The air is thick with disdain. Amy stands in the center of the room, typing on her phone. Her fingers dance across the screen. But when the hairs on the back of my neck rise, I realize she's staring into my soul. Maybe she's a succubus and eats the souls of girls she hates.

Sully sits on the couch and kindly pulls me onto his lap. I sit down stiffly. The back of my brain bristles as the heat of his thighs soaks through my skin and into my bloodstream.

Amy pours herself a cup of coffee, using my mug, and sips it as she tears me to ribbons with her eyes.

"What do you do?" Her voice rumbles the still room, shaking me out of the frozen state I fell into.

Why does she care to talk to me now?

Her shark eyes analyze me. She wants to put me in my place. Prove she's right. I'm just a groupie.

"I'm a model and performer," I say in the most clipped summarized version of my work. If my car would arrive now that would be a miracle.

Amy grimaces, her face twists as if she smells something sour. "Model for what brand?"

Shit. I stepped right into that one.

Sully wraps his arms around my waist, pulling me in closer. "She's a professional mermaid. She does private events, has a show in a popular restaurant downtown, and models for her huge social media following."

She spits out her coffee and wipes her mouth on a napkin. Her frown lines deepen, and a thick green vein bulges in her forehead. I slip off

Sully's lap and sink into the couch cushion, wishing it would eat me whole. My teeth bite into my lower lip as I briefly consider hiding behind Sully, using him as a shield, fearing she'll grab a knife from the kitchen and slit my throat.

"Did I hear you right? A mermaid?" She spews the word "mermaid" like it's a curse, and her lip curls in disgust.

I've had my share of naysayers in my line of work. People mock me for dressing in a mermaid tail, saying it's not a real job, that I'm foolish, a child, or too lazy to get a "real" job. Some even asked if I stayed in a mental hospital recently. But I'm the one laughing. My planned events and modeling gigs pay six figures, and that's before I find sponsors for social media platforms. The thing about money is it goes fast in LA. I have a healthy savings account and another account to keep new tails coming, repair the ones I love, and whatever else I may require. But I refuse to pay crazy expensive rent on a slightly bigger apartment when all I do at home is sleep or watch TV in my downtime, which is rare, depending on the time of year.

A car horn honks outside, and my phone buzzes with a text. My ride is here to save the day. Knowing I have an escape route gives me enough confidence to tell Amy off before taking my leave.

"Yes. A mermaid. My social media has over one hundred thousand followers, and I'm in dozens of magazine articles. Just look up Mermaid Veronica." I stand tall, staring down on this woman who would kill to crush me. "And for the record, I didn't want to go to your stupid music award thing. All I wanted was Sully to give me my ring back." I flash the ring, hoping Amy thought I gave her the bird, and storm out.

Sully is on my heels, preventing me from hearing a satisfactory door slam. He grabs my wrist, but I tug myself free. "Please leave me alone.

You don't think I'm used to people mocking my career choice? I'm a big girl. It was fun whatever we were to each other, but let's face it, we need to get back to the real world where we live two separate lives."

"Don't let her words ruin what we could be."

"This has to be goodbye." I wiggle my fingers in a wave and don't turn back. Once I'm in the back seat of my rideshare, I reply to Alice's text, asking her to grab my red tail, and I'll meet her at work.

The driver curses. I look to see what's the problem. Dead end ahead. There's no way out from the casitas except doing a U-turn and driving past Sully again.

"Hate this place. Damn fire trap," the driver mutters as he pulls into another place's driveway and continues down the road we just left.

Sully spots us and rushes into the road, waving his arms. My driver curses again and comes to a complete stop.

"Please roll down your window and let me explain," Sully begs, knocking on the glass.

I roll my eyes and hit the button to lower the window halfway. "What else is there to say?"

He waves Amy forward. She stops scrolling through her phone and eyes me curiously with a pinch less disdain than before. "After reviewing your...career and showing no interest in perks, such as the music awards, I figure you're allowed to stay."

"Allowed?" I say with bite, digging my nails into my palms, creating perfectly pink crescent moons. Part of me wants to laugh in her face at the ridiculousness, but her face is dead serious.

"As far as the world knows, you and Sully mean nothing. You're nothing..." She pauses, tilting her head, reminding me of Michael Myers studying his victims before slicing them in half. "To each other, I mean."

"I don't know who you are, but you can't control me. How about I—"

The other back door flies open, and Sully jumps in. "Let's go!" he shouts.

"What the hell?" The driver turns around to glare at Sully.

Amy's nostrils flare. "Get out! We don't have time for this."

Sully pounds on the passenger's seat headrest. "What are you waiting for? Drive!"

The driver floors it. Amy shakes her fist in the air, yelling curses at us.

"What are you doing? Trying to get me murdered?" I punch Sully's arm.

He chuckles, turning his phone off.

"Like I said, I'm taking you home, and then I'll go to the studio. They can start without me."

"Well, I'm heading to work. Need to cover for Chloe."

He shrugs. "Then I'm dropping you off at work."

I squint at him. "You know I ordered this ride, right?"

"And I'm stealing it by paying in cash." Sully leans forward and smirks at the driver. "If that's okay with you."

"As long as I'm paid with a good fat tip," he says in a deep smoker's voice.

Sully curls his finger around a strand of my hair. He's close, too close. His hot breath on my neck sends an ache between my legs. I want that mouth on me again, making me come again. Fuck. He's already inside my head.

His hand brushes my breast, and my nipple peaks at the attention. "See. It always works out," he whispers, kissing the sensitive skin below my ear.

A whimper slips past my lips. My entire body betrays me. I want to resist his charm, but I'm mush to his dimples and blue eyes. "What's that witch's problem anyway?"

He scoffs. "Our PR rep, Amy. She's vicious, rude, and like a dog with a bone, but she's good at her job. Unfortunately, she's my aunt's friend and thinks it's in my best interest to look out for me since I'm single and heartbroken. Her words." He slams his back against the seat and pulls on his hair. "She doesn't know when to quit. But she's never been this cruel. I can't apologize more for what she said."

"Whatever. She hates me." My head falls against the seat.

Sully's fingers brush up and down my arm. "She wanted to scare you. I told you how my ex dumped me for another bass player. She doesn't want that to happen again."

"Yeah. Because I just jump from musician dick to musician dick like I have no life." I huff and catch the eye of the driver in the rearview mirror. He winces and his eyes return to the road.

Great. Now this driver thinks I'm a slut. That's lovely.

"She's protective. But I'll get her to lay off."

"And what does that mean for the music awards?" I ask, staring at my mermaid ring to avoid his gaze.

"You can come if you want. They're never as fun as you might think."

"But Gigi would be better PR for the band." I study the hem of my skirt, tracing the stitches with my finger.

"It wouldn't hurt. We are touring with her soon."

"You can take Gigi to that award show. I don't care." I pull on a loose thread, unraveling a few stitches. "I hated how cheap Amy made me feel. I'm not a casual girl. With my ex I had him wait three months before we..." I trail off, remembering we have an eavesdropping driver.

Sully leans over and kisses my bare shoulder. "You're priceless, and I'd never call you casual. Relationships mean something to you. I like that." His words send a zing through my bones.

I turn my head to say something, but he kills it by pressing his lips to mine. Damn it, he can win any argument with those delicious lips.

We make out like teenagers on prom night until the car halts. The driver clears his throat. "We've arrived at The Pearl Kingdom."

"Guess I'll see you later," I say, opening the door. There's a buzzing in my ears as I slip out of the car.

Sully sticks his head out the door and shouts, "I'll pick you up for dinner!"

Maybe it's because I'm swept up in the moment, but I scream, "Okay!" It's silly, but I watch the car drive off, pressing my fingers to my bee-stung lips.

The moment burns off with the scorching sun. After counting to three in my head, I step into the restaurant. To avoid any unwanted eye contact, I tuck my chin into my chest and speed walk toward the breakroom.

My phone rings; it's my mom. I ignore her and make a mental note to call her back later. Out of habit, I open Insta and scroll. There are still a few minutes before my mermaid persona is needed in the tank.

But maybe I should've gone for my tail and not my phone when I see a post from Gigi. She's making a kissy face and wearing a silver crown with pink diamonds. The caption reads, "Can't wait for the Rock Music Awards. Just got my beautiful dress! Who's my date you ask? Only the sexy bass guitarist from Scarlet Failure. XOXO."

Well, this killed my mood. I ditch my phone and try to put on a happy face as I climb the stairs and prepare for my show. Veronica might have a shattered heart that can't repair itself, but Mermaid Veronica has a heart of gold, and nothing can destroy her.

Chapter Twenty-Three

"You have nothing to be nervous about," Alice says, snapping a chocolate chip cookie in half.

"Who says I'm nervous?" I toss a crumpled paper towel at her. "Didn't your mother teach you to eat cookies and not destroy them?"

She narrows her eyes and breaks the cookie into smaller chunks before popping a piece into her mouth. "If you're not nervous, tell that to your hands because if that ring was human, it would be dizzy as hell."

Shit. She's right. I always twist my mermaid ring when I'm uneasy. I wonder if that's why Sully stole it.

"Whatever." I drop my hands to my sides and step into my favorite pair of black stilettos, focusing too hard on the scuff on the inside of the shoe's right heel. I rub it over and over until it fades away.

There's a knock on the door and I almost trip over the couch to answer it.

"Subtle," Alice teases, eating more of that cookie, or its remains. I swear it takes her forever to eat one cookie. She says it makes it last longer, but honestly, she loves to drive me nuts. The girl gets crumbs everywhere and I'm the one who cleans them up.

When I open the door, Sully stands there wearing tight black jeans and a black Def Leppard tour shirt.

"Good show?" I ask, nodding to his attire.

He looks down as if he forgot what he had on and plucks at its collar. "Hell yeah. Caught their last tour in Germany. Have you been?"

"Seen the band, but I haven't had the pleasure of traveling out of the country."

"Not yet!" Alice chimes in, holding the box of cookies and digging out another one.

She chuckles as I shoot daggers over my shoulder. She blows me a kiss and disappears into our tiny kitchen.

Sully offers me a small smirk. "I can fix that. But let's start with dinner."

"What do you have in mind?" I grab my purse and close the front door behind me.

"Actually...I was thinking of cooking for you. I promise I'm an excellent chef."

"Okay," I say, sounding stiffer than I mean to.

The words Amy said, more as a threat than a contract, filter through my head. "*As far as the world knows, you and Sully mean nothing. You're nothing...to each other, I mean.*"

Is that why Sully's cooking? To hide me from the prying eyes of cameras and fans to avoid another argument with her?

A shiver travels through me, almost knocking me off balance. I grab the railing as we walk down the stairs to keep from stumbling and falling onto Sully.

Maybe he's romantic and this is what he does on a second date. It's not unheard of to cook for someone. But it is a little suspicious.

Sully opens the back passenger door and gestures for me to slide in first. I bend my lips into a smile and climb inside. He explains the traditional German meal he's going to prepare and how it's his Oma's special recipe.

"That sounds delicious. I can't wait to try it," I lie through my teeth. Well, maybe it's not a complete lie. What little I heard him say about the food over the voices in my head arguing did sound good and my stomach is growling since I skipped breakfast.

✳ 🎵 🐚 🎵 ✳ 🎵 🐚

The hunger-inducing smell from the kitchen makes my mouth water. Despite us being holed up in his rented condo, he went all out to make it feel welcoming. There are tall, red candles on the table, casting the dining room in a flickering glow. Shadows dance along the walls, reminding me of long fingers reaching out to grab me. To pull me into the darkness and hide there forever.

Sully shatters my thoughts when he places two plates of food on the table. "I hope you like it."

I grab my fork and shove some sausage and noodles into my mouth. "Delicious."

After we finish eating, Sully catches me glancing at the bedroom. The door is shut, but I can still feel the silky sheets against my skin. The warmth of his strong yet gentle arms holding me to his chest. The lingering scent of mint and fresh laundry hanging in the air.

"I can't apologize enough for Amy this morning. Please don't take what she said to heart."

"It's alright." I twirl a piece of hair around my fingers. At least it's not my ring. "I get it." I don't really, but my bad habit is putting on a brave mask and burying whatever hurts me so deeply until the pain gnaws at my bones. "You're the single one in the band and some random fangirl would ruin—"

He reaches forward, placing his finger against my lips, silencing my words. "What if I want you to ruin me?" His voice is deep and his eyes are dark with hunger in the dim light.

"Then I'd say you're a fool."

He smiles, and his hand cups my face. I lean into his touch, feeling like a street cat who found a friendly human with food to share.

"With you, I can be myself. I don't have to pretend." His other hand takes mine; he fingers my mermaid ring. "Amy likes control. It's why she's good at her job."

I move closer, our thighs pressing together, skin on skin. Heat pools in my belly. "Sometimes loss of control is a good thing."

A chuckle rumbles from his chest. "God, with you I want to do bad things."

"Why don't you?" I ask, pressing my forehead to his.

He fists my hair, tugging my face back until we're nose to nose. My breath hitches as his lips brush mine, nothing but a touch of butterfly wings, but it causes a surge of hurricane winds inside my chest.

"Because I'd lose all sense of who I am. I'd blow off my music and ignore my band just to spend one more minute with you." His eyes close briefly, and his lashes splash against his skin.

As if pulled by invisible strings, I'm thrust forward until I'm kissing him. His hands slide along my back until his fingers press into my hip bones. I tug on his hair to deepen our kiss. My nails sink into his flesh. The temperature has gone up ten degrees and we still have our clothes on.

"Should we..." I nod toward the bedroom.

Sully pulls me onto his lap. I can feel his length against my leg, but he shakes his head. "I want to savor you and there aren't enough hours tonight to do everything I keep picturing in my mind."

A blush burns my cheeks. I nip at his earlobe. "Okay," I say, kissing along his throat.

He moans. "You're going to be the death of me."

"You stole my line."

He picks me up like I weigh nothing and switches our positions. I'm pinned against the couch as his legs are on either side of mine, pressing my thighs together.

"This weekend I'm going to take you out for real, and we're not going to stop until you're screaming my name."

My heart somersaults, almost falling out of my chest. My teeth dig into my bottom lip as the corners of my mouth curl into an evil smirk.

"Has anyone told you how devious you are?"

He shrugs. "Once or twice," he says before his tongue darts and licks my collarbone. My hips rock against his, but he braces against me harder until I can't move.

"Patience," he whispers, then bites the fleshy part of my shoulder.

I choke back a moan.

The weight of him is gone too soon. My body is limp and useless without his touch. He takes my hands and pulls me to my feet. "I wanted tonight to be romantic. Let's get you home before I rip those clothes off of you."

✳ ♫♪ 🐚 ♫♪ ✳ ♫♪ 🐚

The next afternoon as I'm fulfilling orders from my website, I receive a text from Charlotte.

> Hey! Sully gave me your number. Actually, I stole it out of his phone. Anyway, the boys are fighting over a new song & I'm about to strangle someone. Wanna hang out to save Sully's life?

I shake my head, only imagining what it's like to hear all three of those guys arguing.

> Yeah. My roommate, her girlfriend, & I are about to watch The Thing. You can come over and hang out.

> Yes! I'll bring snacks.

About twenty minutes later, Charlotte hops out of her rideshare with two grocery bags full of candy, popcorn, and chips. Alice blesses her and takes the food into the kitchen to put into bowls. Emily giggles as she follows to help.

Alice and Emily snuggle on the loveseat under a blanket as they share a giant bowl. Charlotte and I sit on the couch with a blanket and bowl of our own. We laugh throughout the movie as people panic and run for their lives. The graphics from the 1980s are silly, but still damn good.

When the credits roll, Alice and Emily sneak off to the bedroom. Charlotte checks her phone. "Guess I should get back. Hopefully no fights broke out while I was gone."

"It was good to see you." I turn off the TV and put our empty bowls in the kitchen.

Charlotte sees the picture of me as a mermaid hanging on the wall. "Is this you?"

I brush a piece of hair out of my face. "Yeah."

She smiles. "I love it. I can see why Sully likes you. You're sweet, but mysterious."

"Amy doesn't like me," I grumble.

Charlotte waves her hand like she's batting away a fly. "Amy's annoying. We hired her because the band needed someone to run our socials and keep us on track for interviews and such. Sully mentioned it to his aunt, and then Amy popped into our lives. She does help get us seen by more people, but she also likes to comment on things that are not in her job description. Like our cover art. Don't get me started on how she went off on that last year." Charlotte sighs, tugging on her silver hoop earring. "Anyway, we deal with her, but you don't need to take her shit."

"Thanks." Her words don't offer much comfort, but at least I'm not the only thing Amy hates. She's just a control freak.

Charlotte's phone buzzes. "My ride's here. See you later."

We hug, and I open the door for her. She walks down the stairs, and a strange white car catches my attention. It's not her rideshare because she's walking to the idling red car near the dumpster. I don't think I've seen that white car before.

I take a few steps to get a better look, and the car turns before flooring it down the street. For a second, I swear the driver looked a lot like my ex.

My stomach jumps into my throat. That's impossible. I shake off the idea, or try to, and go back into the apartment, locking the door.

Chapter Twenty-Four

THE MORNING SUN BURNS away the fog looming over the city like a phantom. It's Saturday, and my day is booked solid with an hours-long modeling gig. Then dinner with Sully in Beverly Hills, and we might meet up with the rest of the band later for drinks.

But all my joy comes to a screeching halt when I check my phone. Arthur's daughter is sick, and he needs to take her to urgent care. Without my mer-handler, it's impossible to move from photoshoot to photoshoot. Now my pictures will be limited to the first place I drag myself to.

Family comes first, but I rented a lot of expensive photo equipment with a photographer who does video and underwater photography. The goal was to get as many pictures on the beach and in the water as possible, piecing together a calendar for next year and poses to create new merch for my website. Now I'll be lucky to get enough pictures to update the site to get more gigs.

With a heavy heart, I reply to Arthur to spend time with his daughter and not to worry about me. At times like this, I wish there was someone I could call for backup. It's too much to depend on one person to keep my modeling career alive.

As I debate on which of my three tails should be the only one I'm able to use, my phone buzzes. I check it, assuming it's Arthur with his response and apologizing again. Instead, it's Sully wanting my help to narrow down where we're going to eat tonight. I lean against the car and text him back.

> **Seafood sounds good, been a while since I ate decent shrimp. We can meet earlier if you want. My plans went to shit.**

> **What happened? Anything I can do?**

A car approaches. I glance up, seeing the photographer, Peter, pulling into the parking lot. He's usually fully booked, but I snagged him on a last-minute cancellation. I guess Arthur needing to bow out is the universe evening the score.

> **Unless you can be a mer-handler, nothing.**

Peter parks in a spot next to me and waves. I wave back, biting the inside of my cheek. It's going to be months before I can get something on the books with him again.

My phone rings in my hand, startling me. It's Sully. I swipe to answer. "Hey..." I say, failing to hide how weirded out I am that he called.

"What's a mer-handler?" he asks, teasing dancing through his words.

"Did you call to mock me?" I pull off my sunglasses and inspect my tails in the trunk. My favorite—the sunset one with all its reds, oranges, and yellows—will be today's pick.

"I'm sorry, it's just a weird word to use. But seriously." His voice is low and unpolished, with a rasp that clings to every word.

"It's someone who carries me when I'm in my tail so I can travel to different locations without having to crawl and injure myself."

"Oh, I can handle that."

I almost swallow my gum. "Excuse me?" I spit out harsher than I mean to.

"If you need an extra hand, I can help. I've been sitting in my living room trying to write another song, but honestly, I've been watching horror movies."

A whoosh rips through me, sending me into a dizzy spell. "That would be amazing if you could get to Manhattan Beach right now."

"I can get there as fast as my driver can punch it."

"You're a lifesaver!" I must control myself from leaping for joy and screaming woo-hoo. "I'll tell my photographer you're running a little late and we'll get everything set up in the meantime. I owe you big for this."

"I'll have to think of ways you can pay me back," he says, chuckling.

My stomach pings as warmth washes over me. I like the sound of that. Maybe it won't be too bad being his little secret after all.

Peter is a tall guy who is bald but has a long black goatee that comes to a point. His honey-brown eyes have speckles of green in them with the sunlight and he's quick with his hands. He's only been here a few minutes, but he's already gotten out all his equipment and is messing with which lenses would work best.

"My mer-handler will be here shortly. How about we walk and scope out the best places?" I suggest as he pulls a yellow cloth from his back pocket and shines one of his many lenses.

"Wonderful idea." He snaps his fingers and a teenage boy wearing tan cargo pants with a tie-dye shirt steps out of the car looking at his phone. "Daniel put that bloody phone away and watch my equipment while the lovely Veronica and I check out locations."

Daniel mutters under his breath, but he does lose the phone.

"Forgive me for my assistant. He's my girlfriend's kid and I'm trying to teach him responsibility."

"It's all good."

We walk along the beach until we come across a log covered in moss. Peter circles it, forming a square with his fingers and treating it like a camera. "Yes, this will be a great place to start then..." He stalks down to the water. I jog to catch up. "We can have you sit here, right where the water crashes. Now if only we could find a giant rock." He shields his eyes with a hand, scanning the area.

"Yes, this is perfect." He rushes off, kicking up sand.

I linger back, checking my phone. Sully is in the parking lot. My lips break into a giddy grin as my heart soars. I cup my hands over my mouth and shout, "I'm heading back, the mer-handler is here!"

Peter shoots me a thumbs up as he continues his mission.

Chapter Twenty-Five

SULLY IS IN THE middle of a conversation with Daniel when I arrive. When Sully turns his attention to me, I pause. He's shirtless and he must've rubbed suntan lotion on because his skin is golden and gleaming like a Greek god. He's wearing navy blue swim trunks tied in a white bow paired with green and black swim shoes.

"Nice shoes," I say, opening my car's trunk and rearranging my tails. I'm too excited about being able to wear all three now.

Sully kicks a patch of sand, rubbing the back of his neck. "Hey, don't mock the help. I was going to wear flip-flops but remembered how hot the sand can be." He moves in closer, placing his hands on my hips, and whispers in the shell of my ear, "Wouldn't want to drop you."

"No." I swallow my pounding heart and spin around. We're nose to nose. "Wouldn't want that." My voice is low. His eyes lock on my lips. He tucks my hair behind my ear and just as he's about to kiss me, Peter returns, clapping his hands.

"We're losing sunlight, people! Let's move!"

I toss a yoga mat over the sand before grabbing my purple tail and its matching top. "Your first job awaits."

Sully stands beside the car as I change using the yoga mat. I struggle to put my tail on over my hips, but at least with the mat, I don't get sand all over my leggings. Sully is kind enough to hold a beach towel up so I can quickly change my top in private. He's a perfect gentleman, turning his head despite already seeing me topless. When I'm finished, I say, "Okay. I'm ready." I shove my clothes inside my bag and can't help but smirk when Sully whistles, tossing the towel over his broad shoulder.

"Damn, is it weird I like you better this way?" He wiggles his eyebrows.

"Don't blame you. I am hot," I chuckle, tugging on my hip fin. "Now, come on. I'm paying Peter by the hour."

"Bossy. I like it." He scoops me up and I wrap my arms around his neck after hooking my arm with my bag's strap.

I do some shots on the beach and sit on the lone log in my purple tail. Sully is happy to take me back and forth so I can change into my sunset tail. We do a few more different beach shots and then I get into the water. Peter found a rock I can sit on and stare out at the ocean. I run my fingers through my hair and in another, I'm admiring my reflection in a shell-shaped mirror.

After a break, we do underwater videography. I swim in circles and blow bubble kisses. I dive between sea coves and join a school of fish. A dolphin even photobombs us for a few minutes.

We're wrapping up the shoot with me in a red and pink tail. I pose with waves breaking behind me and my fins flying over my head.

Sully eats this up, laughing, and always quick to do whatever is needed. Peter eyes how Sully scoops me from the sand and fingers his goatee.

"Wait. What do you think of having him in some shots? A mermaid and her prince."

Sully shifts his weight and meets my gaze. "I don't know."

"What do you mean? You got the face for the camera." Peter smiles. "Let me take some test shots and you can decide." He starts snapping away without warning and throws his camera's screen into our faces. "See. Perfection."

Sully's jaw clenches. I place a hand on his arm. "It's okay. Sully's in a band and I think he'd need to ask his people for permission before his image can be used."

"Oh." Peter drops the camera to his waist. "What band?"

Sully bursts into a deep laugh. "That's humbling." He runs his tongue over his sunburnt lips and looks down at my tail. "Screw it. We can do some shots."

Peter is about to split in half with joy. "Fantastic! Now hold her over your head like she's the best thing you've ever seen and you must admire her."

Sully lifts me with ease and we can't help but laugh. We do a few more with him holding me close and some with us both lying on the beach with the water all around us. We also do a Little Mermaid pose where it looks like I rescued him from drowning and I'm singing to him.

Peter flips through what he has and nods in approval. "These are amazing. I'll edit them and send you the files in a few days."

"Thank you! I'm grateful you could fit me in today," I say, trying to sit up more in Sully's arms. It's awkward making a business decision while in a tail.

"Pleasure is mine." He barks orders at Daniel on how to pack the equipment back into the car, and they drive off.

"I can say I've never had a photoshoot quite like that before," Sully says, walking us toward the bathroom. Another downside of a mermaid tail is you can never go to the bathroom, not even in the water.

"You're my favorite person." I kiss his cheek. "I wouldn't have been able to do half of what we did today without your help."

His hands shift my body, adjusting my weight. "You still owe me, but I have something else I want to add to your payment."

"What's that?" I ask, flicking my tail and pressing my forehead to his.

"A copy of the best picture of us. Blown-up and framed."

"Oh?" I cup my hands around his face, pulling him in closer. "Anything for my Jolly Sailor Bold," I say seductively and kiss his lips.

He deepens our kiss, setting me on the edge of the sink. I lean back, my ass falling into the large sink bowl and my lower back smacks the mirror. Sully's hands trace my top and migrate down to my waist.

"Umm..." I playfully kick him with my tail. "This isn't the best place to make out." I smile, kissing him again before releasing him. He takes a step back and looks around, sharing a shy grin.

"You're right. This place doesn't seem that clean."

I laugh, pushing myself from the sink and standing on my fins. "That and my legs are trapped."

"Right." He runs a hand along my tail. "Kinda sexy though."

"Maybe we can try that later," I say softly, looking up at him through my lashes.

Blood floods into his cheeks, and he coughs. "I'll let you transform back into human form," he says, and walks out the door.

I change into my shorts and white top with a mermaid shell bikini on the front before relieving myself in a graffiti-covered stall. When I set out with my bag over my shoulder, Sully is sitting on the hood of my car, looking at his phone. I toss my stuff into the back and grab my phone, checking to see if I missed anything since this morning.

My dad texted me an hour ago, reminding me to pick up ice cream for dinner tonight.

"Shit," I mutter, shoving a thumb and finger into my eyes.

"What's wrong?" Sully looks at my phone and then at me.

"My dad. I forgot my parents invited me to dinner tonight. He wants me to bring ice cream. I totally spaced it." I slam the trunk and run a hand over my neck. "I'm going to have to reschedule our dinner."

Sully traces my collarbone with his fingers. "We can have dinner with your parents. If you don't mind."

"You want to meet my parents?" I squeak.

He chuckles, hooking a finger under my chin and closing my gaping mouth.

"Unless you think they'll kill me or something."

"No. They're nice..." I tap my phone against my palm. "Do you really want to come?" I grab my keys and walk to the driver's side.

"I'd love to meet your parents," he says over the car before getting into the passenger's seat.

Butterflies attack my stomach. But something hums in my blood. I like the idea of having someone come to dinner.

It's going to be interesting explaining what Sully and I are to my parents, but at least it gives them something else to focus on than their daughter being a grown woman who is a mermaid for a living. All I need to hear is my mom going off on how I'm wasting my time. Dad doesn't say anything cross, to my face at least, but he doesn't back me up either. He's neutral and likes to keep the peace.

"Okay, great. I'll text Dad and tell him I'm bringing a guest. We'll grab the ice cream and head over."

He clears his throat and plucks at his swim trunks. "Don't you think we should also change?"

"Yeah." I grimace, wrinkling my nose. "That's a good idea and maybe shower. I think there's sand in my hair." I shove my fingers into my hair and shake it and the sand rains down.

"No sand warning in your mermaid handbook?" he jokes, laughing.

"There are pros and cons to everything." I blow a piece of hair from my eye.

His gaze darkens. "What are the pros?"

I bite my lip and back out of the parking spot. "I'll have to show you later."

His eyes blaze into me, but I don't flinch. I may know what his reward is for helping me and it's going to blow his mind. It's fun having Sully around, and he's more reliable than any guy I've been with, and we're not even officially dating.

Sometimes I wonder what it would be like if we could be a couple. Having him hold me and staring into each other's eyes for those pictures were some of the best moments I had posing for the camera. He turned the job into a fun experience. Arthur is a good mer-handler and friend, but he's too professional.

It would be a lie if I didn't admit I like the idea of having a partner. A prince to my mermaid as Peter put it. But we're nothing but friends with benefits. A mermaid and a rock star, what kind of story is that? As we drive toward Sully's place, a voice whispers to let it go. To live in the moment, and for once, I am.

Sully turns the radio on and flips through the channels until he lands on a song he likes. He starts singing, and I can't help but laugh and join in. We belt out the lyrics with the windows down, the salty ocean breeze tangling in our hair and making everything feel a little lighter.

This isn't how I imagined today going—but somehow, it's better.

There's a buzz under my skin every time Sully's arm brushes against mine, a slow, steady warmth blooming in my chest that I can't seem to shake. I just hope my parents don't look too closely and see what I'm afraid to admit...

That I might be falling for him.

Chapter Twenty-Six

I PARK ON THE street in front of my parents' house. Sully grabs the paper bag with the ice cream, and we follow the stone path cutting through the rocky front yard. Mom has little gnomes around with colorful hats. They always gave me the creeps, but Sully points at them with a grin. "Those are kinda cute."

"Please don't tell my mother that or she'll show you the site she buys them from and never let you go."

Sully grimaces and briefly nods. "Noted."

Anxiety pricks at the base of my skull as I walk up toward my childhood home. I've never been on a razor's edge to visit my parents, but I also never brought a boy into their house either. My high school boyfriend honked his car horn when he was outside and my last boyfriend met my parents a couple of times out at restaurants for dinner, but he never wanted to come over, not even for the holidays. Maybe that was a sign he wasn't the one. He always said there were better things to do, but he usually got shit-faced no matter where we went.

I open the door and step in. "We're here!" I shout.

"Hey, honey!" Dad's voice booms from somewhere inside.

We step through the front door and the scent of burning steak wafts through the air. A second later the smoke detector screams and their golden retriever, Bishop, runs out the doggy door next to the back door.

"Welcome to the Gates' house!" I gesture to the couch and take the bag of ice cream from him. "Please wait here."

I rush into the kitchen and find Mom holding a frying pan on fire and throwing it into the sink, dowsing it in water.

"What did that steak do to you?" I ask, putting the ice cream in the freezer.

Mom jumps, clenching the dry towel to her chest. "My goodness, Veronica! You scared me."

"Sorry. I said we were here." I eye the blackened thing that once was food. "But I guess you were busy."

Mom turns the water off and arches her neck to look around the corner into the living room. "Who did you bring? Alice?"

"Oh...no." I focus on folding the paper bag flat against my chest to avoid her questioning eyes. "His name's Sully."

"You brought a boy?" Her voice rises an octave and I want to hide in the bathroom when she breezes past me to meet him.

"You must be Sully," Mom says, acting as if she knows him.

Sully stands and offers to shake Mom's hand. "Guilty."

"We hug in this family." Mom wraps her arms around Sully and he winces when she squeezes too tight.

"I'm sorry," I mouth when his eyes lock with mine.

Mom releases him and shouts, "Honey! Veronica has a date over!" She practically floats to the backyard.

Sully rubs his back. "She popped something."

"She hugs tighter than a python. I should've warned you."

Dad comes in followed by Mom and Bishop at her side. The dog walks over to Sully wagging his tail and smells Sully's shoes before licking his hand. Bishop then goes to his bed in the corner of the room and lies down.

"That means he likes you." Mom smiles, placing her hands on my shoulders. "Can you help me in the kitchen, sweetie?"

"Hey, Ronnie." Dad kisses my head as I walk by him.

"Hi, Dad." I look past him to Sully. He's nervously fidgeting with his hands, unsure what to do with them. He eyes the door, and I don't blame him if he darted out. My dad is a tall and buff man who was in the military. He never told me what he did, but I think it was something off the books, like the missions seen in action movies inspired by true events.

"Do you want mac and cheese with dinner?" Mom grabs the purple saucepan from the pan hook above the island.

"Sure. Sounds good," I reply, lingering near the doorway to hear what Dad is saying to Sully. I can barely see Dad's back, but I can't see Sully.

Mom clicks her tongue. "Sweetie, it's rude to eavesdrop."

"Sorry..." I rip myself away and lean against the island with my elbows, resting my chin on my folded hands. "What do you want me to help with?"

She frowns and replaces the saucepan back on its hook. "Don't worry about it. On second thought, I think it's better if we order out. Your dad almost burned his eyebrows off with the BBQ and you walked in on what happened on the stove." She laughs half-heartedly. "I should wash this frying pan before all this crap is caked on forever." She turns on the hot water and scrapes the burnt pieces into the trash can.

"Let me do that," I say, taking the pan from her. "Just sit down."

She pats my arm and actually listens for once, taking a seat on a bar stool at the island. "Thanks, baby."

As I scrub the pan, Mom clears her throat and asks, "Where did you meet Sully? He seems like a sweet boy."

My muscles lock up in my back and I scrub the pan harder. "He is. We met at a concert."

"That's nice. You have the same taste in music?"

Something like that. I cough to hide my laugh.

"What does he do?"

Here we go. The grilling I always avoided by never bringing boys home. I bet Dad is laying down the law and threatening harm if something happens to me as if I'm sixteen and going on my first date.

The pan is clean, but I keep the sponge going in circles like it's filthy. "He plays the bass guitar in a band."

"Oh," she sighs. One little word and the disappointment weighs heavy on my shoulders.

"He was a great help today. My friend Arthur couldn't come to my photoshoot and Sully volunteered."

"That's nice, dear." Mom stands and gathers her phone from the counter. "I should order dinner or we'll never eat."

Mom loves me in her own way, but how I live my life depresses her. She had big plans for me after I graduated. Honestly, I wish I skipped college and jump-started my mermaid career instead of doing gigs here and there. But that would've gone against Mom's grand plan for me. She wanted me to graduate, get an office job, or something like it that's a steady forty-hour job, then settle down, marry and maybe have a kid or two. Instead, I became a licensed scuba and free diver and grew my mermaid career from a few birthday parties to a gig at a restaurant, to more freelance gigs, and into a blossoming modeling career.

I wait until Mom is finished ordering to say anything else. I wash the pan and leave it in the dish strainer upside-down to dry.

When she sets her phone on the table and grabs a dishcloth to wipe the already clean counter, I ask, "Aren't you going to ask me how work is?"

"Veronica..." She drops her sentence and the dishcloth in the same breath.

Dad walks in, his eyes bouncing between Mom and me. If he notices the tension, he ignores it. "Hey, Sully wants to see the Mustang I've been restoring so we'll be in the garage."

Mom doesn't blink, just returns to making the counter shine. "Dinner will be ready in thirty minutes. Can you pick it up from Tony's?"

"Yeah...I'll tell him we'll check out the Mustang later." Dad slips out and leaves us in a quiet kitchen.

Mom turns to face me, her lips a slash across her face. "Let's drop this, okay? I want today to be nice for all of us."

Yes. Let's ignore my life choices. It's not like they matter.

I follow Mom into the living room. Dad is already gone, leaving Sully to study the family pictures on the mantel. He grabs a framed photo of the three of us at a ski lodge in Colorado about ten years ago. "I didn't know you liked to ski."

"She doesn't," Mom answers for me. "She nearly broke her leg right after that picture was taken. She spent the rest of the vacation in the lodge reading next to the fireplace."

Sully returns the picture. "Guess you've always been more of a beach person, huh?" A smile tugs on the corner of his mouth.

"You have an interesting accent. Where are you from?" Mom pushes forward to move the picture Sully touched a half an inch to the left.

"Born and raised in Berlin, Germany."

"Mom, can you stop with the third degree?" I grab Sully's arm and tug him toward the couch. "How about we play a card game or something until Dad returns?"

Mom wipes her hands on her skirt and grabs Bishop's leash. He hears it and bolts out of bed, running for the front door. "I should take the dog on a walk first. You kids stay here."

Bishop happily pulls Mom outside and they're gone in a whoosh.

"Do I want to know what happened in the kitchen?" Sully hooks his arm around my waist, forcing me to look at him.

"Same old thing. Mom hates my career choices. She doesn't like that you're a musician. Thinks I'm pissing away my life." I shrug. "I'm used to it. How do you think I developed such a thick skin to deal with the horrible comments online?"

Sully presses his lips to my temple and it sends a buzzing through my brain. "Strangers online are always trying to bring down successful people, but mothers shouldn't. She should be supportive no matter what you do."

"Yeah." I bristle and drift toward the rocking chair, wanting to sit alone. "It's a long story. I hope when Dad returns with dinner it won't be so awkward and if it is we'll leave after we eat."

Sully's eyebrows push together in concern. "I don't understand why she—"

I fold my legs to my chest and wrap my arms around them. "She's old-fashioned in what my job should be and how I should live. Being a mermaid seems silly to her. She once told me if I'm not Ariel at Disneyland, how do I get paid at all." I inspect the mole on my forearm to avoid seeing the sympathy in his eyes. "She probably thinks Alice pays most of the bills. Her mind would blow if she knew I paid for almost everything. Alice spends her tips on her ever-changing wardrobe or growing tattoo collection." I drop my legs and lean forward, resting my elbows on my thighs.

Sully sits on the edge of the couch, his knees almost touching mine. "Why don't you tell her? She'll never know you're able to pay your bills and support yourself without communication. It's not easy, but once I told my mother about how our band got a record deal and what benefits came our way after that she didn't worry...as much."

"She never listens." I stare at my hands with my head bowed. "I mean just now in the kitchen I tried and she shut me down. You can't explain anything to a brick wall."

"And now you clam up again for how long?"

My stomach sours knowing he's right, but I can't force myself to face Mom.

"She's angry now. It would be useless to try—"

"All I hear are excuses to sweep this under the rug."

I toe the carpet. "You're supposed to be a rock star, not a therapist." I lean back in the chair, covering my eyes with my arm.

His knee presses against mine. "You're only mad because I'm right."

"Can we ease into it? Maybe we should play a game just me and you. See if she takes the bait and then..."

He nods, standing up and offering me a hand. "See what happens from there."

"Yeah..." I grab his hand, and it's more like a lifeline dragging me out of a self-pity ocean. "What do you want to play?" I walk over to a wooden cabinet and open the doors, revealing shelves of board games and a few different card games.

Sully pauses to scan all the boxes. "I'm not familiar with a lot of these games, but..." He grabs a deck of playing cards. "I think everyone knows how to play gin."

We sit on opposite sides of the coffee table. I rest my back against the couch as Sully folds his legs butterfly-style. Time slows while we play a couple of hands. When the front door opens and Bishop runs in, I jump a little. Sully smirks and draws a card.

Bishop bumps Sully with his golden head, wiping his wet nose all over his cheek. Sully laughs, petting the dog and trying to push him away so he doesn't tower over him.

Mom hangs the leash on the wall hook and places her hands on her hips, watching us. "What's this?"

"Dad isn't back yet." I don't lift my gaze from the cards in my hand.

Sully clears his throat and nods toward Mom. Ugh, he's not going to let this go.

"Do you want to join us? We're playing gin." Sully gestures to the table. "We can start a new game at the dining room table if—"

"That's okay. I'm going to set the table."

Sully is already on his feet, crossing the space to Mom in a heartbeat. "A short game? I'd love to get to know Veronica's mother. I can see where she gets her lovely eyes."

Mom blushes, swatting at the air between them. "Don't flatter me."

"I speak only the truth." He motions for me to join them. "How about we play..." He looks at me. "What's your favorite board game?"

"Clue," I say, gathering the cards into a stack and wrapping a rubber band around them.

"Excellent. How about we play before enjoying a delightful meal?" He lifts a brow and tosses his dashing smile at Mom.

She giggles, wiping her palms against her pants. "I suppose one game will be fine."

Sully does have the magic touch when it comes to Gates women. His accent could talk us into almost anything.

Fifteen minutes later, we're deep into the mystery when Dad wanders in with two bags of food. "Who's hungry?" he says, holding up the bags.

Mom tosses her cards and check sheet down. "Time for dinner," she says, walking over to the island and helping Dad divide the food onto plates.

"How is this helping?" I whisper to Sully. Since playing we only spoke when it related to the game, whose turn it was, or showing a clue when someone entered a room. We didn't chip away at the dysfunction between Mom and me at all.

"Patience. Ease her into it. Right now, she's not upset anymore. Later maybe you can talk, and she'll listen."

I squint at him. "How are you this wise?"

He shrugs, putting the game pieces away and folding the gameboard.

For dinner, we all have ribs with sides of mac and cheese and corn on the cob. Classical music plays softly in the background as we eat. Dad and I finish first and take our dishes to the sink.

"You have any plans after dinner?" he asks, rinsing off his plate and placing it in the dishwasher.

"No. It's been a long day. I'll probably drop Sully off at his place and then go home."

I might have sex with Sully, but I will not discuss that with my father.

"I'm glad you're getting some work done." He takes my plate and rinses it off, placing it in the dishwasher too. Vague as ever. But at least he doesn't insult me.

"What about you and Mom? Going to watch a movie tonight?"

Dad dries his hands on the dish towel. "No. We'll probably read in bed."

"That sounds nice."

He places his hands on my shoulders and kisses the crown of my head. "One day you'll know what it's like to share your life with someone. Your mom is my favorite person."

My heart sinks, but I put on a happy face. "I should get back."

Sully and Mom are laughing as he shows her something on his phone. It's almost as if I walked into a parallel universe where Mom is warm and open to who I bring into this house. What if Sully is right? Maybe better communication is what Mom and I need to be on the same page and not have this rift between us. It would be nice to feel like we weren't on two different continents anymore.

Chapter Twenty-Seven

WE EAT ICE CREAM and then play board games for three hours, and I can't believe how time flies. It's like we're a happy sitcom family from TV performing for an audience of millions instead of a family who only gathers maybe once or twice a month. I don't remember having that much fun with my parents since I was a child.

Dad yawns, checking the time on his watch. "I better take Bishop for his evening walk, and then I'm crashing for the night." He pats Sully on the shoulder. "It was nice to meet you, son. Next time I'll show you the Mustang."

"The pleasure was mine," Sully replies, smiling.

Dad grabs the leash, and Bishop doesn't miss a beat. Mom pushes her chair out and stands. "I should clean up—"

Sully rushes forward, blocking her path. "Allow me."

"You're our guest. I can't—"

"Please. I want to. *Meine mutter* taught me manners, might as well use them."

Mom caves, sitting back down. "Thank you."

Sully eyes me and motions to Mom. "Talk," he mouths before slipping into the kitchen.

I focus on stacking the boxes of games on top of each other and closing the cabinet's doors. "Mom, can we talk?"

"About what, sweetie?"

"My life…" I dig deep for my courage, preparing to bare my soul. "You never ask any more since I passed on the job at your friend's firm. When we were at the mall we almost got into a fight."

She focuses on shoving her thumbnail into each cuticle on her right hand. "That's water under the bridge. You know—"

"No excuses or slipping away. We need to have this conversation. Everything needs to be out in the open for once."

She slaps the table, anger spiking, and her top lip quivers. "You know perfectly well what I think about your career choices, Veronica Anne. How can anyone take you seriously when they ask what you do and you say you're a damn mermaid? It's something a little girl would say."

I lick my lips and press my back against my chair, trying to keep myself calm and not lash out. "On the surface, I can see that. It does sound ridiculous and I do have my share of teasing when I tell a stranger what I do. But you've never taken the time to see what I've accomplished. To see any of my achievements. My career has evolved so much since my college years."

She wrinkles her nose like she smells something rotten. "I know you work at that restaurant downtown. Pearl something."

"The Pearl Kingdom," I say with a heavy sigh, exhausted from this conversation already. "You and Dad have been invited countless times to come down to the restaurant for a free dinner and watch my show, but you've never taken the time to see how much joy I bring to others. How much joy my job brings me." I close my eyes, settle my nerves and push past the lump forming in my throat. The fear of breaking whatever branch our relationship is barely hanging onto these past few years. "Can I show you something?" I grab my phone and pull up my website. It takes all my concentration to keep my hands from shaking.

Mom studies me for a moment, considering, but gives in. She shifts in her seat, moving closer and eyes the door, probably waiting for Dad so she can excuse herself and disappear. With the door closed, she sucks on her teeth and finally says, "Fine. Show me."

I place my phone in front of her where my photo gallery is lazily playing a photo at a time with a five-second time lapse. "Look." She does and interest sparks in her eyes. She accepts the phone and tilts her head as she watches the slideshow.

"When were these taken?" she asks, curious.

"They are from a few different shoots throughout the year. Half a dozen companies booked me for their corporate meetings and afterward, I passed out countless cards. Some people promised to book me again for their holiday parties. A few scheduled me to do their kid's birthday or for a pool party. At some parties I teach the kids how to swim in mermaid tails and at other times, I'm there in character to entertain them. Throughout the summer, I was doing at least one party every other day. To the point where I started recording video messages personalized to kids and even started my own merch line."

"Hmm," she says, clicking on a video of a party I did three weeks ago. She turns the volume down. She then enters my store where I sell pictures of myself as wall art, pillows, and shirts. More merch is coming soon is what the site reads on the bottom. "And these pictures in your little shop are taken at the beach around here?" Her eyes are glued to the screen.

My hopes soar, but I try to keep level-headed. In the past, I've fallen for her traps where she acts interested in my activities, such as being in the school play in high school, but when it came to opening night, she never came to claim the tickets I had on hold for her, claiming a charity event popped up and that was more important than my short career in the arts.

"For my social media, I hire a highly recommended photographer to take my pictures at beaches, mostly all-over Southern California, but we've traveled for shoots too. He also specializes in underwater photography and videos. I already have over a hundred thousand followers and have been featured in two magazines so far. Fingers crossed for even bigger sponsors. Right now, I do have two local sponsors and an online store that makes and sells mermaid tails—they give me a phenomenal discount and I'm one of the main models on their site. My other sponsors are a seafood restaurant near the Santa Monica Pier and a surf shop on the Venice Boardwalk."

I brighten, remembering the good news I saw this morning—something that got lost in the chaos of today's photoshoot drama. "Oh—and a cruise line just picked me up! They want me to star in a commercial early next year for their newest ship. I'll be swimming as a mermaid right alongside it in open water. It still feels surreal."

I reach for my phone and show her the email. "There are a ton of other mermaids like me too." I quickly find another professional mermaid's social media. I show my mother her account. She has over two hundred thousand followers. "This woman is a friend of mine and she recently signed with an NFL team and they gave her a tail, and matching leggings, with their team logo. She does short videos for them right before they play a game. Some mermaids have been given free trips to destinations to help advertise resorts and beaches. With my cruise line commercial, I'm sure those doors will be opening for me soon."

Mom nods, setting my phone down. She interlaces her fingers together, resting them in front of her like we're in the middle of a company merger agreement and not a conversation about her only child's life. "And how much does it cost for a company to book your services?"

Her words slice into me, cutting my heart to ribbons. I swallow the sharp retort rising in my throat and force myself to stay calm, even though shame and frustration twist in my stomach. Instead, I dive into the details—explaining how someone would go about making arrangements to work with me, trying to sound composed even as I feel like I'm being judged.

"Let me show you." I grab my phone, find the price sheet and booking section on my site, and hand her back the device. "It depends on how long the event is and if I will be sitting in one place for the entire time or if they have a pool and want a show. For kid parties, I also have an additional package where I teach them about how to be a mermaid and provide tails for them to use."

She glances at the price sheet and sets the phone face down on the table. Her soft but firm hands take mine in hers. She squeezes my fingers. "I had no idea there were so many parts to your career. You figured it out beautifully."

It's good she's holding my hands because if she wasn't I probably would've slipped out of my chair and fell onto the floor. She's never said a nice word about anything I've been interested in. At least not about anything I can recall.

"I also plan to grow my online store where people can buy calendars and coffee mugs. I'm working on getting a stuffed doll designed in my image. Next year, I'm co-hosting a mermaid convention in Florida where hundreds of mermaids from around the world will be meeting."

"Wow," she sniffs, rubbing her nose.

I've been focusing on the China cabinet behind her most of the time, when not finding something on my phone, but when I take in her face, I see she's crying. She wipes away a tear and holds my hand with both of hers. "Veronica, I'm sorry about what I've been saying these past few years. I never took the time to listen and learn what you do. You're building quite the business empire for yourself. I'm so proud of you for all the hustling you must be doing to get yourself to where you are. It takes a lot of guts and courage to start a company from the ground up."

My eyes burn and my vision blurs as tears blind me. "I learned how to hustle from the best." My eyes flutter closed for a second as I gather my strength. "My life could never be spent sitting at a desk five days a week. Clocking in and out, doing their nine-to-five, with weekends and holidays free. I need to see the world and meet new people. Have my weeks be different from each other where I have a set schedule, but my life isn't day-to-day predictable. It's not the most orthodox way to live, but I have a healthy savings account and I won't quit. I'm determined to get what I want."

Mom stands and walks around the table to crush me in a hug. My rib cage cracks, splintering bones pierce into my heart, but I don't fight. It's the first time I feel like my mother loves me for me and not out of some obligation, a little box she needs to check off. For once she accepts me and there's no shame in her watery eyes when she looks at me.

"I love you, baby girl. I'm sorry for not being there for you. It's clear, you're strong. Never stop what you want in life, even when your old-fashioned mother tries to strike you down with cruel comments to kill your passion."

A wall in me breaks, and I sob on her shoulder. All the pain and sorrow flood out of my system. The front door opens, and Dad pauses after letting Bishop off his leash.

He joins us in our hug. "My girls," he whispers.

I love how he has no idea what's going on, but holds us together all the same. Mom lets me go and leans against Dad's chest. "Thank you for coming to dinner."

"Thanks for listening," I say, straightening up and wiping my eyes with the back of my wrist.

Sully exits the kitchen. "Everything's all cleaned up. If you don't mind, I'd like to take Veronica home."

Mom nods. "Go ahead, kids. We'll see you at dinner next month, right honey?"

"Yes." I nod, blowing kisses. "See you then."

Sully holds his hand out, and I'm too tired to fight. I hand him the keys and slip into the passenger's seat.

He starts the car and turns the radio off. "Looks like you and your mom had a moment."

I laugh, but it gets trapped in my swollen throat. The sound comes out strangled and garbled, like a small animal dying. "You could say that."

He flashes his cute dimples, watching me.

"Your parents weren't bad. I liked them."

"Of course you'd say that." I nudge his arm.

He tightens his hold on the steering wheel and clenches his jaw like he's battling what he wants to say next.

"Veronica, seeing you in your tail at the beach, living in your element and then coming here to see where you grew up. I'm thankful to be a part of that." He swallows, his Adam's apple bobs.

"Spending this time with you makes me want it to never end. I think I may be fall—"

My heart will burst if he says what I think he might be saying so I kill his words with a kiss.

"Let's go." I drum my fingernails on the gear shift. "I want to end tonight with something extra special." My hand trails down to his thigh and brushes his dick.

His eyes darken as he shifts into drive. "Say no more."

Chapter Twenty-Eight

WE WALK UPSTAIRS, AND I unlock my apartment's front door. "Alice? Alice?" I look around the cramped apartment and poke my head into her room and find it empty.

"We're alone," he says darkly when I return to the living room. He watches me with his hooded eyes as he leans against the front door, turning the lock without breaking eye contact.

A thrill zips through me like being on a fast roller-coaster, dipping up and down hills at lightning speeds. "What should we do?"

He places his hands on my hips and brushes his nose against mine. "Can you put your mermaid tail back on?"

I laugh, shoving his chest, but he doesn't move. "You really want all this tied up?" I bend my knee and stroke my thigh.

He groans. "Never mind. I want you naked."

"So, demanding..." I kiss his mouth and wrap my arms around his neck.

He picks me up effortlessly and we enter my room. He gently sets me on my bed. "I have a gift for you."

"Oh?" I move back to rest against the pillows. "It's not even my birthday."

He pulls out a velvet box from his pocket. "Don't get too excited, *Schatz*."

That nickname sends tingles between my legs. I inhale a sharp breath and stop breathing as he hands the little box to me.

"Open it." I flick my gaze up, watching how he bites back a smile waiting for my reaction.

Exhaling and trying not to choke on air, I reply, "Alright." I crack it open and see a pair of silver starfish earrings.

"Thought they were fitting for my mermaid," he says, giving me a wolfish smirk.

"They're perfect." I close the box and wrap my arms around his neck. "Thank you!" I kiss him and pull him onto the bed with me. My legs wrap around his until we're entangled in each other.

He kisses me and where his lips touch ignites into flames. His phone goes off, but he ignores it, tossing it onto a random pile of clothes, and presses me onto the comforter. He's on top, kissing my collarbone as his hands tease my breasts.

The phone draws questions, but I don't dare ask them. Instead, I enjoy Sully's firm yet delicious touch and close my eyes. He's tender but rough and I watch the fireworks explode behind my eyelids.

Hours later, Sully snores beside me. I pad into the bathroom to freshen up and check my phone. Alice is crashing at Emily's and she sends kissy faces. It's like she knew what this night would bring.

There's a strange message on my Insta. Someone requesting to chat. It's usually fans or people asking advice on how to kickstart their mermaid careers.

My stomach plummets to the floor when I see the name Amy and the picture is of the same stone-cold bitch I met at Sully's. The message is simply: call me and her number.

How did she find me? Oh, I was a smartass and told her my damn handle. Good job, Veronica.

Crap. I pace in the living room as panic builds behind my eyes.

Why should I call her? I don't answer to her. But Sully turned his phone off. Could something have happened and they need to get a hold of him and they can't? Maybe it's an emergency.

I'm about to dial her number when Sully stalks out of the bedroom, rubbing his eyes. "Do you want to go out for breakfast or do you have anything here to eat? I'm good with cereal or..." He rubs his jaw and notices my phone. "What's wrong?"

"Amy sent me a message on Insta to call her."

"The band's Amy?" he asks, confused.

"Yeah...I don't know anyone else by that name unless you count the singer of Evanescence, and I doubt she wants me to call her."

"Don't worry about it. She's just pissed my phone is off." He strolls into the kitchen. "I need coffee before I talk to her."

"What if something bad happened?" I set my phone on the counter and watch him fill the coffee machine with water.

"She makes everything sound worse than it is. I'm needed at the studio. That's all."

"Hmm..." I steal the coffee can from him so he'll look at me. "You can't blow off your band for me."

196

"Watch me." He takes the can back and pours three tablespoons of grounds into the machine, closing the lid and turning it on. "Why do you think Scarlet Failure hardly tours? I don't have it in me anymore, and they won't find another bass guitarist because of the deal we made—that we'd stick together or the band's dead."

I cross my arms, studying him. "What about the music awards tonight?" My voice comes out sharper than I mean it to—part accusation, part wounded hope.

He pauses, glancing at me over his shoulder like he can feel the shift in the air. For a second, something flickers in his eyes—regret, maybe.

"We'll see," he says with a shrug, too casual. He turns and opens the fridge. "You need to go grocery shopping. Your milk's gone." He tosses the empty container into the sink.

"Yeah. Alice does that." I roll my eyes. "But don't change the subject."

He closes the fridge and kisses my lips. "Don't worry. I'll sort it out after we eat. Now help me find food."

"Okay," I mumble, caving in.

We find cherry pop-tarts and eat at the two-seater table drinking coffee. He does what he promised, calls Amy, and orders a ride to the studio to meet up with his band.

"Do you want to come?" He offers me his hand.

I interlace my fingers with his and we climb into the car.

We arrive at the studio and Amy's fuming when she spots me. I hold my head high and enter with Sully.

Charlotte sits on a stool next to the producer as Ben and Lars lounge on the couch.

"Hey, Veronica." Charlotte greets me with a hug and ushers me to the soundboard. "You have to hear this track." She motions for the producer to play something. He nods and music starts. The song is heavy and the lyrics deep, about being lost in a world you don't understand.

"Wow. I love it," I say once it's over.

"Thanks. It's going to be the first single off the new record."

The door opens again and slams closed. When I look over my shoulder, the temperature in the room drops twenty degrees. Gigi shrugs out of her black fur coat and tosses it at Lars like he's part of the furniture.

"Great. She's here early," Charlotte mutters.

"Why is she here?" I whisper.

Charlotte rolls her eyes. "Amy and her PR games. Talked Gigi into singing on one of our new songs and dragging poor Sully to the award show tonight." She grimaces. "I'm sorry. I said Sully should take you, but—"

"It's fine. It's for the upcoming tour. Nothing personal." *Right?*

Gigi spots Sully sitting in the corner on a stool with his guitar. He's been holding it silently as if he didn't make a sound, he'd turn invisible.

"Sully! There you are." Gigi floats toward him in her seven-inch heels like she's walking on air.

He adjusts his guitar and strums the strings. "Hey. I'm tuning this and then I'll be ready to play."

She pouts and runs her thumb under the thin bra strap on her shoulder. Amy rushes to Gigi's side. "Can I get you anything?"

Gigi blows a bubble with her gum and pops it loudly. "Coffee." That's when Gigi's eyes fall on me. "Is that your job?"

I stiffen. "No."

Amy waves a hand at me. "She's nothing."

Sully stands and sets his guitar on its stand. "Veronica is my guest."

A ping hits my heart. What's this weird feeling taking over me? Is this jealousy?

"Oh." Gigi steals the seat next to the producer and scrolls through her phone. "Someone getting that coffee?"

Amy nods. "Yes. Right away."

Charlotte touches my arm. "Don't worry about her. She's a diva."

I nod and glance at the clock on the wall. "It's okay. I need to be at work soon anyway."

Sully cuts in, cupping my face in his hands. "I'm coming over after the show, okay?"

"I'll see you then."

He kisses me and I wave my goodbyes to the rest of the band.

I walk to the diner around the corner and ask Alice to come pick me up. As I lean against the brick wall, I glance up at the video billboard promoting the award show. To my surprise Scarlet Failure is on there with a bunch of other artists, including Gigi.

My insides feel hollowed out thinking of Gigi hanging on Sully tonight. I hate Amy and PR. I hate games to make sure bands get more exposure. And despite my best efforts, I *am* falling in love with Sully, and it makes me ill knowing my heart is placing itself on the chopping block once again.

Chapter Twenty-Nine

THAT NIGHT ALICE AND I turn the breakroom TV on to the music awards. My mermaid show is starting soon, but I'm sitting on the bench with a nervous stomach waiting to see Sully. Alice opens a snack bag of goldfish and sits beside me. She loudly comments on everyone's wardrobe during the red-carpet walk.

"Work it, work it!" she shouts as a rapper and her girlfriend walk arm in arm wearing colorful blazers.

"What is this?" Alice snorts, throwing goldfish at the TV. "Did a sewing machine blow up on your ass? Who is this clown?"

I glance up from my phone. No new texts. Of course, Sully is busy, but I sent him good luck and told him I'll be watching.

Alice waves a hand in front of my face. "Veronica? Are you watching this? You know I hate these things. I'm here for support and you are not laughing at my running commentary."

"Sorry." I set my phone facedown next to my thigh. "Just seeing if Sully replied. You haven't seen him yet?"

"No. Just been a bunch of people I don't know and a few I recognize."

A chill blossoms inside my core, turning each bone to ice. Any blow will shatter my entire being.

"Lady Gaga, I love her sparkly dress. Definitely a step up from the meat dress so many moons ago." Alice laughs. "Do you remember that?" She drapes her arm over me and rests her head on my shoulder.

"Yeah. We saw that dress in that pop-up thing near the merch booth at Gaga's concert."

"Just making sure you're with me."

"Yes. We'll suffer through this together."

About five minutes later, a car pulls up and Scarlet Failure pours out. Sully is the last member and offers his hand to someone hiding inside. I bite my thumbnail as a woman's arm shoots into view and takes his hand. Gigi is wearing a short vibrant green dress with her breasts pressed up so high they look like a mini butt. Her legs are miles long and perfect like all singers with nine-inch heels and green sparkles. Her platinum blonde hair is wavy and perfect like she just stepped out of a model shoot.

"Gigi looks...like a walking Christmas tree." Alice munches on a few goldfish and adds, "Her hair is so shiny it could be the star on top."

Gigi is gorgeous and there's nothing we can say to deny that. Alice tries to spare my ego from being bruised and distract me from that woman clinging to Sully's arm. But there's not much we can say to bash her looks. I can see why Amy wants to pair her with Sully. They do look perfect together.

Sully is wearing a black tux with an emerald green tie to match Gigi's dress. She sticks to him like they've been hot and heavy for months.

"It's all for the camera." Alice's voice pulls me out of the storm clouds forming above my head.

"Oh...yeah. For their next tour." As I keep reminding myself but it never helps.

Out of habit, I spin my ring around my finger. Sully likes me though. We're more than a simple fling, or so my idiot of a heart whispers to my frazzled brain.

But seeing him with Gigi and kissing her cheek for all these flashing cameras is a blade to the gut.

It should be me standing beside him in a beautiful gown with him kissing my lips in front of the world. To make every Scarlet Failure fangirl curse my name and prove Sully belongs to me.

Only yesterday, I was in his arms. The prince and his mermaid. What a cruel trick.

Arthur clears his throat. "Hey. There are people wondering where the mermaid I introduced is. I told them she's stuck in a net and needs to be saved..."

"Shit." I leap to my feet. "I'm sorry! Give me a minute and I'll be there." I dash for the stairs leading to the top of the tank.

✳ ♫♪ 🐚 ♫♪ ✳ ♫♪ 🐚

My fans lift my spirits as they smile and watch me swim in amazement. I blow them kisses and twirl. It's true, keeping a smile on your face does something odd to your mood, making you happier.

But it all goes to hell when I return to the break room and grab my phone. I flop my fins on the floor and search for Gigi and Sully hashtags online. It's worse than I thought.

Everyone's gushing about them. How the tour is a cover for them to date. How the songs are about them. It makes me sick.

I watch a couple of videos and one pans to Sully and Gigi in the audience and she wins Best Single of the Year. She kisses Sully hard on the mouth, like she's trying to eat his face.

"Bitch," I mumble, tossing my phone onto the towel I dropped on the floor.

Alice breezes in and frowns. "What's wrong, pretty little mermaid?"

"You know." I run my hands over my tail. "What if we go out tonight?"

"Are you serious? Don't screw with me." She points a finger at me as she toys with the silver chain around her neck.

"Yes. Let's go to one of your favorite haunts."

Anything to get my mind off Sully and Gigi. I need something to focus on and to stop doom-scrolling. He's coming over later. Sully will be in my bed, not hers. Why does that make me feel warm and tingly inside?

"Hell yeah!" Alice smacks my thigh. "Get out of that tail! We're going to hit the town!"

Chapter Thirty

ALICE DRESSES ME IN an off-shoulder black dress with a heart-shaped necklace and lets me borrow matching heels. She pours herself into a red dress with a see-through back and fire-red heels.

I curl ringlets into my hair and add dark eyeshadow, giving myself a smokey eye. My self-image is already improving while I twirl in front of the mirror.

Alice orders us a car, and it drops us off at her favorite club, The Rainbow Pony. She knows the bouncer, and he waves us in without checking IDs or forcing us to join the line wrapped around the building.

"Good to know people," she shouts as she tows me toward the bar.

We grab the first two stools available. Alice sits on her knees, leaning over the counter to grab two glasses and the closest bottle of liquor, whiskey.

"To us!" She pours us each a double shot and lifts her glass in the air.

I laugh, clinking my glass with hers. "To us!"

We drink. She pours us more as my body shivers with the warm liquor burning its way through my organs.

"Can't we order something?" I ask, accepting my glass.

She sticks her tongue out. "I'll get the bartender if you need your drink watered down."

Alice slams her hand on the bar and beckons the bartender a few feet away. He glares at the bottle of whiskey in her hand and takes it back. "Alice, you can't take over. You don't work here."

"Damn right, I don't. This bar would have top-class service if I did." Alice smacks her lips. "Can you make my best friend an adios mother-fucker?" She rips the bottle out of his grasp and pours herself another shot. "I'm good for now."

He shakes his head as his hand wraps around the whiskey's neck and he places it as far from Alice as possible.

Alice checks her phone and grins, a wicked spark in her eyes. "Emily's already here!" she shouts over the music.

As a new song by Sabrina Carpenter blasts through the speakers, Alice practically vibrates with excitement. She leans in close, her voice loud in my ear, "I'm going to dance. Find me after you grab your drink!"

She gives my arm a playful punch before vanishing into the crowd, her body already moving to the beat.

The bartender returns with my blue drink. "Alice is a spitfire. Always in here trying to do my job. You know last week she hopped the bar and was serving people while I was in the restroom?" He whisks away the empty whiskey glasses. "She's determined to get me fired."

"She's passionate," I say, biting my tongue. I'm terrible at defending my bestie.

"Yeah." His nostrils flare and he turns away to help someone else.

The music rocks the building as I sip my drink and search for Alice on the packed dance floor. A group of girls grab me to join them as they bounce and shimmy their hips. For a minute, I'm theirs until they drift off, and I'm free to wander again. I locate Emily leaning against the wall, smoking her vape, but Alice isn't with her.

"Hey," I say, my voice cracking. Her hazel eyes widen when she sees me.

"You look different with that eyeshadow," she says. "Are you looking for Alice?" She blows white smoke over her head. "Didn't believe her when she said you wanted to come out tonight. You seem like such a workaholic. No offense."

"Yeah, well." I shrug. "Thought it was time for a change." What I needed was an excuse to get out of my head. I step closer to the wall to avoid a group of girls heading toward the bathroom.

"How's it going with your rock star?" Emily offers her vape to me. Against my better judgment, I accept and take a puff. It tastes like cotton candy and cherries.

The smoke curls out of my lips. "It's been fun but—"

"Oh…" She takes another drag and blows the smoke behind her shoulder. "You're using the death words, past tense, and the dreaded *but*."

"It's complicated." I toy with a strand of hair, coiling it around my finger until my pulse thuds in its tip. "There's never a story about dating a musician and it not being rocky."

She nods. "True, but are you talking Courtney Love and Kurt Cobain kind of fucked up or Bon Jovi and his high school sweetheart?"

"Too early to tell." I rub my temple. This drink is going straight to my head. "Where's Alice?"

Emily points to the cage dancers. "She pulled out one of the girls and took her place. You know how she can't stand not being the center of attention."

I glance up, and sure enough, Alice is shaking her ass fifteen feet in the air inside a steel cage. "Naturally." I bow my head and tap my heel against the floor, enjoying the annoying clicking sound.

"Gotta love her spirit. She always gets what she wants."

"Agreed..." I finish my drink and watch the ice spin inside the glass. "Despite the cost to others," I mutter, pushing off the wall and entering the crowd again.

One of the reasons I never go to clubs is no matter how many people surround me, I never feel more alone. I leave with bruised arms and sticky shoes but inside I'm empty.

The alcohol buzzes inside my head and turns my blood into sludge. My thoughts spin and my vision warps.

There must be something between going to clubs and staying home. Though you'd need more of a social life to be invited to things or be in a relationship with someone who wanted to be seen publicly with you.

A giant hand falls onto my shoulder and for a heartbeat I think it's Sully, finding me like some fictional hero who can't stand being away from his love interest.

"You're not leaving, are you?" the stranger beside me asks. His dark hair is swept back by gel, and his skin is sun-kissed. By the looks of his body beneath his tight tee and jeans, I'd bet he's a surfer.

"Don't have a reason to stay," I say.

"Let me change your mind. One song?" He offers his hand and a shy smile.

My eyes flick to my phone. No new messages.

"Okay. One song," I reply, letting the stranger lead me into the crowd.

A new catchy song hits the speakers and we dance. His hands slide from my sides to my hips. I swing around him, and he twirls me. I laugh, allowing my nerves to drift away. Trying to live in the moment and have fun.

"Veronica!" I hear Alice shout.

I scan the area and spot her in a cage hanging above us to the right. She waves, then shakes her ass, whipping her hair like she owns the place.

"Friend of yours?" the guy asks, his grin too wide, too eager—like he's already unwrapping me in his mind.

"Yes," I reply, dragging my hand down his sculpted chest. He's all muscle and show, but there's nothing—no spark, no heat, just a cold flatline.

He finally looks away from Alice and fixes his eyes on me. "How about you hop in the cage next?" His fingers trail along my collarbone, rough and intrusive, like they're staking a claim that doesn't belong to him. A chill runs through me, like my skin's trying to crawl away from his touch.

"Gotta go." I duck away and weave through the crowd until I reach the bathroom. I slam a stall door shut and lock it behind me. Girls yell, pounding on the door, but I press my back to the wall and try to breathe.

With a shaky hand, I check my messages again, and nothing. I search online, and my heart dies as my stomach falls to the floor. Gigi won Artist of the Year, and during the after-show, she kissed Sully again. But this time, she has her arms wrapped around his neck. His hands locked on her hips. His head tilted like he was enjoying their embrace.

Screw him. I wipe away my tears and order a ride home.

Fuck him for cracking open my world and basking me in light. The darkness wasn't so bad, not when I had a career to pour all my energy into. Now my heart is exposed, and it's his fault.

When my ride is nearby, I throw open the stall door and text Alice, telling her I'm leaving. My fury must radiate off my skin because people move out of my way so I can exit this despicable club without tripping over anyone's feet or being pushed in a different direction.

Chapter Thirty-One

MY FIRST INSTINCT WITH Sully was correct, and I shouldn't have believed anything different. All we are is a fling and nothing more. These past two weeks, I've been living in a dreamland.

Seeing Sully and Gigi super cozy tonight and the media frenzy after the music awards with fans buzzing as if they're already an item hurts on a deep level. One reporter is ballsy enough to ask if they've been secretly dating for a while and might already be engaged. I refuse to stand in the way where his people don't want me anywhere around.

Scarlet Failure will not lose Sully because he chose me over them. It would be to spite them, and he'd grow to hate me for ruining everything he's worked for. A girl you barely met is not worth throwing away your life. If he wants to leave, I won't stick around just to be the excuse when it all collapses.

It's too risky for my career. I'm part of the mermaid community, and no big-time sponsor will take me seriously if I get wrapped up in a celebrity scandal. It was hard enough to recover after "the incident" with my ex that went viral. At least his following was nothing compared to a globally known band.

Sometime after midnight, Sully finally replies.

> **I'm so sorry! I lost my phone! I didn't kiss Gigi! I can explain.**

A few minutes after that, he sends another text.

> **Please, I hate these after parties. They create so many rumors.**

I leave him unread and go to bed.

When I wake up, he sent me another message, inviting me over for breakfast. I toss my phone onto my bed and follow the scent of coffee into the kitchen. Alice stands slumped over the counter waiting for the coffee machine to finish brewing with her mug in hand.

"How long did you stay dancing in that cage?" I ask, grabbing my mug beside her.

"Shh!" She covers her ears and slowly pulls herself together, standing up mostly straight. "I have a pounding headache."

"A long time then," I say, clicking my tongue.

She grabs the coffee pot and pours herself some liquid heaven and then sets it on the counter for me. "Shut up, Miss I-want-to-go-out-but-leave-within-the-hour."

"Hey, I stayed longer than an hour...I think." I shrug, grabbing the creamer from the fridge and stirring it into my coffee.

"Not according to Emily, but I'll take your word for it."

"Whatever." I absorb the warmth through my mug before taking a sip and bumping my hip against the table.

Alice leans against the opposite chair. "What happened with Sully?"

"He texted me after midnight, but I haven't replied." I fall into the chair, resting my arms on the table.

She watches me over the rim of her steaming mug.

"Not planning to either. It's too much. This push and pull. This should I or shouldn't I. It's exhausting."

Alice squishes her lips to the side but doesn't say anything. She doesn't need to. Her watchful eye says it all. She doesn't believe me.

"Don't look at me like that," I say, running my finger along the rim of my cup. "I'm not going to cave. We had a fun fling, but a real relationship is too...messy."

She raises her hands in mock surrender. "I didn't say a word."

"Your face says enough." I trace the scrape carved into the table's surface. "You didn't see how their PR lady looked at me. I felt small and disgusting, a cockroach who they think is riding on his coattails for fame. Sully wanted to invite me as his plus one to the music awards and she nearly bit his head off. Then Gigi stopped by the studio and acted like she already owned the place. Scarlet Failure is going on tour with her. I don't stand a chance."

"Did Sully stand up for you or did he sit back and let these people treat you like dirt?"

"What does it matter if he did or not?"

She drags the chair out and sits down, slamming her empty cup onto the table. "I'm asking if he had a spine or not. If he has one then there's still a chance, he will fight for you, but if he allows them to run his life then I agree, cut your losses and move on."

"Umm." I tug on my earring. "He told Amy to back off. At the studio he barely acknowledged Gigi. But..." I gesture toward the TV. "Gigi was on his arm and I was swimming in a tank miles away."

"I don't want to see you go through what happened last time. But Sully doesn't seem to be like he who shall not be named."

"There's a fine line. Sully could hook up with Gigi. I mean his PR rep basically blessed it right before my eyes and turned around to toss me out." I shove my mug away and cross my arms, resting my chin on top of them. "Maybe it's true what they say...you shouldn't meet and then fuck your favorite musicians. It's too...murky."

Alice snorts. "That's not the saying and you know it." Her face falls as she studies me. "Be honest. Is he worth all this trouble?" For a second, I think she's being genuine. "How is he in the sack? Do you come or do you fake it?"

And...there it is. I can't have a heart-to-heart with Alice to save my life.

I stumble away from the table, almost choking on my gasp. "I'm not going there with you."

She shrugs, running her tongue along her top teeth. "Just something to think about. You're a real tight ass when you're not getting any."

"Screw you." I flip her the bird, and she chuckles, gathering her cup to grab more coffee.

"So, your brilliant plan is to ignore him forever? You know he'll show up here again or at work. What will you do then?"

I want to crawl into a hole and hide for a month. "This is all your fault. If you didn't—"

"What?" Her joy is gone, replaced with red-hot rage. "If I didn't get tickets to my best friend's favorite band to cheer her up? Did I force you to hang around an alley to meet the band in the middle of the fucking night?"

"Okay. That's on me..." I wrap my arms around my waist, shielding myself from her verbal blows. "But you don't—"

She shoves her finger into my chest and it feels like the barrel of a gun. "No. Don't you but me. You met the band and you chose to text Sully. Without telling me, you went to meet him at his hotel and then you went to Vegas! You! The girl who thinks serial killers lurk in the shadows and doesn't allow me to open windows past ten o'clock despite us being on the second floor and the whole city in the middle of a heat wave."

"Okay, fine." I rub my chest where her finger dug a hole. "It's my fault. Is that what you want to hear? After spending all this time with him, I learn he's sweet and strong. He supports my mermaiding and doesn't make me feel foolish. Fuck. He's in some of my modeling pictures now!"

Alice blinks at me for a moment. "I don't know what that means, but screw you."

"No..." I tug on my hair and spit my next words, "You didn't want to hang out at home with your heartbroken best friend but didn't want to feel guilty going out either. So, if I had someone then you were off the hook."

"I'm not going to keep doing this with you." She hits a vase of flowers, and it crashes to the ground, exploding into pieces. "You want to be a miserable workaholic and piss away the rest of your life be my guest!" She stomps on the broken shards and swings open the front door.

Her sudden exit sucks all the oxygen out of the room. I stand there in shock, staring at the gaping hole to the outside world. The sky is a bright blue with no clouds in sight. Birds sing and people honk car horns down below on the street. Life goes on, but I'm stuck in this moment. Speechless and glued to the ground.

It's not unusual for Alice and me to fight. Being roommates and best friends does equal a kind of sisterhood. And sometimes sisters argue and turn nasty at times. But this is different. Alice never got in my face like that. Her words never cut me so deeply that my skin felt raw and bleeding. I didn't want whatever was going on with Sully and me to ruin the only friendship that lasted more than a few years. We've been there for each other since grade school. I'm the first person she came out to. We share a whole history.

After a few crushing moments, I push myself forward and close the door. Alice is too far away to do anything. At this point, I'm not sure if an apology will help smooth things over, but I need to do something. The more time we spend apart angry, the more our friendship cracks and splinters.

"What the hell am I doing?" This is so me. Burn anyone too close. No one can hurt me if I cut off their legs and abandon them first.

With a heavy heart, I scoop my phone off my bed and send Alice a text. Asking her to lunch and sending a white flag emoji as an olive branch.

A moment later my phone lights up with a call. I don't look at the name on the screen, I just hit answer.

"Alice. Please come back and we can—"

"It's not Alice." Sully's voice slices into me deeper than a razor blade.

I remove the phone from my ear, muttering swear words under my breath. Why didn't I look before answering? I'm a damn fool.

"Veronica?" he asks, pain leeching into his voice.

Ice climbs up my spine. My thumb hovers over the end call button.

"Sully, I can't do this anymore. Can we just—"

"Please. One last date. Then if you don't want to see me again, I'll respect your wish." His voice is rough, thick with grief. If I close my eyes, I can almost see him—the way his lips would pout, the deep frown lines creasing his forehead.

I clutch the phone tighter. "Does Gigi know you're calling me? Did you ask Amy for permission?" My voice cracks at the end, exposing too much.

Sully lets out a low, frustrated breath. "Gigi doesn't control me. Amy doesn't either. Last night at the award show...it was a setup. They've been trying to pull this shit for a while. I'm the only single one in the band, and they think that makes me easy to manipulate. Like some kind of trophy to parade around."

My heart stutters.

"She kissed me without permission, Veronica. I didn't want it. I pulled away the second it happened. But Gigi and Amy—they're playing a different game. Gigi wants some hot bass player on her arm to boost her image for the tour. Candy for the cameras. And Amy..." His voice darkens. "Amy's on a power trip. She thinks managing us gives her the right to manage everything. Even our personal lives and with everyone else being married...she's hooked her sights on me."

I stay silent, my mind racing to keep up with the new version of events.

"I'm easy-going, yeah. Always have been. But people take advantage of that." He pauses, voice raw. "I don't want anything to do with Gigi, or her power-hungry bullshit. I just want you."

The air leaves my lungs.

I glance at the signed Scarlet Failure setlist taped to my bedroom wall next to the mirror. It's now or never. Do I throw whatever is between us to the wind and watch the ashes scatter, or do I play Russian roulette with my heart one last round and pray it doesn't explode in my chest?

I remember the way Sully's hands moved over me—slow, deliberate, like he was learning a song he never wanted to forget. His mouth on mine. The weight of his body against me. In those moments, everything else disappeared. No stage lights. No lies. Just us, tangled in something too intense to name.

"One date," I say, collapsing onto my bed and staring up at the ceiling, my heart beating too loud in the quiet room.

"Is tonight too soon?" His voice is full of glee, and I can't help but smile.

"Please. One last date. Then if you don't want to see me again, I'll respect your wishes." His voice is rough, thick with grief. If I close my eyes, I can picture his perfect lips pouting and the frown lines on his forehead.

I turn over, kicking my legs behind me. "I'm off, so tonight works."

"*Wunderbar*! I'll pick you up at seven. Wear comfortable shoes."

The line clicks before I can ask why.

"God, I hope he doesn't want us to hike." I sigh and pinch my nose before checking my messages with Alice. She hasn't replied.

To keep my mind off Alice—and to stop myself from spiraling into a depression—I head down to the pool and slip into the water. I spend the afternoon pushing my body through mermaid training drills, swimming lap after lap until my muscles ache and the sting of worry fades into the rhythm of movement. It's easier to lose myself in the water than face the knot tightening in my chest. Before I know it, the sun dips low, and it's time to get ready for what might be the last night I ever spend with Sully.

Chapter Thirty-Two

SULLY PICKS ME UP at seven sharp. He's wearing black skinny jeans with a red and black plaid long-sleeve shirt. He eyes my silky pink top with white polka dots when I slide into the passenger seat. "You might want to grab a jacket."

I wipe my palms against my jeans, enjoying the friction. "We're in LA. I don't think there's snow for—"

"We're not going to the mountains, or I'd question your shoes." His thumbs drum against the steering wheel. I glance down at my flats but let the comment go. He adds, "Let's just say the air conditioning can be chilly where we're going."

"Okay, I'll trust you." I jog back inside to grab my gray jacket from my closet and return to sit beside him. "Better?"

"Yes. You hungry?"

"What do you have in mind?" Since my fight with Alice, who still hasn't responded, I forgot to eat. All I had today was coffee. No wonder my stomach is turning on itself.

He changes lanes. We're driving toward the beach, and traffic picks up. "There's food where we're going, don't worry."

Part of me wants to pepper him with questions, but I don't have the energy. Sully pulls into a parking garage, and I catch the name. We're going to the local aquarium.

"Aren't they closed today?" I ask, checking the hours on my phone.

He waves at me, forcing my phone away. "Don't look at that."

Sully hands the parking agent folded cash, and we're in with a parking tag hanging on the rearview mirror.

We find a spot on the third level near the elevator. Sully kills the engine and turns toward me, holding a silky blue blindfold. "I want this to be perfect. Can you put this on?"

My mouth goes dry. I want to say a kinky joke, but my throat closes. All I can do is nod, accepting the blindfold and placing it over my eyes. Sully ties it.

"That's not too tight?" he asks, running a hand through my hair.

"No. It's fine." I can't see anything. It would be hard to tell if my eyes are open or closed if it wasn't for my eyelashes brushing against the fabric.

Sully gets out and walks around to open my door. I take his hand, and he patiently leads me toward what I assume is the elevator.

"Don't bump me into any poles or let me trip over any parking blocks." I drag my feet, worried he'll guide me to the edge and I'll fall to my death on the street below. Unrealistic, but it's hard to have faith when you're blind.

"You're acting like a cow being taken to slaughter." He drops my hand and moves behind me, guiding me with a gentle hand on my lower back.

"For the record, I'm not a fan of surprises. If someone pops out, fair warning, I'll punch them in the throat."

His chest rumbles with his laugh. "I'll cancel the clown then."

I freeze. My blood turns to slush, picturing a clown waiting for me. One of my ultimate childhood fears that linger on forever. "Please tell me that's a joke."

His hands slide up to my shoulders, squeezing them in a caring gesture. He whispers, "Yes. I promise to keep the evil clowns away." I hear elevator doors slide open, and we enter. Sully hits a button, and we go up.

When the doors slide open again, we're greeted with a blast of cold air. It tosses my hair back and raises goosebumps on my arms. The smell of salt and fish lingers in the air. Our steps echo as we move deeper into the room.

"Now look," Sully says cheerfully, taking off my blindfold and wrapping his arm around my hips.

I blink a few times, allowing my eyes to adjust to the dim lighting, and look around. To our left, there's a line of waiters dressed in black and white uniforms. A lone table sits in the middle of the room washed in dark blue, the light shining down and bouncing around the walls made of glass. I look up and my lungs squeeze out all their breath as my heart leaps out of my body.

Countless fish in different colors and sizes swim above us in a domed tank. I spot a hammerhead shark in the back corner. I twirl, laughing as the water's reflection dances around us.

"I love it! This is so magical," I say in a rush, grabbing Sully's arm.

"Only fitting for my beautiful mermaid." His lips meet mine before his mouth travels down my throat.

Classical music floats above us as the waiters move, grabbing our chairs and gesturing for us to take a seat. The tablecloth is soft and feels like handspun cotton. In the center is a vase of blood-red roses with fat pink candles in golden candlesticks on either side. One of the waiters lights the wicks as another pours white wine into our glasses.

Fresh salads with the greenest lettuce I've ever seen are placed in front of us.

"I didn't order yet..." I say, confused, picking up a fork.

"Don't worry. I planned everything." Sully's head darts around the flowers, trying to see me. He's more of a floating head coming in and out of focus.

"Can we lose the roses? They're a bit much," Sully says, giving in.

A waiter whisks them off the table and rearranges the candles without a word.

"There's that smile I love." Sully's voice is low and warm, sending a shiver across my skin. I bite my lip to hide the shy smile tugging at my mouth as a flush creeps up my neck. Needing something to steady myself, I take a giant sip of wine, hoping it will calm the jittery excitement dancing in my chest.

Above and all around us, fish glide by, moving idly through the water with nowhere to go.

"Have you ever swum with a shark?" Sully asks, gesturing to a nurse shark cruising to our right.

"I have in Fiji and Costa Rica. I was supposed to last year in Hawaii, but my dad got sick, and I canceled to stay here to help take care of him."

"And he's doing better, right? When we saw them, he—"

"Yes." I dab my mouth with a cloth napkin. "It takes more than pneumonia to extinguish his fire."

Sully nods, his crooked grin sending my heart into flips. If I'm not careful that damn smile of his will send me into v-fib. "I'm happy to hear that."

The waiters take away our salads and place steaks with loaded mashed potatoes and buttery green beans in front of us.

"What about your family? You haven't told me much about them." I glance up from cutting my steak, cooked to perfection with a warm pink center, to see Sully freeze mid-cutting his steak.

He shoves a bite of potatoes into his mouth, chewing the bite slowly, buying time for a response.

I finish my wine and the waiter behind me is quick to refill the glass. "I didn't mean to step into something uncomfortable. You don't have to talk about them if you don't want to."

Not to sound like a stalker, but I read about Scarlet Failure online and tried to learn more about each band member years ago when I first discovered them. Clicking on their names brought up pages about their personal lives—a few paragraphs about their families, where they grew up, and where they went to school. I learned that Charlotte and Ben founded the band when they were eighteen, and that Lars married his high school sweetheart, someone completely outside the music industry. But when I clicked on Sully's name, it was mostly blank. All it said was when and where he was born—and that after their first album, he became the one who writes most of their songs.

His personal life is a mystery. Maybe it made him a bit more interesting. A spark of the unknown hides behind his blue eyes.

He gulps his wine and waves his hand, slicing into the tension building between us. A pained expression crosses his face. "It's okay. I knew you'd ask sooner or later." He straightens his plate and places his black cloth napkin onto his lap. "*Mein vater* left us when I was five. Started a new *familie* and then died in a car accident about four years later."

My heart cracks, seeing a small Sully with wildly curling hair drowning in his tears. His beautiful smile with deep dimples wiped away for what probably felt like forever.

His attention remains on his mashed potatoes, his fork stabbing at them. "*Meine mutter* did her best to take care of my *bruder* and me. She had to jump from job to job and never had time to date. I think it's partly because she didn't want to give her heart away again."

I run my fingers through my napkin as my chest tightens, a vise grip twisting until my breath hitches.

"Betrayal is one of the hardest things to recover from," I say, voice hollow.

"Agreed. After graduating from *voortgezet onderwijs*..." He looked at me for the words. "What do you call it here?"

My thoughts whirl, trying to understand his words. "High school?" I guess.

He nods. "Yeah, that. I used to play my songs at local pubs. One night, this guy told me about a band looking for a bassist. I found their flyer tacked up in a coffee shop and decided to try out. Charlotte and Ben had already started Scarlet Failure. They took a chance on me."

He shrugs like it's no big deal, but I can hear the weight behind the words.

"I worried about losing control of my songs," he admits. "At first, I didn't know if they'd want to rewrite everything or turn it into some-

223

thing fake. But after the first album, they trusted me. Now I write most of what we put out."

Sully goes quiet, eating his dinner, and I respect the silence.

I never thought about it before, but maybe that's why his music always hit me so hard. It wasn't just sound or words—it was him bleeding through the speakers, raw and real.

Their first album still lives in my bones. Rage pulsing through every track, heartbreak stitched between every line. Songs that didn't just ask you to feel—they demanded it. I practically wore out my headphones after my last breakup, clinging to those lyrics like a life raft, letting them scream for me when I couldn't find the words.

And still, even after all that, Sully once said in an interview that his favorite album was their second record—the one where the anger hadn't fully faded but hope had started slipping in through the cracks.

Maybe, deep down, he's always been someone searching for the light too.

Chapter Thirty-Three

WHEN WE FINISH, SULLY takes my hand and guides me on a private tour of the aquarium.

"This place is ours," he whispers, kissing my temple.

"This is the best date I've ever been on." I twirl around him and kiss his lips.

He brushes his thumb along my jawbone. "I'm pleased my romance game beats your previous experiences with your exes."

"They could never compare," I say, looking up through my lashes.

"Any of them take you to the Hollywood sign? I sense that's a big make-out place in this town."

I drift away from him and place my hand against the glass of the jellyfish tank, watching them float. "Maybe in the movies but in real life it's fenced off with a security alarm that calls the cops if you go anywhere near it. Kinda kills the romance."

He rubs the back of his neck. "Damn. That's worse than learning it doesn't light up at night."

"Yup. All the houses on the hill ruined that."

"The ugly underbelly of LA revealed."

We walk to the eels hiding in their holes. Their little heads poke out with sneers to stay away.

"You have no idea how terrible LA can be. There's this lookout place where you can park and make out while being above the city, if the smog isn't hiding it, but it was also a hot spot for serial killers in the seventies and eighties."

"I'm not sure if I'm impressed or concerned you know that fact," he says.

"Sometimes the true crime junkie in me comes out." I shrug. "LA was a big place for it. Countless stories of girls who came here for fame and ended up dead."

Sully tugs me toward his chest. His arms twist around me. "Why do you stay here if it's all darkness and struggling to survive? For your family?"

"Partly, but this is my home, born and raised in this city. That's rare if you ask around, most people are implants." I pause, stopping to look at the octopus in the corner of its tank. "I thought of moving to Florida in the past. I have a few mermaid friends who live there, and we could perform shows together..." My sentence dies as I open the door to the Arctic part of the aquarium.

"Why don't you?" Sully queries, sitting on the bench in front of the penguins. They wander around the ice and dive into their chilly waters ignoring us.

"It's something I push off." I sit on the other side of the bench, leaving enough space for an invisible third person to sit between us. "Always had an excuse to stay here. This past year, I've had tunnel vision about my social media, trying to gain traction so I can travel the world. Fill my life with adventure and new places, forget about the past."

Sully moves closer, capturing my chin in his cupped hand. "Is this about the ex who can't be named?"

"You don't want to hear any more about him."

He gingerly wipes a tear that escaped my hold. "I want to know everything about you."

The memory of my ex tangled in someone else's embrace clouds my mind. It was so easy for him to move on, to hook up with one of my so-called friends while he was still with me. It was as if I meant nothing, just a placeholder until it was convenient for them to rip the rug out from under me.

It doesn't help he sent me that looming text a while back or that I swear I've seen him around. Like that suspicious car the other day at my apartment complex. The driver looked so much like him, but why would he come back around? I told him my peace. There's nothing left for him.

Sully drapes his arm over the top of the bench and stares at the penguins. "After our first record was released, I went home to spoil *meine mutter*. I wanted to spend my first check on her. She didn't answer when I knocked. I had a spare key and walked in, thinking she was taking a nap or out. What I didn't expect to see was her lying on the couch. I touched her hand. She was cold and stiff."

A gasp rips from my throat. I dig my fingernails into my thighs to keep from crushing Sully in a hug. He needed to get this off his chest and I needed to remain still until he finished.

"Later, I was told she'd been gone for two days. No one cared to check in on her. Said it would've been at least a week before anyone bothered to visit or for the smell to alert anyone."

"Where was your brother?" My voice is a grave whisper as I place my hand on top of his thigh.

He spits on the ground. "Damn him. He didn't bother coming to her funeral. Too busy with his new family. Just like our *vater*. A rotten seed." He shoves the heel of his hand into his eye and releases a shaky breath. "When we went on tour, I'd get blasted on our days off. It was only a handful of times, but it was enough to spread rumors I liked to party. That I was like all the classic rock stars before me. A player, a drunk, a man with talent but not a lick of sense."

"For the record, I never viewed you as a player."

He smirks, but it doesn't reach his eyes. "I wanted a *familie* too. Someone to help me move on, but girls only wanted to be with someone famous. When I tried to connect or to learn anything about them, they'd grow restless and they'd leave for the next band blowing into town." He cracks his knuckles. "Figured love wasn't for me. I'd be forced to see it from afar. Write about it, the highs and lows, but never obtain it."

His honest words chip at my armor and the walls I kept building come crashing down. "My high school boyfriend left me at a dance because I refused to sleep with him. He called me a tease and spread rumors I was a terrible lay. But I got over him in college. That's where I met...the ex...*Teddy*." I flinch saying his name after so many months. It hurts to think about how much I loved that fuckface. "He was a baseball player and swept me off my feet. Thought I'd spend the rest of my life with him, and then...the incident happened. He turned me into a joke, and I buried myself in work, thinking no one could hurt me if I became an ice queen."

Sully takes my hand in both of his. "Christ, what *arschlöcher*."

"Maybe it's extreme after only two failed relationships, but I don't want to waste time kissing a hundred frogs for a prince. I just want someone to love and who loves me. So, I moved in with Alice and she drags me to things so I don't turn into a hermit crab or run off and try to become a real mermaid." I laugh, but it's too hoarse and humorless.

"All I wanted was something real like my parents." I glance at our combined hands and trace my fingertip over the vein crawling up his wrist. "They met in high school, were crowned king and queen at prom, and the next year they married. Two years later I was born. Sometimes they get on each other's nerves, but they're always there no matter what. I'm starting to think people aren't like that anymore. That they use you until something better comes along."

Sully stands and pulls me to my feet. "Veronica, I never want you to feel that way. You're an extraordinary woman, and there's a fire burning bright inside you. You don't take shit from anyone and say what's on your mind. I can't tell you how amazed I was watching you put Amy in her place the other day at my casita." He entangles his fingers in my hair, pulling me in close. "I want to show you something." He kisses my lips and then takes my hand, guiding me into the next room. I'm breathless as my heart beats in my head.

Chapter Thirty-Four

THE ROOM IS DIM, and the water dark. Above us, the small pinpricks of lights almost look like stars. "This is where the deep-water fish live." His voice booms around the small space.

I'm puzzled why he wants to bring me here, but when his lips meet mine, the answer scorches my skin. I rip at his shirt and toss it onto the ground. His skin is warm. I sink my fingernails into his back, and he moans my name.

He presses me against the cool glass, and his lips tickle my ear. "I only want to see you happy...and naked." His hands move underneath my shirt and run along the rim of my pants.

"Aren't there cameras?" I whisper as between my thighs throb.

He presses me against the wall and chuckles as his fingers unbutton my pants. "Don't worry. They're all turned off."

Sully eases my jacket off my shoulders. He's gentle when he grabs the hem of my shirt and tugs it over my head. The freezing temperature causes my nipples harden, and my breath hitches as his hands unhook my bra. His warm touch on my breasts sends a shiver through my body.

He kisses my throat and licks my right nipple, teasing it as his hot breath unravels me. My hands fumble with his zipper. He's already huge and bursting at the seam.

"*Schatz,*" he rumbles as I tug his pants and underwear down his thighs. I brush my thumb over his tip and slide my hand down his shaft, giving him a lazy pump.

His hands hitch me up high until I'm at the perfect angle for him to slide into me. All my walls crumble as he fills me up. He nips at my neck as he fucks me hard against the wall. I tug on his hair and he bites my shoulder, a moan spilling from my lips as my eyes glaze over.

Breaths come short and heavy. I hook my hands behind his neck and kiss him, pouring every fractured part of myself into him as he comes undone inside me.

✳ 🎵 🐚 🎵 ✳ 🎵 🐚

We finish the tour and conclude at the gift shop. Our hair is a mess and our clothes are wrinkled. I grab a stuffed orange fish because it reminds me of Nemo. Sully laughs and buys it for me. "Something to snuggle with when I'm not lying beside you," he says, placing money on the counter with my new stuffed animal's tag.

We walk along the moonlit garden outside and sit down on the edge of the stone water fountain.

I find two pennies at the bottom of my purse and hand one to Sully. "Close your eyes, make a wish, and toss it into the water."

He closes his fingers around the penny as I pinch mine between my thumb and forefinger. A rush of nerves flutters through my chest as I scramble for the right wish. Water splashes as Sully tosses his in.

I wish to stop sabotaging myself.

My penny flies and plops into the fountain, sinking to the bottom with countless others.

"Before I left the last after-party, I learned we're going on tour a lot sooner than I thought," Sully says, staring hard at the fountain. His words force my heart to fall into the water, destroying my wish.

"When are you leaving?" I ask, hoping my voice doesn't sound broken like my heart feels.

He pushes a hand through his hair. "We're leaving for Europe as soon as we finish recording the new record. In a week or two maybe?"

"Ah." I draw circles in the dirt with my shoe, avoiding his gaze. "I hate to say goodbye, but you're more known there. I'm sure—"

He presses his lips to my ear. "Come with me."

"What?" I move away and lock eyes with him. "You can't be serious."

"You want to travel for your social media. This could be a fresh start for us. We won't be lost if we have each other."

"I can't leave without notice. It's not going to be for a weekend like Vegas was." I sweep my hair away from my face. "How long is the tour?"

He shrugs. "Dates are still being discussed but it's usually three months give or take."

The world sways and gravity becomes too light. I feel like I'm about to float away and burn up in the sun. "I can't. Not with Alice and me in the middle of a fight. I can't leave the restaurant on such short notice. The restaurant only has me, Chloe, and Rachel. And I don't want to sound vain, but I'm their best mermaid."

"I understand." He picks a yellow wildflower and tucks it into my hair. "We'll postpone the tour then."

"You can't do that."

He traces a finger along my collarbone. "Then they can find a new bass guitarist to take my place. I don't mind sitting this one out."

I press a hand to his chest and tip my head back to kiss his cheek. "When would this tour start?"

His brow wrinkles. "I don't understand."

"If you give me time to make up with Alice and find a replacement at the restaurant, then I'll go. Like you said, I've always wanted to travel more. Between the cruise line commercial at the beginning of next year and the chance to be a mermaid in multiple countries, this could boost my career."

"Really?" He lifts me and spins. "Are we doing this?"

"It's about time I take more chances so I say hell yeah!"

"We need to make a list. During the band's downtime, I can take you to all my favorite haunts. We can explore new places together. I'll even pose as your prince in pictures if you want me to."

"What are we waiting for? Let's go to your place and figure out how this will work."

He hugs me until my ribs crack then releases me. I glance at my phone and see a text from Alice. "I have an idea on how to mend things with Alice."

It'll cost me, but if I pull the right strings, I can make some calls and get her tickets to her favorite Broadway play that's in town and sold out.

"Hell of a date," Sully says, snickering, and envelops me in his embrace. I inhale his scent of fresh pine and musk.

We drive to his place and dive deep into web searches. With a blank notebook, we fill the pages with places to visit, restaurants to try, and beaches for me to scope out. I'll have to find connections and see if anyone knows a good photographer I can hire. This could be the perfect excuse to create that travel blog I've wanted to but never have since I don't leave southern California often enough.

I didn't know pennies held this much magic. Or is this the universe finally shining its light on me? I can't question it, or I'll unravel this gift. For now, we will plan and bask in the joy of living our dream and being together.

But I will not say I'm in love. No, this is a harmony between us, the right chords and musical notes that create a song. Yet a voice in my head tells me I'm lying to myself. I should let the final impenetrable wall inside me collapse and face the truth. I *am* falling in love. And at breakneck speed, leaving me dizzy and lightheaded. It has me throwing caution to the wayside and makes me want to believe in happy endings again.

Chapter Thirty-Five

I'm LYING IN BED with Sully's oversized white t-shirt on, scrolling through different travel blogs on my laptop to get an idea of unique things to do in Europe. I made a list of all the restaurants we should try and which beaches I want for my photoshoots. It'll take some time, but I have a list of photographers to contact. The only issue is finding a good and reliable mer-handler. Sully might have to pull double duty if I can't find one.

Sully pads into the bedroom with a pink box of doughnuts and two cups of coffee. I close the laptop and move the pillows around to make room for him to sit beside me.

"You're my hero," I say to the coffee, taking a loving sip.

Sully chuckles, biting into a chocolate-glazed doughnut. "Should I be offended you're saying that to your coffee and not me?"

"A good man knows when to accept defeat," I tease, grabbing a strawberry doughnut with rainbow sprinkles and taking a giant bite.

He swipes crumbs off my lips and licks his thumb. "You know—"

His phone rings. He pushes ignore, but it rings again.

"It's fine. You can answer it."

"Just one second." He grabs the phone and hits the speaker. "What do you want?"

"You were supposed to meet me an hour ago!" a woman screams.

He rolls his eyes and bites his doughnut. "Told you last night, Gigi. I'm not coming to the studio today."

Shame creeps into my veins. I run my fingers along the list of places I wanted to see in Paris. How could we run around Europe without answering to anyone? He'd be too busy to do half the things we discussed. I close the notebook and kill the dream of us traveling across the ocean.

"It's okay, Sully. I should get going." I gather my clothing and walk toward the bathroom.

"Who are you with?" Gigi demands, venom dripping from her words.

Sully places his hand over the phone's mic. "Veronica. Please stay."

"I have to go to work anyway," I lie, locking myself in the bathroom to get dressed and brush my hair.

"I'm not going to make it, and if you call me again, I'll turn my phone off. Goodbye." Sully hangs up.

He knocks on the bathroom door. I open it and slide past him. The warmth of his chest is almost enough to tempt me back into bed and to forget that phone call.

Sully runs a hand through his hair. "Sorry about that. I don't know why she wants to meet at the studio. We're done recording. I think Amy's filled her head with lies."

"Amy's looking out for the band, I guess. Thinks it will hype the tour if you're dating."

236

He nods. "I thought being single meant independence, not having a matchmaker. Especially when I found someone I like spending time with." His hands cup my hips, pulling me closer to his chest.

"Oh?" I gasp as his hands squeeze my ass.

Sully's lips brush against my cheekbone to my ear. He nips at my throat and hikes me up. I wrap my legs around his hips. He kisses me as my back meets the wall.

I claw his shoulder blades as he pins my arms above my head. His other hand works my buttons. My black lace bra peeks through, and his hips rock against mine. I can feel he's ready to throw me onto the bed and screw my brains out.

"Can we put a pin in this?" I ask, between breaths.

He pauses, lips still on my chest. "Why?"

"Because I need to go home and make up with Alice, and you need to deal with this Gigi issue."

"Do I?"

"Yes. She's not going to..." My sentence fades as Sully frees my left breast, teasing the nipple into a hard pebble.

Desire builds in my core, and I'm about to tell him to forget it and rip his pants off when he releases me. My swollen lips ache for his as I tuck myself back into my bra and fix my shirt.

"We'll resume later tonight." He glances around and finds his shirt. "Don't worry about the tour, and keep that notebook close. I told you before, and I'll say it again, I'm not going anywhere if you're not with me."

He moves closer, and I press two fingers to his lips. "If we kiss again, I'm afraid we'll end up on the bed, and we'll never leave this room."

Sully laughs, kissing each finger before walking over to pull on his shoes. "Don't you find anyone else while I'm gone."

"No promises." I toss my hair over my shoulder. "You know how many men I beat off with my tail?" I joke.

His gaze darkens as his jaw clenches. "Don't say shit like that. It makes me never want to let you out of my sight."

"Don't worry about me. I've taken care of myself this long. I think I can handle one more day."

I'm not ready to face Alice yet, so I head down to Santa Monica to walk along the beach and clear my head. It's a weekday, so there are only a few people lying on the sand or hanging out in the water. I spot a handful of surfers out catching waves.

This time of day, no shells wash up on shore to collect. Instead, I walk in ankle-deep water, listening to the waves crash while the seagulls cry out.

"Veronica!" a male voice shouts behind me.

I ignore it. There must be some other girl here by that name. Maybe a child who ran off from her dad.

"Hey!" a breathy voice says as a hand grabs my shoulder.

I whirl around and choke on my tongue. My ex stands with a smile like we're old friends who haven't seen each other in ten years. He opens his arms to hug me, and I stumble back, shoving my hands in front of me to keep him at bay.

"What are you doing here, Teddy?" I rasp. My voice isn't as strong as I want it to be. Saying his name feels like I activated a terrible curse.

He smirks, placing his hands on his hips. He's wearing a surf shirt and black swim trunks. "Saw you walk by and wanted to talk. I've been texting you."

"Yeah…" And I've been ignoring you. Hoping you'd fade away like the horrible memory you are.

"Please. Can I buy you a cup of coffee? I want to talk." He holds his hands up in surrender. "That's it."

He gestures to the little coffee cart past the sand parked on the sidewalk.

"I guess," I sigh, following him to the cart.

I'm so going to regret this.

Chapter Thirty-Six

WE ORDER OUR COFFEES, and Teddy tries to pay for mine. "We're paying separately," I say cooly to the cashier. The cashier looks at Teddy and then me before nodding.

"Still as independent as ever," Teddy tsks.

"That's why I owe no one anything," I say flatly.

When our drinks come, we grab them and walk over to the closest picnic table. I sit across from him, and my right leg won't stop bouncing. It takes all my energy not to leap across the table and strangle him. Instead, I hold my coffee cup between my hands and study him as a lioness sizing up a zebra.

"What do you want?" I ask, trying to sound nonchalant.

He clears his throat and flashes that dazzling smile of his. It used to make my heart stop, but now all it does is encourage me to punch him until his teeth fall out.

"No, how've you been? I haven't been that great." He sips his coffee and shifts his weight.

"Just cut to the chase," I reply, hoping my voice has some sting in it.

He nods. "Veronica. We should get back together. We were so good, and I—"

It's hard to hear what else he says because I can't stop laughing. He looks appalled at my reaction. I used to apologize when I hurt him, but now I don't feel the urge to.

"Veronica. Please." The tips of his ears redden.

I wipe a tear with the back of my hand and settle down. "Maybe you thought we worked. But we were oil and water."

"Come on. We're both social media influencers. We're both..."

"I'm a professional mermaid who uses social media. There's a difference. I don't post stupid pranks for attention."

He winces at my verbal dig.

"You cheated on me. Publicly humiliated me, and I had to sue you to take down the video, and now you come crawling back months later licking your wounds. Why? Did your new girl ditch you for someone better?"

His gaze drops to his coffee cup. He's never this quiet.

"Ha! I'm right." I shake my head. "Wow."

Does Teddy think I'm that damaged? That I'd take him back after everything? I'd rather drown.

He licks his lips, searching for the right words as his brow wrinkles. "Please listen. It was all a mistake. I should've never done any of that to you. You were so kind to help me build my following, and I threw it in your face. Jessica was a temptress. A she-devil. I thought she loved me.

But while in New York, all she cared about was money. Nearly bled me dry! I had to leave. The apartment lease alone got to the point where—"

"Poor you. Used. Beaten down. Made a fool of. I wonder how that feels. Oh, wait, I know."

"Can't you just—"

My blood turns to fire. I want to pour my hot coffee over his head and leave, but I'm better than that. "What do you think will happen? I'll be so happy you want me back. I'll cry and leap into your arms. We move back in together. Get fucking married? What? And then another girl bats her eyelashes at you or says your channel is amazing, and you chase after her. Leave me to clean up the mess again. Maybe you post it online again for all to see. Yeah. That's never going to happen." I stand and plant a hand on my hip. "I never want to see you again."

"We could work this out. I'd be loyal. I swear." There's a wobble in his voice. He's full of crap. He knows how to act like a kicked puppy, and I will not fall for it.

Not when he dissed my mermaiding. He'd say little jabs about how silly it was. He had real fans, and mine were simple-minded children and their parents. He claimed he'd have to support me when I built his following from what I learned from my career. He never spoiled me. Made me feel special. Never came to a mermaid event. Told me how hot I was in a tail. Held me in his arms. Hell, he never shared more than a couple of dinners with my parents.

But Sully has. He makes me feel seen. He takes my career seriously.

Teddy catches the flicker of doubt in my eyes. He pushes up from his chair, reaching out like he might actually care—then stops himself, his hand dropping like dead weight. "Figures. You're tangled up with that rocker now, huh?"

A wrecking ball slams into my chest. I heave as my heart restarts. "What? How do you know about him?"

Teddy shrugs. "You wouldn't answer my texts. I was worried, so I came around a bit..."

My anger shakes my bones. It takes all my strength to keep from strangling him in public. "You followed me? It was you in that car at my apartment complex."

He nods. "Guilty. I was at the restaurant once and maybe a few other places." He shrugs like it's nothing to worry about. He's being protective. "And I don't like that guy. He's not even American. He's stringing you along."

"Unlike you?" I bite back, throwing most of my coffee in the nearby trash can. I walk toward my car.

Teddy trails behind me. "I love you. He just likes fucking fans."

I pause, sinking my fingernails into my palms, and take a shaky breath. He smiles. He doesn't know I'm about to snap. "Go to hell and stay there." I turn my back on him.

Teddy cuts me off. "Look at this." He shoves his phone under my nose. It's a picture of Sully and Gigi. They're somewhere dark, but I can see they're close, too close.

"He's with her. She's his type. What does that make you?" Pity drips from his voice.

Confused. Lost. Hurt. But I'll never admit that to Teddy.

"I don't believe you. You think showing me this terribly lit picture will send me into your arms?" I push past him and don't stop walking.

"Text me when you realize I'm right!" Teddy shouts.

I clench my teeth to keep from shouting back obscenities. Hot tears slip down my cheeks, and I wipe them away before anyone sees. Sully wouldn't be with Gigi. He said he wasn't. I want to believe him—I do—but the sting in my chest says I'm scared. Scared that I'm wrong. Scared I'll get burned again. I might be falling for Sully...or maybe I'm free-falling into something that'll leave me shattered.

Chapter Thirty-Seven

WHEN I ARRIVE HOME, Alice is cooking hamburger patties while Emily prepares a Caesar salad. They're laughing and singing along with Taylor Swift until I close the front door. Someone cuts the music, and the apartment becomes uncomfortably quiet.

"Sorry…" I say, rounding the kitchen table to see them past the wall. "I'll be in my room. Continue your date." I offer an awkward smile and turn toward the hallway.

"Wait," Emily says. I stop and glance over my shoulder. "You two need to work this out." She gestures between Alice and me. "Best friends shouldn't give each other cold shoulders. That's how I lost mine, and I wish someone would've told me to kill my stupid pride and just talk to her. Maybe we'd still be friends." Emily lifts a shoulder as hurt etches across her face.

Emily grabs a paper towel off the roll and wipes her hands on it, stepping out of our mini kitchen. "The salad is finished. I'll see you tomorrow." She kisses a stunned Alice on the lips.

The kiss snaps Alice back to life. "Babe, you don't need to go. We can—"

"It's okay. I'm not watching a friendship explode if I can help it."

Alice nods, giving in. They kiss again, more passionately. Alice squeezes Emily's ass. "See you later."

Emily offers me a wave and walks out the door.

Alice turns her attention to the hamburger patties, flipping them and adding pepper.

"Well," I say, rocking back and forth on my feet. "Guess we should address the elephant in the room."

Alice lifts her gaze and then glues them to the burgers, adding too much salt. "You mean my stuffed elephant, Blueberry?"

That was a curveball I didn't see coming.

"Umm...what?" I say, a laugh slips from my lips.

She gestures behind me. I turn to see a little stuffed elephant on the kitchen table. "Ah. He's cute. From Emily?"

"Yeah. She won him from a claw machine at The Rainbow Pony."

An awkward silence threatens to take over. I sigh, pouring my heart out. "I'm sorry for yelling at you. I know it's not your fault..." I take a breath while digging tickets out of my purse. "And I got you something to make up for it."

She walks over and accepts the tickets. Her eyes widen when she reads "Mean Girls" written in bold on the top. "Oh my God! You didn't have to but thank you!" She crushes me in a hug. "All's forgiven and forgotten. Okay? I'm not losing my BFF over this crap."

I hug her back. "Good. Because I need you."

She pulls away and brushes my hair from my face to meet my gaze. "What happened?"

"So much. Do you want me to start with me answering the phone, thinking it was you, but it was Sully, or how my evil ex ambushed me?"

"At the same time?" Her eyes widen in horror.

"No. But it's been a hell of a long day."

She guides me to the kitchen table. We sit. "Spill. Start with Sully."

She nods as I tell her about the aquarium date, the romance of it all, even the sex. Down to us lying in bed planning our little getaways between his European shows. Until he had to go.

"Wow. The aquarium was..." She makes a chef's kiss motion. "But of course, that spoiled bitch had to ruin it." She shakes her head. "Now what happened with that assface ex of yours?"

"He ambushed me at the beach," I sigh, shuddering as I remember. "Claimed he loved me and that leaving was a mistake, blah blah."

"That rat bastard. Do you want me to gut him?"

"You haven't heard the worst part. He's been following me. Lurking around our apartment parking lot. Even showed me a dimly lit picture of Sully and Gigi and said he was cheating on me."

"What the hell!" She stands, pacing the floor.

"I told him off." I shift my weight uncomfortably. "He's not worth thinking about."

Alice takes my hand and squeezes it. "Veronica. You're special. Don't let anyone dim your shine. Not that asshat ex or even Sully."

"I know. But I—"

The smoke alarm goes off. Alice leaps to her feet. "Crap!" She turns off the burner and rinses the pan in the sink, but it's too late. The burgers are charred pieces of meat.

She chuckles nervously. "How about we order in?"

I laugh, grabbing my phone. "Sounds good."

✳ ♫♪ 🐚 ♫♪ ✳ ♫♪ 🐚

It's seven in the morning, and still no word from Sully. A heavy, twisting knot settles in my stomach. I can't shake the thought that something terrible might have happened. If he'd been in a car accident or rushed to the hospital, no one from his world would bother to let me know. Well—maybe Charlotte would, if it was serious. But even that feels like a long shot. I searched his name online, but nothing came up.

"Do you want to drive to his place?" Alice asks, sliding two blueberry pop-tarts into the toaster.

I glance at her and stop paying attention to the orange juice I'm pouring into a glass. "I'm sorry, did I just have a mini-stroke?"

"Watch it," Alice says, pointing.

The juice overflows. I rush to grab paper towels and mop up the table. "Did you really suggest driving to his place?"

She inspects her fingernails. "It's suspicious you haven't heard a thing from him. Based on his history, he usually replies with something."

I nod, sipping my juice. "I hope Gigi isn't there because I'm going to throw up."

The pop-tarts pop up, and Alice wraps them in paper towels. "Let's go."

I drive to the hotel, and as we drive down the road going around to the private casitas, there's a roadblock ahead and a man dressed in black slacks and a red coat with the hotel's logo in gold on his chest.

He walks over, and I roll the window down.

"Hello," he says, leaning in and looking at Alice and me. "Are you two guests?"

"No. We're here to visit a guest. His name is Sully Graham."

"We have no guests currently staying in the casitas. The last guest checked out this morning, and he gave me a note to give to someone." The man checks all his pockets and finds an envelope. "What's your name?"

"Veronica Gates."

He nods, offering me the envelope. "He left this for you. You can turn around if you pull forward into the dirt. Have a nice day."

I drive to the front of the hotel and park the car in the back of the parking lot, where the parking agents can't see us or bother us about not having reservations.

"You open it." I shove the envelope at Alice.

She opens it and unfolds the letter inside. First, she reads it to herself. Part of me wants to rip it from her hands and read it myself. The other part wants to go home and draw a warm bath and hide underneath all the bubbles.

"It's short," she says, after what feels like an hour. "Dear Veronica. I'm sorry I couldn't tell you this in person or by phone. My team forced me to move to the house in Beverly Hills with the rest of the band late last night. Claims it will keep me on track. I owe you dinner. Please forgive me. I'll make this up to you. I promise. Love, Sully."

Alice folds the letter and shoves it back into the envelope. "Well, then..."

I shift into drive and put as much distance between us and the hotel as possible. I press my foot on the pedal and drive, no destination in mind. Alice shrieks and shouts, "Watch out!"

My vision sharpens just in time to realize I'm in the wrong lane—and a truck is barreling straight toward us. I swerve hard, jerking the wheel and veering into a grocery store parking lot. Tires squeal as I throw the car into park. We're both breathing heavily, my chest heaving, and my hair is damp with sweat.

"Can I drive?" Alice asks, clicking her seat belt off.

"Yeah. That's a good idea."

Alice walks around the car, and I hop over the center console into the passenger's seat.

That night, I throw myself into work. My show doesn't suffer, but I'm not as happy or as bubbly as I usually am. For the first time, I decline a meet and greet, which is okay since there aren't too many kids tonight.

Arthur carries me into the break room, and when he sets me on the bench, he asks, "Why the long face?"

I run my hand over my tail, admiring the pattern of purple and pink to avoid his searching gaze. "Just having an off day."

"It's because of that rock star, isn't it?"

"You can say that."

"Do you want to talk about it?"

"No." I flop my fins on the floor. "Not really."

He rubs his hands against his jeans. "Okay. I'll leave so you can change."

I watch him retreat.

Against my better judgment, I check Insta and go to Sully's page. He's tagged in three new pictures with Gigi. I flip through them. They were posted two hours ago at some fancy restaurant in Beverly Hills. In the first picture, Gigi's smile sparkles and Sully looks at the camera stone-faced like always. But his hand rests on her hip. In the second, Gigi offers a spoonful of cheesecake to Sully, and he leans forward, mouth wide open to accept it.

The final blow that forces me to drop my phone and screw my eyes closed is Sully and Gigi standing outside the restaurant by a wall with string lights, as her arms snake around Sully's neck, and her left leg is popped up behind her as she kisses him. He has his hands on her waist and his eyes closed as if he's enjoying their intimate kiss. The comments are blowing up. Already gushing about how they're meant to be.

I lean forward. My hands slide over my tail as my head rests where my knees are to keep from heaving. Was Teddy right? That fucking bastard.

Alice walks in and falls to my side, rubbing my back in gentle circles. "What's wrong?"

"Check phone," I mumble, whisking away hot tears with my wrist.

She opens my phone and sees the pictures. "That prick," she hisses.

There are no words. I'm empty. Completely hollow inside. Right now, I need my best friend to keep me from crumbling into a million pieces on the floor.

"You want to get out of here?" she asks.

"Mmm." I nod, wiping my hands on my tail. "Crap. I still haven't changed."

"Let me help you, and then we'll do whatever you want."

"Emily won't be mad? I thought you two had plans."

She shakes her head. "No. I'll send her a text. She understands when a BFF is needed."

Alice grabs my fins, tugs my tail off my hips, and hands me my clothes. I change, despite the numbness in my limbs. She treats me to Mexican food for dinner and a slasher movie. She tries to cheer me up, but I can't crack a smile. My face has turned to marble. My heart freezes in place. There's a block of ice where it once was, and no one will stop the blizzard roaring in my soul.

They say the third time is the charm. But for me, there will never be a third time falling for someone. It's too late. I'm already dead inside.

Chapter Thirty-Eight

TWO DAYS FADE BY without Sully, and I'm finding my rhythm again. I perform at the restaurant and do my events on the side. At night, I'm working on my website and fulfilling a ton of online orders. I'm booked for the rest of the year. Maybe next summer, I'll travel to Europe alone or with a group of fellow mermaids and visit all the places I wrote about in my notebook. Who says I need to go with anyone special?

Alice and Emily watch a horror movie, snuggled on the couch under one blanket. They laugh at the actors and yell at them for their dumb mistakes, like running upstairs and not out of the house.

Screams come from the TV. I've had enough of their movie marathon. I appreciate Alice staying here and not going out partying so I'm not home alone, but honestly, it's better when I'm alone. Having them kiss and giggle just reminds me of what I don't have.

I check my email, and Peter sent me copies of my last photoshoot. I flip through them, and they are vivid and breathtaking. The underwater ones are my favorite. I look like a real mermaid. I grab a few and create online posts for my social media handles. It's hard to pick which ones should be printouts and used in my store.

A knife pierces through my chest and twists my gut. The images of Sully and me are at the end. He's cradling me, and we're staring into each other's eyes. He's holding me above his head. He's saving me from a net. I rescue him from the water.

It's overwhelming to see him looking at me like I'm precious and kissing me like I'm the only woman on Earth, but Insta paints another story.

I'm the other girl, and what's worse is no one knows we were ever together. I'd sound like a crazed fan if I told anyone. These photos could be evidence to prove I'm not lying, but people would claim I faked them with Photoshop somehow, and with me being a mermaid, it's not a great defense.

Besides, I don't want to be involved in an online war. I can't do anything that could damage my name or image. Mermaid Veronica is a brand, and nothing can taint her.

I email Peter back, telling him I love the pictures, thank him again, and then finish saving them to my desktop. I close my laptop and lie on my bed, preparing to read a book, but my phone buzzes. My heart sinks knowing who it's from.

> *Veronica, please answer me! I need to see you. I never kissed Gigi! Those pictures are fake!*

My lungs tighten, like I've been holding my breath too long. My eyes blur with tears I don't want to shed. I want to believe him—God, I do—but it's getting harder to hold onto hope when every day brings a new reason to let go. I'm tired. Tired of wondering if Gigi's stealing him from me piece by piece. Tired of feeling like I'm the one he hides instead of the one he chooses.

> **I'm at the studio right now but after I'll swing by your work. Will you be there?**

I silence my phone and pick up my book, pretending the words on the page matter more than the ache in my chest. Tomorrow, I'll tell Arthur and the rest of the security team at The Pearl Kingdom to keep him out. Not because I hate him—but because I need space to breathe. He's leaving to go on tour soon anyway. Maybe it's better if he doesn't see me at all. Maybe that's how I'll finally let go.

Chapter Thirty-Nine

COMPANIES WITH BUSINESS MEETINGS who hire me are some of my easiest jobs, but they can also be the most awkward. I dress in my blue tail, and Arthur pulls me to the ballroom on a flatbed cart. I hug my tail to my chest to keep it from dragging on the ground. When we arrive at the event, Arthur helps set me up on a table decorated with sea shells and starfish. I have a matching crown on my head, and I wave to every guest, welcoming them and handing them a fancy gold gift bag.

Arthur wanders off to sneak some appetizers while he waits to move me to the next area.

Later, as a man in a navy-blue tux stands in front of the room talking about numbers and stats in a mic, Arthur wheels me to another table. I lie on my stomach with my tail flipped up into the air. I greet and briefly chat with anyone who comes to the dessert table.

People find me charming, asking me about my tail, and some joke, asking how the ocean is these days. I play along, and they laugh as they grab their treats. Arthur stands a few feet away with business cards if anyone asks about my services for their next gathering.

When closing remarks are made, I'm back on the cart, waving at anyone who notices me on the move.

I change inside an empty business meeting room with a large circular table surrounded by chairs. My calf cramps from the angle it's been held in for such a long time. I bite my hand and flex my foot, slowly easing the pain.

Arthur knocks on the door. "Everything alright in there?"

I rub the muscle in spasm, trying not to cry in pain. "Yeah," I say, voice breaking.

My phone buzzes. I grab it and read the message.

> **Can u meet me 2day? I'll send a car. It's important.**

His brief words smack into me and throw me off. I fall out of my chair.

"Ow," I mutter, rubbing my tailbone.

"Is someone beating you in there?" Arthur's voice is low and deep, like a cop about to knock someone out.

I picture Arthur grabbing Sully and punching him in a dark room before kicking him to the curb.

"No. Just slipped," I reply, standing and pulling my jeans on. My leg still aches, but putting weight on it helps. I chew on my inner cheek and type my reply.

> **Give me a good reason.**

He replies within a few heartbeats.

> **I'm sorry...let me make it up 2 u.**

My gut tells me I'll regret it, but my heart controls my thumbs.

> **I'm finishing a gig. I'll be home soon. Send the car there.**

> *C u soon. xx*

The two kisses in his text are odd and he never uses shorthand. He's never done that before. Maybe I'm looking for red flags when there aren't any.

I open the door, and Arthur smiles, taking my bag. "You ready?"

"Yup. Let's go."

We walk to the car, and I can't shake the sinking feeling in my stomach. It's like watching the water pull back from the beach, and you can't see the giant tidal wave coming to crush you and everything in its path until it's too late.

Chapter Forty

W H E N I A R R I V E H O M E, I put away my mermaiding stuff and knock on Alice's bedroom door. I need advice before seeing Sully again.

"Enter," she cheerfully says.

I open the door to find her sitting on her bed with her legs crossed and her laptop on her lap, a worn purple Tarot deck resting nearby.

"What's up," I ask, lingering in the doorway.

"You look like crap, sweetie." She closes the laptop and pats the bed next to her. "Care to explain?"

I lie down, draping an arm over my eyes. "Sully texted when I was finishing the Cooper and Associates event. He's sending a car so we can talk in person and—"

She smacks my thigh. "Girl, when will you open your eyes and see that bass player has it bad for you?"

I sit up too quickly, giving myself a head rush. "Does it matter? He's going on a European tour soon."

"Did he ask you to come?"

I focus on my hand running over the sheet, smoothing its wrinkles.

Alice inhales sharply, bouncing on the bed. "He did, didn't he?" she shrieks in joy.

"He did after the music awards, but then…" I trail off. Then Gigi happened.

"He doesn't want her. Not to be cliché, but it's plain as day with him texting you. Needing to see you."

"He's acting weird and…" I shrug. "Plus, I can't hop on a plane and go on tour. Saying it out loud doesn't even sound real." I bow my head, covering my face with my hands. "A weekend in Vegas is one thing, but an entire tour! I can't. What about my life here?"

Alice rubs small circles on my back. "Your life? What life?"

I glare at her, but she's right. Other than work and hanging out with Alice, I don't do much, and I live in one of the most exciting cities in the world.

She takes my hand and squeezes it. "If the restaurant is holding you back, don't worry. I'll help find someone to hold your place. But traveling will be good for your brand. I'm sure whatever events you have scheduled can go to another mermaid. I keep saying you need sisters. A mermaid pod so you don't work yourself to the bone and you still make money even if you don't personally attend every gig."

I lift my head and dare to meet her gaze. She smiles, but there's a flicker of sadness behind it. "And if it's me in the way, I'll be okay. Maybe Emily can be my new roommate." She hits her leg with mine. "Kidding."

Alice stands and stretches, then snatches up her Tarot deck from the bed.

"Want me to pull a few cards for you?" she asks, fanning them out with a little flourish. "Might give you some clarity before you see your man."

I shake my head quickly, laughing nervously. "Thanks, but no. I don't think I can handle any more mysteries today."

She shrugs and drops the cards onto her dresser. "Suit yourself, mermaid. But when you're ready, the cards are always ready too. But I think this would be an amazing opportunity. Especially for your career. All those beaches. So many pictures to post on your socials. New things to post in your store. You can blog about your travels. I'll be with you in spirit."

The anxiety building within my chest causes pressure on my heart and my left leg to jiggle uncontrollably. "I have a list of all the places I want to visit."

"See." She grabs my wrist and pulls me to my feet. "It's time to see your boyfriend and make those plans come true."

Alice shoos me out. "As for me, I got a dinner date to get ready for." She winks and closes her door.

I shuffle into my bedroom and change into a cute little black dress with matching heels. I reapply my makeup and brush my hair. A car horn honks, and I drift downstairs.

When I slide into the car, I find myself alone. "Where's Sully?" I ask the driver.

He pulls onto the street and glares at me through the rearview mirror. "At the house in Beverly Hills." His voice is cold and stiff like steel.

"Oh…" I sink into the leather seat and watch buildings and cars whizz by. The sickness in my stomach burrows deeper. I swallow the nervous fear and close my eyes, picturing Sully shirtless and kissing me. His hands on my waist, cupping my breasts, making me shudder and come apart as his body molds to mine. It's only been a few days, but I already miss him. His scent, his warmth. Just him.

✱ ♫♪ 🐚 ♫♪ ✱ ♫♪ 🐚

The closer we get to Beverly Hills, the more I debate leaping out of the car at every red light and stop sign. Something tells me this is a trap, and I have no idea why. I squirm in my seat, knowing the rest of the band is there, eavesdropping on us.

My hands shake as I send Sully a text.

Almost there.

He replies within a few moments.

K.

What the hell? The dreaded one letter with a period? What's going on?

The driver stops in front of a massive mansion with a fountain with an angel holding a pot where the water spills out. I missed the drive up by staring at my phone like it would decode Sully's very short reply.

I step outside and look up at the stone fortress with ivy crawling its walls. It looms in the distance like Dracula's castle, and I'm the victim about to be eaten.

The pink and purple flowers leading to the wooden door aren't inviting. The singing birds sound like a warning. Even the sun's warmth chills my blood.

The door opens before I can knock. A twenty-something woman in a black pencil skirt and white blouse waves me inside. I follow her wordlessly through the gorgeous living room with antique furniture and a giant picture of Marilyn Monroe above the brick fireplace. She leads me into the dining room and points to a chair. "Sit," she orders as if I'm a dog.

I linger but give in, dragging out a chair and sitting on the edge of its cushion, ready to bolt.

"Where's Sully?" I ask over my thundering heartbeat.

The woman sighs as if my question inconveniences her. "He will not be joining us. Please wait here." It's the wickedness of her smile, the evil gleam in her eye, and the sharp echo of her heels that send my soul flying to the ceiling. If he's not here, why am I?

My gut was right. Something is wrong.

A door opens somewhere inside the house and heels click on the tile floor. I look up to find Gigi grinning at me, her cat-green eyes blazing beneath thick black lashes. A red dress hugs her perfect figure, pushing up her breasts and complementing her glowing skin. Gigi's like a model who just stepped off a billboard or glossy magazine cover. She's all glamorous with a stone-cold bitch glare directed at me.

"It was you who texted me," I say, trying to keep the surprise from my voice and failing.

She scoffs. "You're smarter than you look." She takes Sully's phone out of her bra and tosses it on the table.

Sully would never send Xs as kisses. I should've known. But if she has his phone, then where is he?

"Did you steal his phone?" I stand firm. "Why can't I speak to him?" I demand, sounding stronger than I feel.

She rolls her eyes. "Enough of this." She snaps her fingers, and the pencil skirt woman reappears with paperwork in her hands.

"This is my assistant, Laura." She gestures for Laura to set the pile of papers in front of me. "I want to make you an offer." She snags a pen from her bra and tosses it in my direction.

I cackle, shaking my head. "You sound like the mob."

"I'm worse than the mob, honey. I can do more things than they ever could," Gigi says, her cold glare slicing into me, drawing blood.

I shift in my seat, my foot tapping anxiously against the floor. I glance around, but the rest of the house stays hidden from view.

Are we alone? Where is the band? Why do I feel like I'm about to be eighty-sixed?

"Here's the deal." Gigi smacks her lips, glancing at her phone like she has a million better things to do. "I'm ready to support your little mermaid gig Amy told me about—I'll invest forty thousand dollars to kickstart your brand. Consider it a generous donation."

Laura brushes her hands down her perfectly smooth skirt to avoid my gaze. It's like Gigi's offering me a full-ride scholarship to the dream university I'd never afford to get into myself. "Allow me to boost your career. You could be famous by this time next year."

As if I need her help. I'm already creating my own splash. But I doubt she cares.

I leaf through the papers, beyond confused. Why on Earth would she want to give me fortune and fame? We don't even know each other. Unless it's a buyout. Hush money. A parting gift from Sully.

My heart leaps into my throat, and I must speak before the words choke me. "What's the catch?"

Here we go. They'll say to leave Sully alone, and he'll find out about this conversation and go off on them again. This is a never-ending battle.

Gigi nods at the paperwork. "It's all there. I help you, and you kill this...thing between you and Sully." She wrinkles her nose as if our relationship smells of rotting garbage. "Liquidate your relationship. Never tell a soul you were with him."

"You can't be serious. This is—"

She holds up her hand. "I'll spell it out for you. You were never his girlfriend or fuck buddy. Yes. You met him during a meet and greet with your favorite band. Lucky you."

I clench my jaw to the point my teeth might break. They don't know about Sully posing with me during my mermaid shoot. What would they do if they saw those pictures posted online? Could they sue me?

"I have more than just one photo."

Gigi leans forward, resting her palms on the table across from me, and stares into my being. "Whatever other pictures you have must be deleted."

My blood boils, but I hold my tongue. I skim the words before me, and it's like I'm signing divorce papers. The phrases are all legal terms that make my brain pound. Do I need a lawyer for this shit?

"Where's Sully? I need to speak to him." My voice cracks, betraying me.

Gigi nudges the pen toward me. "He's busy. Just sign the papers and go. Your ride's waiting."

"This is insane," I whisper, my pulse pounding. "You have his phone and he's not even here. It's like you've—" I swallow. "It's like you've made him disappear."

She lets out a cold, humorless laugh. "Sweetheart, he's not dead. He just can't stand the sight of you."

My fingers tighten around the pen. For a brief second, I imagine stabbing Gigi in the neck, then smashing the chair into Laura for looking so damn smug.

But I stay still. I won't give them the satisfaction.

"And if I don't sign?" I lift my chin and stare at the back of Gigi's meticulously braided bun, avoiding her eyes. If I look at her, I might scream. Or cry.

But I won't break.

Gigi moves around the table, appearing like she's floating in that long red dress. "I'll ruin you." Her words twist the knife in my gut, but I won't show the pain.

Her lips turn into a sneer as she sits on the table a foot away and taps her scary, long, blood-red nails on the papers. "I don't know what you thought you and Sully had, but it's over now. I'm offering a clean break. Now be a good little fangirl and sign these papers."

The base of my skull prickles, and it spreads along my spine. Gigi may have a model face and an angel's voice, but staring into her eyes is like seeing the devil. My body goes cold.

"I'm not doing anything until I speak to Sully in person."

Gigi moves faster than a bullet, pulling my chair away from the table with me in it. How is she this strong? Maybe she is a she-demon.

"He's off-limits. You're dealing with me now." She crosses her arms and narrows her eyes. "Now sign these fucking papers."

I find my voice hidden underneath all my hurt, confusion, and spite. "You can shove those papers up your tight waxed ass." I stand and push the papers with such force they flutter to the ground.

She sighs, tsking. "Haven't you seen us online? We're meant to be. That's what our fans say. You can't come between us."

She moves closer, and I'm frozen in place, turned to stone by her glare. "He's mine. He could never be yours. All you are is a woman playing make-believe. And as a mermaid!" She cackles, shaking her head. "How pathetic."

Gigi grabs the blue pendant hanging around her neck and idly runs it along its silver chain. The massive sparkling diamond ring on her left-hand glints in the light, deliberately catching my eye.

"You see this?" she purrs, holding up her hand like a queen showing off a crown jewel. "Sully gave it to me last night."

The room seems to tilt, but I lock my knees, refusing to stumble.

A lie. It *has* to be.

But for a split second—only a split second—the old wound reopens.

The memory of Teddy and his cruel prank. The hope that twisted into heartbreak when he ended things, and tried to ruin my career, instead of proposing.

I shove the memory away, blinking fast.

"That's funny," I say with a tight smile. "Sully never mentioned being anyone's fiancé and he said those pictures of you were faked."

Gigi's laugh is like shattered glass—sharp, cruel.

"We're keeping it private. For now." She winks. "Can't risk the media getting too wild before the tour."

My mind races.

Sully had just asked me to *come with him*. Would he really do that if he were engaged to someone else?

But the doubt—tiny, toxic—creeps in anyway.

Men have lied to me before. Played me before. Maybe I was being played again, too foolish to see it. Still, I meet Gigi's catlike gaze head-on. "Until Sully tells me himself, I don't believe a damn word you say."

Her smile fades, just a crack. She slides closer, her expensive perfume coiling around me like smoke.

"You poor thing," she says softly, almost pitying. "Still clinging to a fantasy. Still thinking someone like *him* could ever choose someone like *you*."

Each word strikes like a whip. She wants me to break. She wants me to run.

But I stay frozen, fists balled so tight my nails dig into my palms.

I don't know what the truth is yet. But I know I'll find it—from Sully. Not from her.

Gigi circles me, her heels clicking a slow, mocking rhythm. "You have two choices, little mermaid. Walk away with a career and a nice fat check." She nudges the papers with the toe of her designer shoe. "Or stay...and be crushed. Trust me, love, you don't survive long standing in my light."

I smile, sweet and slow, even though my heart's shattering inside.

"Guess we'll see," I say.

Game on, bitch.

Chapter Forty-One

SOMEONE BOOKED ME LAST minute Saturday morning at a resort's pool in Burbank. I change into my blue tail with purple fins, and Arthur wheels me toward the pool area.

And it's a ghost town. There's a sign hanging on the gate claiming it's closed for a private event, but there are no signs of life. No tables, food, or decorations in sight.

Arthur checks his watch and whistles through his teeth. "This kind of seems like the Twilight Zone to me. Should we cut our losses and leave?"

"Can you give me my phone? Maybe we're at the wrong hotel."

Arthur digs in my bag for my phone and says, "But the pool sign says there's a private event happening. But if any private event is happening, I have a feeling it should cost a lot more and be in a suite..."

I click my tongue and shiver. God, I hope someone didn't book me for a one-on-one, thinking they'd get lucky and screw a mermaid. That happened once. Someone tried to book me to their room, and it gave me hooker vibes, and I blocked their number.

All the details on my phone match up. We're in the right place; it's just empty.

"Let's give it another five minutes, and then we'll go." I hug my tail to my chest and shift my weight to keep my ass from falling asleep on the cart.

The gate swings closed, scaring me. Arthur and I whip our heads toward the sound, and Sully walks forward with a guitar strapped to his back. "Please listen before you bolt," he pleads, pulling a chair from a nearby table.

Arthur cracks his neck and steps forward, but I place a hand on his arm. "Wait," I say, eyes locked on Sully.

He pulls a guitar pick from his pocket and does a quick strum check for the strings, tuning it. He meets my gaze briefly before his attention falls to his guitar.

"I just wrote this. Please be gentle." He clears his throat as his fingers fall into position on the guitar's neck, and a soft rift begins. "One look and I'm yours. I need to kiss you, but your lips are a drug. One taste, and I'm hooked. My veins are on fire with this damn desire. I don't want to break these chains. The pain is all I have left to keep me sane. I need to touch you, but you're only a dream. Nothing can save me from this living hell." He strums for a beat more and presses his hand over the strings.

The silence is stiff. Arthur backs away. "I'll be in the car. Text if you need me." He takes the long way around the pool and exits through the gate.

Pain zings from my tailbone, but I ignore it by straightening my spine. "What is this?" I motion toward the empty pool area. "Did you seriously book a mermaid encounter to ambush me, knowing I can't leave?" I swing my tail off the cart, push the brake on with my hand, and use the cart's handrail to stand up. "Please. Just leave me alone. Gigi confronted me, threatened me! She claims you're engaged. What do you want from me?"

His eyes widen in alarm. "What? We're not engaged. I swear." He sets his guitar back in its case. "Gigi had someone Photoshop pictures of us. I'm not with Gigi and I never will be. I don't care about my image. I only care about you."

A weight falls from my heart. I'm lost for words.

Sully pulls the chair he used around and sets it behind me. "Please sit. You're making me nervous standing in that thing."

I want to argue, but this tail isn't meant for standing like some of the others. I fall back into the chair and cross my arms. I wake up my phone and tap on Arthur's number.

Sully squats to my left and places his palm over my phone's screen. "What Gigi did was unspeakable. I should've known Gigi had something wicked cooked up when Amy ordered me to move into the Beverly Hills house, saying it would be better for the band and I was bleeding unnecessary money. My phone disappeared, but every time I tried to look for it, Amy shooed me into the recording studio, saying she'd find it." He rakes his fingers through his locks. "If I would've known Gigi planned to ambush you, I would've—"

"You would've what? Swooped in and rescued me like my prince charming?" I rub my palms against my scale-covered thighs. "We are not meant to be. Don't you see all the signs the universe keeps throwing at us? Don't you know we're living in the definition of insanity? Doing the same things over and over and praying for different results."

Sully takes my hand in his. "I think the opposite. The universe wants us to be together. It's just showing us some tough love first. Nothing worth having is ever easy."

I lift an eyebrow. "What are you going to say next? That our horoscopes line up?" I fidget with my silver crescent moon pendant, running it up and down its chain. "I'm a spiritual person, but this is exhausting." I click on Arthur's name and text him to come back. "And I'm not having this conversation painted into a corner with a damn tail on so I can't leave."

If this tail wasn't one of my favorites, I'd peel myself out of it and storm away in my leggings, but I'm afraid if I'm too rough I'll rip the material, and then it's toast.

Sully stands and stares down at the water. "You're right. I wasn't thinking. This was a terrible idea. I wanted to see you again. Your website was in my recent history. My phone is still missing. I think Gigi tossed it."

Arthur returns, and Sully lifts his hands in surrender. "I'll let you go, but at least let me say this. I quit the band this morning. No more Amy. No more Gigi. No more nothing. I did it for me. It's time I figure out what else I am besides a quarter of Scarlet Failure."

"I hope you find what you're looking for." I nod to Arthur, and he helps me back onto the cart and pulls it toward the exit.

My heart splinters. It's broken again, and I can only blame myself. To keep from choking on my words and saying something I'll regret, I bite the back of my hand and allow Arthur to take me to the bathroom so I can change.

When I step out with my bags in hand, Arthur cracks a smile. "That was the quickest gig we ever did."

I nod but can't play along.

As we walk through the lobby, I spot Sully sitting on the couch next to the fireplace with his head in his hands. I steer Arthur toward the glass doors when Charlotte enters in a vision of purple. Her dress flows around her, and her high heels click with determination.

Arthur is already outside with the bags. I linger by a fake fig tree and watch her confront Sully. She places her hands on her hips and says something venomous sounding in German. Sully drags a hand down his face and waves her off.

She stomps her heel and continues to speak, attracting the eyes of everyone passing by. She glares at anyone who stops to gawk. My phone buzzes in my hand, surprising me. I yelp and drop it. I try to catch the phone, but it falls with a loud crack.

I reach to grab my phone and hear heels coming my way. Fear paralyzes my body as blood freezes in my veins.

"Veronica," Charlotte says, her accent thick. She pauses in front of me and sighs. Her anger fades. "He's different with you," she says softly. She looks at him over her shoulder, but he's already gone. "Ich schwöre, ihr seid füreinander geschaffen." She gently pats my arm and leaves.

Despite numbness spreading throughout my limbs, I walk toward the exit.

I jump into the car, and Arthur eyes me. "Just drive," I huff, putting on my seat belt.

Arthur pulls onto the main road and turns up the rock radio station, nodding to the music. I repeat the phrase Charlotte said into my phone to translate. It means I swear you were made for each other.

My heart melts as I sink deeper into my seat and close my eyes.

To get out of my head, I should book a trip to Florida. Alice already called for someone to replace me for a while just in case, and I could hook up with fellow mermaids. It could be the distraction that will turn my heart into stone and allow me to become nothing more than Mermaid Veronica. The human Veronica will be shelved for good.

I open my airline app and search for the soonest flights. It's time I move on and let Sully become a bittersweet memory. There's irony in wanting to meet someone so bad you'd stay up all night and then weeks later flee to the other side of the country to avoid running into them. My life is nothing but a cruel cosmic joke. Leaving LA might be the push I need to get my priorities straight.

Chapter Forty-Two

I'M PACKING MY BEST tails and their matching tops when Alice comes home, slamming the front door and skipping down the hallway. "Emily's gotta work tonight. You wanna order in?"

"Sounds good," I shout, zipping the suitcase.

She opens her bedroom door to toss her shoes inside and then peeks her head into mine. "Chinese sound good?"

"Yeah. Our usual?"

She types on her phone. "Ordered. Umm..." She sits on my bed and pushes the pile of jeans back before it tips over and spills onto the floor. "You going through your closet?"

"Something like that." I nod at the suitcase in front of my dresser. "Decided to take that time off after all."

She brightens. "Did you make up with Sully?"

I shake my head. "God, no. I'm going to Florida for a month or two. I didn't buy a return ticket yet."

Alice purses her lips and crosses her legs. "It's that bad?"

I let out a sharp breath that sounds like a cackle. "That event I had today was him. He wanted to talk so he scheduled a mermaid at a resort pool. How twisted is that?"

"When you cut someone out of your life, you don't leave any opening. I'm not saying it was right, but I can see why he went to that extreme. What did he say?"

My walls fly up fast and hard, but it's the only way to protect myself. Love isn't for me. Time and again, I've learned that, and I'm finally accepting my fate.

"He wrote me a cheesy love song. Claimed Gigi stole his phone and created all this drama to drive me away. He also quit the band." I study a strand of hair, looking for split ends to avoid her piercing gaze.

"Then what?" She grabs my arm and tugs me to sit next to her.

"I yelled at him for trapping me into a meeting, and Arthur took me back to the bathroom to change. When I was leaving, I saw him slumped forward in the lobby, and Charlotte marched in to chew him out. Naturally, I hung back to eavesdrop and drew attention to myself when I dropped my phone. Charlotte saw me. She came over and said a few words, then left." What those words were, I don't want to share.

Alice stands and hooks her arm with mine. She drags me to the kitchen table and forces me to sit down. "So, to recap. Sully booked a one-on-one with you to tell you that he quit the band and to sing you a song before adding he loves you after that shitstorm happened at his place. That a psycho pop star tried to control him and stole his phone. And your reaction was to brush off his feelings and then spy on him until you were spotted. Now you're planning a last-minute trip across the country with no return date because you can't face your emotions."

"When you say it, I sound like a bitch." I cross my arms and cradle my chin in my hand. "Everything is too heavy here. I'm walking around in a fog, and the cliff's edge is too close. Maybe a change of scenery will bring clarity and—"

"Bullshit." Alice grabs the purple Tarot deck off the table and starts shuffling with a sharp snap of her wrists. "I'm happy to help you leave LA for your career or for love, but not to run away and keep your head buried in the sand." She fans out the Tarot cards in front of me, the vibrant images like a secret language I'm finally ready to hear. "It's time to find answers that are not from a place of fear."

My heart jumps into my throat. I stare at the cards, suddenly willing to listen, to believe that they might offer the guidance I've been too scared to find on my own. "What if I'm not ready?" I whisper.

"When is anyone ready?" she says, her voice softer now. She motions for me to choose.

I pull three cards from the pile with a shaky hand, flipping each over one by one, laying them in a row. My blood whooshes in my ears, my anxiety pounding like a second heartbeat.

Alice leans forward, studying them, then taps each card as she explains. "The sun upright—positivity and success. Followed by the lovers reversed—self-love. And lastly, the devil reversed—exploring dark thoughts and releasing limiting beliefs."

She says this like it's obvious, but I blink at her, needing more. "Please, none of your vague answers," I say, biting my lip. "Just tell me."

Alice gathers the cards and reshuffles them slowly, giving me a second to breathe. "It means you should focus on the good things in life and stop spiraling into the darkness." She places the deck aside and levels me with a look. "And the cards think Sully's a good match."

I narrow my eyes at her, but deep down, I believe her.

The doorbell rings, and Alice jumps up. "I'll get it."

Sure. Avoid my death gaze. The reading echoes what I already knew but was too afraid to admit to myself.

Alice dashes into the kitchen, opening containers and eating orange chicken with chopsticks.

She points at the container in front of her. "I got you the pot stickers you love."

"Thanks. And thanks for the reading." I grab what I can carry and sit at the table. We eat, switching containers every few minutes.

"You might bite my head off for saying this, but I think you're in love with him." Alice steals a spring roll and bites into it. "You already had a crush before you spoke to the guy, and now...it's..." She pauses to finish the spring roll. "Magic."

"Huh." I stab the last pot sticker. That's what Sully called it. Magic.

I swallow my bite and grab the mushroom chicken. "Maybe I did fall for him, but now it's a mess. You know what? Serves me right thinking love could be something I could have."

Alice slams her container down, and rice goes flying. "I'm sick of you sabotaging yourself. Stop shutting out the universe with any sign of trouble. Open up, dammit!"

My stomach twists as a cold sweat breaks on my forehead. "I need to finish packing."

I lock myself in my room, sorting through the clothes I want to bring with me. I grab my folded underwear, and a note floats to the ground. "What's this?" I drop the underwear onto my bed and pick up the note.

In a world of chaos, you're my beautiful peace
In a world of agony, you're my sweet release
Veronica, my favorite mermaid
For you, my love will never fade

A red-hot blade pierces my chest. Despite trying to turn my heart into a black hole, it's still beating in its bony cage, raw and bleeding.

I stumble into the living room and fall beside Alice on the couch. "I found this..." I hand her the lyrics.

She squeals in delight, waving the paper in the air. "You can't deny fate now! This is like a car running you over."

Definitely feels like it.

"What now?" I ask, picking at my thumbnail.

"You risk it all, girl! Life is a game of poker. You gotta be all in and risk losing everything with the cards in hand."

I smack her thigh. "Stop sounding like a fortune cookie and tell me what to do."

"Get dressed and put on your war paint. It's time we fight back." She waves her phone. "And I may have cyberstalked Sully and pinned his location."

"Where is he?" I ask, surprised.

She pushes me to my room. "First things first. You get ready, and I'll come up with the plan. It's going to be insane."

Fear burrows in my gut and blooms doubt. But I resist the urge to tuck my tail and run. That's what I've done my entire life.

I can't run off to Florida—not when the man who wrote that note is still here, just miles away. What's wrong with me? Am I really so broken that I can't let myself be happy? My ex twisted me up so badly I barely recognize myself. But Sully...Sully showed me something different. He's better. He's *real*.

And I'll be damned if I let Amy and Gigi win.

Alice is right. I can't let Sully slip away. Not without trying. He only wanted to help me, and I pushed him away like everyone else.

This time it's do or die. I can't just survive anymore. I need to live my life and face the pain and heartbreaks that come with it. Scarlet Failure has a song about walking through hell for love, and I'm about to blast open the gates of Hades to see if what's between Sully and me is the real deal.

Chapter Forty-Three

ALICE PULLS ME BEHIND a concrete column and sneers at a group of girls passing by. We're standing in front of a venue, and Gigi's name flashes on the marquee sign. I punch Alice's arm and hiss, "What the hell are we doing here?"

"Calm down." Alice rubs her sore arm and lowers her voice. "Gigi posted that she has a surprise for fans tonight. On Charlotte's Insta, she posted being at a restaurant around the corner. I know a bartender who works here and asked if Scarlet Failure was spotted. He said yes and confirmed seeing Sully. Though he was moody and told anyone who spoke more than three words to piss off."

"Why would he be here? He told me he quit the band."

Alice shrugs. "You said that Charlotte confronted him in the hotel lobby. Maybe they made some kind of deal?"

"Deal with the devil," I mutter, wishing I could smash Gigi's name off the building. How dare her terrible name be in lights.

"What's the plan? We go inside, and what?" I tug on my hair. "Please don't say you're going to have us meet them after the show because—"

"No. I won't force you to relive that little meet cute you had. My plan is more devious." She grabs my hand and pulls me around the corner. "We are going in through the service entrance." She sends a quick text and shows me the screen. "My friend, Randy, is coming."

A dark cloud hovers over me. We're sneaking in and about to ambush Sully like he did me at the pool. Crap. I need to take calming breaths and center myself. If I knew sneaking around was in our plans tonight, I would've worn quieter shoes and something more blending in, not a short blue dress with a sweetheart neckline. I would've dressed the part of someone backstage.

"Okay, you found us a way into the venue, but how are we getting backstage and finding Sully without being caught?"

She laughs, flipping her hair back. "Bitch, this is backstage. Once we're in, we zip our hoodies and keep our heads low. Grab anything you can hold and act like a roadie."

I want to wring her neck when the door cracks open. A guy wearing a beanie steps out. "Hurry," he says.

Alice and I slip inside, and she high-fives Randy. "Thanks, man. You're helping my friend's Cinderella story in the making." She gives me a side hug, squeezing me too tight.

"Just don't get caught. If you do, I know nothing." He points to our left. "I saw Scarlet Failure over there about fifteen minutes ago. You should find Sully easily. He's the one yelling."

"Maybe this is more like Beauty and the Beast," Alice mutters, zipping her jacket and popping up the hood.

I mimic her, and we grab the stands next to a drum set. "Stop naming Disney movies and tell me the rest of the plan."

"That's easy, V. Don't draw attention and find Sully. Talk to him, and then...I don't know...it's up to you."

"I can't believe we're doing this." I bite my lip until the pain is unbearable. Alice hugs the walls, but the coast is clear. She moves forward, and we freeze when we hear voices.

"The lights are off. We need to reset them," the guy in blue jeans says then looks at a clipboard.

"We're already running late. I'm fucking tired of these delays." He grabs his radio and says, "Jimmy, reset the lights, and God help you if you screw this up again."

They see right through us and keep walking. A weight falls off my shoulders, and I lean against the wall.

"It's a maze back here. Maybe we should—"

"Give up? Crawl under a rock again like you always do? Yeah, okay. You can keep living how you were and pretend Florida will change everything."

I set the stand down and wipe my sweaty palms on my jacket. "Are we going to search room by room? I don't think—"

"Randy said Sully was yelling. We can walk until we hear his voice. This place isn't that big." She touches my arm and smiles. "We're rewriting your story. Remember that."

"Okay." I grab the stand, and we're off. Lars and Ben exit a room, and I turn around to face Alice. "Shit," I mouth.

She and I huddle next to black containers of gear as they breeze by talking about pizza. We both sigh in relief when someone clears their throat behind us.

"What do you think you're doing? Those stands don't go there. Why is everyone here a moron?"

"Sorry, we'll move them," Alice says, grabbing her stand and nodding for me to follow.

"Wait. Forget the stands." The woman snaps her fingers, and a tall, skinny boy hurries over, wiping his brow and smearing black grease across his forehead. "Take these to where they belong." He rushes off to do what she said, and she clicks her tongue at us. "As for you two, I need you to help set up Gigi's wardrobe changes."

I fight the instinct to gag and dig my fingernails into my arm.

"Of course," Alice replies, grabbing my wrist and dragging me down the hall.

"I hate LA," the woman mutters too loudly and then walks away, barking at someone on a radio.

We are going in the opposite direction the arrows are pointing for the stage. The hairs on my arms rise when Sully's voice booms in the distance. "I can string my own guitar. Get the hell out!" A boy yelps and runs down the hall, shoulder-checking me, and doesn't look back.

"We found him." Alice gasps and pulls me behind a tower of crates. "Gigi at ten o'clock."

"She can't see me, or we'll be tossed out before I can say anything." I hang my head. "This was a long shot anyway."

"What are you saying? We found him! I'll distract Gigi, and you sneak into his room. Be sure to lock the door if you can."

I lick my lips and ball my hands into fists to hide their tremors. "What if he chews me out, too? He doesn't seem to want to be around anyone right now. This mission could be for nothing and—"

Alice slaps me across the face. "Snap out of it! He will take one look at you and thank his lucky stars or some romantic crap like that." She tugs on my sleeve. "After you lock the door, take your hoodie off. He needs to see how hot you look, and he won't be saying anything." She giggles and covers her mouth.

She shrugs out of her jacket and tosses it on the ground. "You'll do great. Text me if you want me to stick around or go, okay?"

I nod, too nervous to speak. She hugs me and disappears. Her voice echoes as she speaks to Gigi, complimenting how gorgeous her hair is. She's able to pull Gigi into another room as they talk about outfits and lipstick color.

"Just do it," I say to myself and beeline for the room Sully's voice came from. I look around and spot him sitting on a couch with his back to me, strumming his guitar. My heartbeat is louder than the soundcheck on stage as I close and lock the door. I slip off my jacket when he snaps, "Why doesn't anyone understand I want to be left alone?" He places the guitar next to him and turns to sneer, more angry words on his tongue, but he goes mute when he sees me.

"Veronica? What are you doing here?" He scratches his head. "I knew there was something in that cookie. Fuck."

"It's me. I found this." I pull his note out of my bra and set it on the table in front of him. "And decided it's time I stop running. I'm ready to hear you out if you still want to talk. If you don't, I understand." I wrap my arms around my torso, unsure what to do with my hands.

Sully flies to his feet and holds me in his arms. "I'm so happy you're here." He kisses me. It's deep and hard, full of hunger and lust.

I run my fingernails down his back, and we fall onto the couch. The guitar slides to the floor, but we don't give it a second thought.

"How did you get back here?" he asks breathless.

I smile at him big enough to crack my face. "Alice is scarily good at getting what she wants. She should've been a spy."

"How do you know she isn't one?" he snickers, wrapping his arms around me. "I'll have to thank her. I was afraid I'd never see you again."

"I don't want to be in this world without you," I whisper, looking at his lips to avoid his searching gaze.

He tips my head back with a curled finger. "Let's get out of here. Where do you want to go?"

I laugh, lying my head against his shoulder and interlocking our fingers together. "You can't walk out on this show. We can do something after."

"Screw this gig. I only agreed to get Charlotte off my back. I owed her one." He traces the freckles on the back of my wrist. "I was serious about giving everything up for you. All I wanted was to write music and have it change one person's life. I've done that tenfold, and I can still be a songwriter. But none of this means anything if I don't have you."

"You're okay leaving Scarlet Failure and the fallout you'll face on social media? Fans will attack you online."

He bends forward, picking up the guitar and examining its neck. "I never wanted the fame. It's a pain in the ass. I'd love to be another face in the crowd walking down the street." He leans the guitar against the table and turns to face me. "I'm fine fading into the background and having you be the star. I'll be your...what was it?"

I laugh. "Mer-handler."

"Yeah. I'll be your mer-handler, and we'll travel around the globe. On the side, I can sell songs. Sounds like the perfect life."

My phone buzzes. It's Alice asking if she needs to stay because Gigi is forcing her to watch a fashion show about what she should wear on stage, and her eyes are bleeding.

"Crap. I forgot Alice was distracting Gigi," I say.

Sully sucks on his teeth. "She better run. Once Gigi gets her claws into someone, they're scarred for life."

"I'm going to tell her it's okay she leaves. I'm in good hands."

He pulls me close to his chest. "Damn right, you are, *Engel*." His husky voice rumbles through me, and all I want to do is jump his bones. I text Alice, freeing her from friendship duty, and she sends me a thumbs up with a kissy face emoji.

"How do we get out of here?" I step back to keep myself from climbing on top of Sully and kissing him until we're dizzy. "Pull the fire alarm?"

"We can't go that far, but we could create a diversion." He grabs a radio and switches channels until he finds the one the crew uses. "What should we say?"

I pace the room, thinking. "Groupie on the loose? A spill?"

He nods. "Okay. I got one." He presses the button and speaks in a thicker German accent says, "Pizza guy's here, but he dropped some boxes. Giant fucking mess."

"Son of a bitch!" comes blasting over the speaker.

We laugh, and he ditches the radio onto the couch. He grabs his guitar and nods toward the door. "Let's run for it."

People buzz around, but we slip out the exit door without anyone stopping us. We run to the coffee shop down the street, and I order a ride while Sully gets us a couple of drinks to go.

We're finally free.

Chapter Forty-Four

"THE CAR WILL BE here in five minutes," I tell Sully when he returns with our coffees. He rests his arms on the standing table and grins.

"We're going to need to pack my shit fast before anyone realizes I'm gone and sends someone to check the house," he says.

"Of course." I sip my coffee. "Do you think they know where I live?" Fear pricks across my skin like bugs. I'd hate for Amy or Gigi to chew out Alice or catch me off guard...again.

"No idea. I wouldn't doubt it. We need to hide out until they leave town in three days."

"Oh, sure, no problem," I mutter, rolling my eyes. Finding a place to lay low without using credit cards—just in case his team has someone who can track that stuff—totally simple.

My phone buzzes. I read Alice's message and my heart plummets.

> *They found me! I hope you're far away because they're searching for Sully!*

"Crap..." I click my phone off and eye the door. "We need to go. There's no time for the car."

"What's wrong?" Sully grabs my arms. "Tell me."

"Alice was found. They know I was there, and you're gone."

"Shit." He shoves the coffee shop's door open and looks down the street. He returns, his face drained of color. "The entire band, Amy, and fucking Gigi are headed this way. Do you think there's an exit in the back?"

I look behind us. The place is small with three tall tables to stand around and a cramped area to order and pick up. Three people stand in line and the only way out back is through the employees-only area. Our only Hail Mary is to hide in the single-person bathroom.

"I have an idea." I grab Sully's wrist and tug him toward the tiny bathroom, but the damn door is locked. I knock with no answer. "Shit. You probably need to ask for the key."

"Our executioner is coming." He shields me from view as six people file in. Alice is in the center of the group with a deep frown and lines on her forehead. She's their hostage and this is all my fault.

"What do you think you're doing?" Amy spits, poking Sully in the chest with her finger. "You leave without a word and with this...*groupie*."

That word is a knife to the gut, but I can't react. I won't fall apart and lash out. The only way out of this is if we remain level-headed and try to compromise.

I gently push Sully to the side and step forward. "Why can't we just—"

"Don't you say another word." Gigi's eyes cut into me sharper than razor blades. "I should call the police on you and your friend for trespassing. For stalking." Her eyes blaze with fire. She smacks Amy's arm. "Can you report them?"

Alice stiffens her spine and bursts through the crowd. "I need caffeine dealing with you fuckers." She marches to the counter without a glance behind her.

Amy nods at Gigi, typing something on her phone. "Yes, of course. We need to keep the show on track and away from these nobodies," she says.

Gigi claps. "Well, then. Let's get back. The venue is losing it with all their artists missing and the doors opening in less than an hour." She frowns, looking at her phone. "But devoted fans know how to wait for a good thing. I'm planning a duet cover." Gigi reaches for Sully's wrist. "And we can finally publicly announce our engagement." She looks at me when she says that.

Sully yanks his arm back and slams it around my waist, anchoring me to his side. "That's enough." His voice is low but thunderous, vibrating through his chest like a warning growl.

"I don't know what kind of delusion you're living in, but I never proposed to you. Not then. Not ever." His eyes burn with fury now. "We were collaborating on two songs. That's it. It was business. Creating buzz for the tour. Nothing more."

He turns, locking eyes with Gigi. "But that's over now. I'm done playing polite. Being nice has only let people walk all over me and twist my silence into consent. I'm not your damn puppet, and I'm sure as hell not a trophy you can drag out when it suits you. I'm done letting other people dictate my life."

Gigi flinches, her perfectly painted smile cracking just a little. "Sully, baby...you don't mean that." Her voice trembles, not with fear, but with disbelief—like she's not used to being told *no*. "You're just upset. You're letting *her* twist things."

She steps toward him, but Sully tightens his grip around me, like a physical declaration of where he stands.

"I mean every word," he says coldly. "And don't you dare blame her for your games."

Gigi's eyes dart to me, venomous now. "You think she's not using you? Don't be stupid, Sully. She's a phase." Her voice gets sharper, more desperate with each word. "You *need* me. Your image, your tour—everything we built—"

"We built *nothing*," he snaps. "You built castles out of PR stunts and lies."

Gigi's jaw tightens. The façade slips entirely now, revealing something hard and bitter underneath. "Fine," she spits. "Burn it all down."

Sully doesn't flinch. "I'd rather crawl through the ashes than live another second under your thumb."

Amy moves forward, snapping, "Stop it! This little tramp—"

Sully clenches his teeth and shoves a finger into Amy's chest. "Don't you call Veronica anything else. It doesn't matter everyone else is married, and you think your PR powers can turn me into a meat stick to sell this band. I'm in love with Veronica. She's not a fling or a crazed groupie. This might be something real, and I wish you'd respect us enough to allow us to figure it out for ourselves without all these lies and deceit."

My breath hitches at the word *love* and I can't help but smile. We never said the words to each other, but I've never felt this safe around someone before. It's like he's been in my life longer than a few weeks. I spent too much time worrying about my heart and keeping my walls up, but he found a way in. He supports my career and gets along with my parents when no one else tried. I could picture us going on double dates with Alice and Emily.

"Let me walk away. Come up with whatever story for my departure. Just let me live my life in peace, please."

Amy squints at Sully and then sneers at me. "You'd leave without a penny?" she asks with disdain. "If you're that naïve and foolish about this so-called love then—"

"We're not standing by and letting Sully walk away…" Charlotte pipes in, interlacing her fingers with Ben, and they stand beside us. "Ben and I created this band, and we're taking back control."

"Yeah. What she said." Ben smiles at his wife.

"I'm with them," Lars says, hitting Sully's shoulder. He stands on the other side of Ben.

"Damn," Alice cuts in, leaning against a wall and sipping her drink, watching us as if we're an improv show.

"This is ridiculous." Amy stomps her foot, acting like a child who couldn't have dessert before dinner. She waves her hand in the air.

Charlotte steps forward and smirks. "We no longer require your services."

Amy blinks and bares her teeth. "Come now. You wouldn't be anywhere without—"

Sully motions to the door. "That means you're fired. Leave." His voice is full of bite, and she moves back as if she can feel the pain in her flesh.

"Screw you! Tank your band. See if I give a rat's ass," she snarls and pushes her way out the door. The glass door swings open and smacks the brick wall, but it doesn't shatter.

Gigi stands alone, fuming. Her face is scarlet, and her eyes bleed black, it's like she's possessed. "You'll be sorry you ever fucked with me."

Charlotte rolls her eyes. "I doubt it. We're no longer using your song and please feel free to drop the song we're on from your album. We'd hate to be tainted by you any further."

"Rot in hell," she spits, and her evil eyes fall on me. "How does it feel to ruin a band with your magical pussy?"

Sully pushes Gigi out the door. She stumbles backward and falls on her ass on the sidewalk. "Say another word to her and I'll rip your tongue out. Now get lost!"

She scrambles to her feet and flees down the street.

Sully turns to everyone. "I'm sorry about that. I snapped. She didn't deserve—"

Lars laughs. "Dude, chill. It's okay."

Alice claps. "Ding dong, the evil witches are dead! We gotta celebrate."

Charlotte sighs and gestures toward the venue. "Guess we should go back to pack our crap and tell them we're not playing tonight."

Ben clamps a hand on Sully's shoulder. "You can stay here." He offers his hand for the guitar. "I'll treat your guitars real nice."

"Not a scratch," Sully says, giving him his guitar.

Charlotte hugs me and kisses my cheeks. "Be good to our Sully." She kisses Ben on the lips, and they leave together.

Lars pulls his phone out. "This makes me want to call my wife. See you later." He follows his bandmates.

Alice tosses her coffee cup in the trash can and winks at me. "See. I knew this plan would work. No problem."

I chuckle, shaking my head. "Thanks."

My phone buzzes as a call cuts through. It's the driver for the ride I forgot about. "You ready? Our driver has been circling, pissed they can't find us."

Sully kisses my temple. "Yes. I'll go anywhere with you."

We flag down the car and hop inside.

Once we get to my place and close the door, our mouths slam together. We fumble to my room, peeling off our clothes along the way.

He sweeps my hair over my shoulder to kiss my neck. "You're mine, *Schatz,*" he growls.

I run my fingers along his jaw and pant, "Forever."

Sully palms my breast. I arch at his rough touch. He gently tosses me onto the bed and licks his lips, watching me for a second. His dick is hard and ready. I can't wait any longer and grab his wrists, pulling him onto me.

I suck on my bottom lip as he sinks into me. At first, he's slow, teasing me. I dig my fingernails into his shoulder blades and rock my hips, wanting more of him. Needing him to fill me up.

He holds my hips and pumps into me, going harder and faster. My eyes roll back as my moans grow louder and louder.

"That's it. Scream for me, *meine Liebe.*" He cups my breast and nips at the other one.

The headboard pounds against the wall. A framed picture above my nightstand falls to the floor and shatters. But it doesn't matter, not when this orgasm has me seeing stars.

My breath hitches as I feel him come too. Tremors rock my body as he falls to my side, breathing hard and covered in sweat.

Sully is my Heaven on Earth, and I will never let him go. Never again.

Chapter Forty-Five

SULLY AND HIS BANDMATES decide to finish recording their new record in LA before flying home. One of the songs sticks out from the album, and Sully suggested a music video to help promote their music after canceling their European tour.

As they plan the video, Sully smirks at me and shows his band something on his phone. The four of them stare at me. My skin itches under their inspection.

"Why do I feel like a zebra about to meet the wrath of a pride of hungry lions?" I chuckle, gritting my teeth.

Charlotte walks over and circles me. "Sully showed us the video he took of you at the restaurant."

"As a mermaid?" I ask, voice barely above a squeak.

"It'll be okay." Sully captures me in his arms. "I already see the music video in my head. Do you trust me?"

I pause, meeting everyone's gaze. They nod, encouraging me, and I fold faster than a house of cards in a high wind. "Yes."

The song is about a long-lost love reunited. The band plays together on a stage on the beach, where the story follows a mermaid who is in love with a human. Sully plays the part of the human, and I'm the mermaid.

The mermaid calls to her human love every night from shore, but he never shows up. Then he's seen coming off a plane. He sees a postcard of the ocean, and it calls to him.

The words, "She longs to see me, but I've been gone so long. How will she recognize me with everything gone so wrong?" are sung when the mermaid is caught in a wave and dumped onto the beach tangled in a fishing net.

He frees her, and they hold each other. The video zooms out and cuts to black.

Ben is already editing that night, and it's online within twenty-four hours. I hold my breath as I watch the final cut at home.

Alice crushes my bones in a hug. "That was epic! Right, Emily?"

Emily smiles over the rim of her wine glass. "Yes. A great twist on a classic love story. The song is catchy too."

Alice bounces on the couch cushion like a child. "You're about to go viral! I can feel it!"

Sully steps out of the bathroom, drying his hair with a towel. "What's going on?"

Alice rips the phone from my grasp and rushes over to show him. "Your music video already has five hundred thousand views!"

"Damn. And Amy thought we needed her. Ben is better at PR than she ever was." He high-fives Alice.

Emily swirls the rest of her wine in its glass, saying, "We need to celebrate."

✳ 🎵 🐚 🎵 ✳ 🎵 🐚

The four of us go to The Pearl Kingdom for dinner. I couldn't think of a better place to enjoy the spoils of the music video than the place that helped me most.

A shy little girl hugging a stuffed blue octopus wanders to our table while we're drinking and enjoying appetizers. I wipe my hands on a napkin and press a finger to my lips to pause Alice's story. To the little girl, I ask, "Hey, sweetie, are you lost?"

She shakes her head no and points to the water tank by our table. "I know your secret," she says softly and looks around. "Promise I won't tell."

"Awe," Alice says, running her fingers up and down Emily's arm. "She's too cute."

I lean closer to the little girl and smile. "Thank you. Who's your friend?" I tap the octopus's head.

"Ollie," she says, hugging the stuffed animal tighter.

A woman rushes over, taking the girl's arm. "Holly, there you are." She picks up the girl and smiles at us. "Sorry."

I wave. "Don't worry. She's a cutie pie."

The woman eyes me, and then her gaze flicks to Sully. "I'm sorry, but are you in the video 'Soul of Mine'?"

Is this what it feels like to have fans? What an odd sensation. My stomach flips as my heart races.

"Y...yes," I finally say. It comes out more like a question than a statement.

"I love that song," she says, and the little girl drops her stuffed animal.

I pick it up and stand to hand it back to her. "She's really a mermaid," Holly says, then covers her mouth, "Sorry."

The mom looks at me, and I motion to the tank. "I'm one of the mermaid performers here."

"You perform beautifully. I work in marketing. I'd love to meet with you sometime." She sets Holly down and digs into her purse, handing me a business card. "It was nice to meet you." The little girl waves as they return to their table.

I fall back into my seat and flick the card like I'm someone famous. "How about that?"

"Didn't I call it? I knew those Tarot cards were right," Alice says, raising her glass. "To Veronica!"

Sully kisses my cheek before raising his glass. "It's hot seeing you meet fans, but do you think you could find the band some love, too?" he jokes, winking.

I shrug. "I'll try." I click my glass with everyone, and we finish our drinks.

When we return home, Alice checks the music video again, and it hit over a million views. Sully group texts the band the good news. The exposure is helping them thrive as well.

I scan through the comment section, and every doubt I had about Sully and me wash away. The fans are rooting for us. They love us together, and now I want to share the pictures of us from the mermaid shoot. They are even using the hashtag "Verlly" for us.

Chapter Forty-Six

Three Months Later

I BLOW BUBBLES AT Sully and Alice as they sit at the closest table to the water tank. I give my all to the last show at The Pearl Kingdom. In two days, Sully and I will fly to Germany to meet with his band and go on tour. I already have gigs lined up in a handful of countries. Since the music video, Sully and I have spent a few weeks together off and on as he needs to travel home for various reasons. I can't wait to see all his favorite places like I showed him all my stomping grounds in and around LA.

When I change into my regular clothes and leave the break room, the entire restaurant stands and applauds me. I blush, waving, and sink into a chair. My parents are there, and Mom wipes her eyes. "Sweetie, I loved your show."

Dad nods, smiling. "You're wonderful. A real-life mermaid."

I couldn't function for a moment. They've never seen my mermaid shows live. I don't know if they've even seen any videos of mine without me shoving them under their noses before I gave up. I choke on my words but manage to say, "Thanks for coming. You don't know what this means to me."

Alice stands, tapping a spoon to her glass to settle everyone, and nods to give their attention toward Sully.

He smiles his thanks and takes my hand. "Veronica, since I've met you, it's been the best part of my life. You're magic, fierce, and fearless. I love everything about you and..." He falls to one knee and pulls a gorgeous ring out of his pocket. It's blue sapphire with silver shells on both sides. "Will you do me the honor of becoming my wife?"

I gasp, my hands instinctively flying to my mouth. The room goes eerily quiet, and time feels like it's holding its breath. Every gaze is on me, the weight of their attention undeniable.

I used to believe I had to face the world alone, that I was my own force of nature, invincible and self-reliant. But that version of me—the strong, independent woman—has faded, crumbled, and been left behind.

Now, everything feels different. With Sully, I see the world in vivid color. We share nights of passion, city after city, as he performs and I stand by his side. He's my equal, my partner, helping me with my career as much as I help with his. We fit together like two pieces of a puzzle, and it feels like fate has woven us together.

"Yes!" I say, and he places the ring on my finger.

He stands, and I kiss him fiercely, almost catching the room on fire with our passion. The restaurant is loud in applause, and someone in the back whistles.

Sully whisks me off my feet and spins me around. I giggle, wrapping my arms tighter around his neck. "I can't wait to start my forever with you."

He whispers in my ear, "You're all I ever wanted, and I can't wait to wake up to you every morning for the rest of my life, *Schatz*."

We kiss again. I'm eager for our journey abroad. After the tour and my cruise line commercial, I'll plan our wedding, and then everything else can come as it may because I have my mermaid dreams and my handsome bass playing prince. The future is wide open. I'm about to dive in for the first time with a giant smile and someone amazing holding my hand.

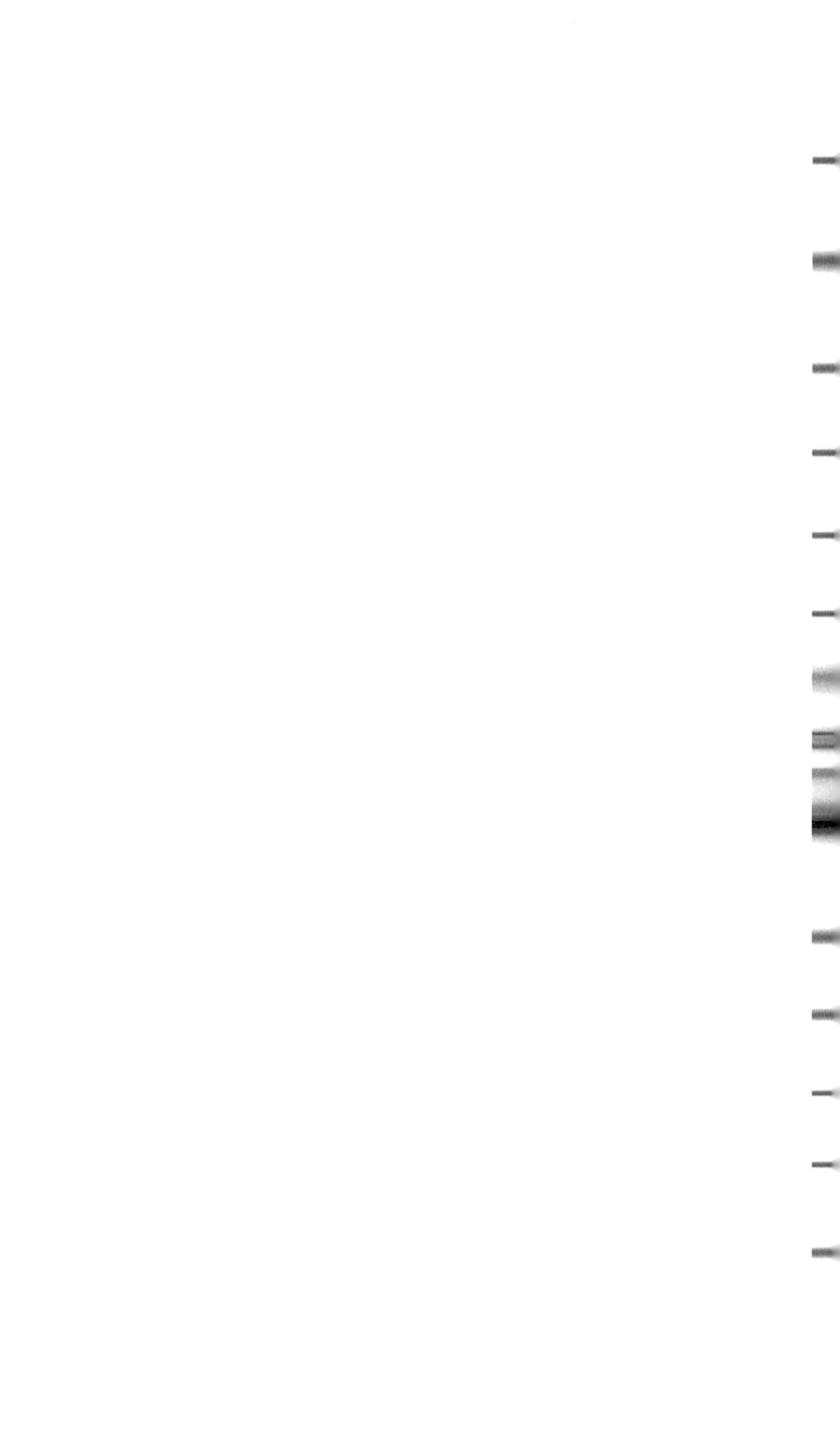

Enjoy After Finding You?

If you enjoy reading this book, please leave a review!
Reviews are important to authors. They help books reach new readers.
I really appreciate it and I'd love to read your thoughts.

Playlist

Covered by Roses • Within Temptation

Sing Like A Siren • Within Temptation and Jerry Heil

Don't Pray For Me • Within Temptation

Find You • Ruelle

Blow • Eva Under Fire feat. Spencer Charnas of Ice Nine Kills

ihateit • Underoath

Dying in LA • Panic! At The Disco

Immortal • MARINA

Masterpiece • Motionless In White

Die With Me • Gemini Syndrome

Unholy • Lilith Czar

Messy • Conquer Divide

Don't Hate Me • Badflower

Truth • Godsmack

Poison • Alice Cooper

MAGNETIC • Wage War

Also by Brittney Coon

Shades of Sydney – A Sydney West Novel, Book 1
Breaking Down Sydney – A Sydney West Novel, Book 2
Piecing Together Sydney – A Sydney West Novel, Book 3
Don't Let Go (YA Mafia Romance)

Coming Soon:
Like A Villain (Vampire Romance)
Melting Points (Hockey & Ice Skater Romance)
Drown In Me (Mermaid Romance)

About the Author

BRITTNEY COON GRADUATED MAGNA Cum Laude from Arizona State University with a Bachelor of Science in Communication and a minor in Film and Media Production. Brittney has always been creative and turned to writing to share the stories playing through her head. In her spare time, she reads, attends rock/metal concerts, watches *Friends* or *Twilight* depending on her mood, and writes horror features. She currently lives in Arizona with her spoiled rotten cat.

You can follow Brittney on Instagram, TikTok, Facebook, and Twitter/X by searching @BrittneyCWrites

Visit Brittney's Website for updates at https://brittney-coon-writes.mailchimpsites.com/

www.ingramcontent.com/pod-product-compliance
Lightning Source LLC
Chambersburg PA
CBHW030624110726
47901CB00002B/304